RACE
to the
BOTTOM
of the
SEA

RACE

to the

BOTTOM

of the

SEA

LINDSAY EAGAR

CANDLEWICK PRESS

Copyright © 2017 by Lindsay Eagar

First paperback edition 2019

Library of Congress Catalog Card Number 2017956984
ISBN 978-0-7636-7923-1 (hardcover)
ISBN 978-0-7636-9877-5 (paperback)

19 20 21 22 23 24 BVG 10 9 8 7 6 5 4 3 2 1

Printed in Berryville, VA, U.S.A.

This book was typeset in ITC New Baskerville.

Candlewick Press
99 Dover Street
Somerville, Massachusetts 02144

visit us at www.candlewick.com

For my editor, Kaylan,
the wind in my sails

With its astounding monopoly on the earth's surface—some 80 percent of blue—and its collection of our most beautiful, bizarre flora and fauna, it's a wonder we don't rename our planet Ocean.

—*Exploring an Underwater Fairyland* by Dr. and Dr. Quail

Two scoops of mashed fish guts. Four gallons of blood.
Mix together in a barrel, then pour into the ocean.

The recipe in Fidelia Quail's observation book was for chum, and at eleven years old, she could recite it by heart.

This smelly pink slick took to the waves, spreading half a mile in the seawater. Sharks in the bay would take it as the perfect invitation to swim past the research boat, the ancient brown-and-beige refashioned trawler appropriately named the *Platypus.*

Measure the regulars, tag the newcomers, and hopefully find out which ravenous shark had been munching through entire schools of halibut . . . Fidelia's favorite days were shark days.

A spray of seawater hit her face, rinsing off the homemade sunblock she'd just applied to her fair skin and peppering her square-framed glasses with briny speckles. She smeared another layer of the sea slug slime–based mixture over her face, then wiped the lenses on the hem of her pinafore and quickly replaced them; without her glasses, she was as good as blind.

One time she'd dropped her glasses during a routine reef check. In the underwater haze, she'd reached out to find them and accidentally grabbed the snout of an ill-tempered gator fish.

"Holy hammerhead," she muttered now, catching sight of the bib of her once-white pinafore. It was an abstract masterpiece of pink and brown splotches: faded bloodstains, the juice of fish innards, a spot of engine oil, and other fluids from various sea creatures.

An entire summer of research, displayed in a collage on her clothes.

Leaning over the port side, she dumped a sticky scoop of chum into the water. "Calling all sharks! I made chum with tuna, your favorite. Come and get it!"

A frozen mackerel stared at her from inside an icy cooler. She looped a rope through its gill and threw it overboard as extra incentive. Now the sharks could have hors d'oeuvres and dessert, if only they'd hurry up. Right now the sky was striped in the fuzzy, lazy blues of late afternoon, but once the Undertow hit, all would be gray.

Arborley Sea's frigid waters teemed with sharks, large and small, during the summer months. Schools of fleshy white cod bred and swam in a ring around Arborley Island, drawing the hungry predators in. Usually checking the sharks' tags was easier than milking a sea snake, but today, she couldn't tempt the sharks with any of the usual bait.

Fidelia knew the culprit—the Undertow. It always gave the marine life a bit of stage fright.

She tapped the Hydro-Scanner. The silver circular radar detector was a Fidelia original; the university didn't have an accurate fish-finding device, so Fidelia had built one herself last spring.

Fidelia had taken her invention to the patent office on the mainland, but the clerks hadn't even been subtle when they rejected it. "A child's contraption," they called it, right to her face. "We're not in the business of patenting home-made doodads. This is nothing more than a toy for bored schoolgirls who like to play at science."

Play at science . . . as if Fidelia's whole life were nothing more than a tea party.

Ridiculous. She couldn't help being eleven years old, could she? Child or not, her Hydro-Scanner had never missed a fish.

Its red needle quivered, swept across the screen, then dropped. Not a fish in the vicinity—not so much as a sea horse. Fidelia gave the Hydro-Scanner a dirty look, then pushed the sleeves of her dove-gray frock above her scabby elbows.

She moved the mackerel line to the starboard side and looked down into the water. The chum spun and frothed in the chop, making salty, fish-flavored bubbles.

"Hurry your gills up," she called to the sharks. *Before the Undertow hits,* she added silently. Hands curled around the *Platypus*'s railing, her eyes peeled the surface for any telltale dorsal fins, or boils in the water, or strange blue shadows.

But she was alone.

Until the radio buzzed.

"Quail? Quail, do you copy?" Her mom's chipper voice crackled on the speaker.

"Quail here," Fidelia said. "Any sharks in sight?"

"Nothing from our position," her mom answered.

"Not nothing!" her dad said. "The mermaid's wineglass is blooming. Steer us a bit closer there, dear. See if you can snag a bouquet to take home." Mermaid's wineglass, a marine plant with delicate green tops shaped like little cups, would be displayed not in a floral vase on the mantel but in the terrarium on the Quails' dining-room table.

Fidelia's parents were the internationally acclaimed biologists Dr. and Dr. Quail. They were currently hovering fifty feet below the *Platypus* in the miniature aqua-blue research submarine, the *Egg* (another Fidelia creation).

Arthur Quail was a marine botanist, easily excited by the colorful flora of the watery deep, and Ida was a gill-, fang-, and fur-loving marine zoologist. Fidelia, their only loin fruit, was the perfect blend of both—with a knack for inventing that was entirely her own.

The *Platypus* rode a wave high, then bounced down with a thwack.

"How's topside?" Fidelia's mother asked.

"Nothing yet—oh, wait! Stand by." Fidelia tracked a flurry of bubbles through the blood-slicked water. Bubbles could mean sharks.

But a party of seagulls landed in the water and picked at the chum.

Birds wouldn't land if they sensed sharks nearby. "False alarm," Fidelia sighed.

"How close is the storm?" Ida Quail asked.

Fidelia wiped a smear of sweat from her neck. "Oh, we have . . . a while." Luckily, her parents were down in the *Egg* and couldn't see the swirl of black clouds inking the otherwise pastel horizon. Dr. and Dr. Quail would be zooming to the docks if they knew how dark the sky had dimmed.

But it was the last day of September, the last day of summer. The last day to tag sharks. Their last chance to collect data before the Undertow left them stuck on the island for the long, cold winter. Nothing to do except write up their summer notes and wait for the Undertow madness to end.

Fidelia wanted to make sure they used every last available second before they were landlocked.

"Maybe I should put out another mackerel?" Fidelia asked. "Or take the *Platypus* farther out to sea?"

"Relax," her father said jovially. "Let the chum do its job."

Fidelia begrudgingly sat on the *Platypus*'s bench and leaned back, stretching her legs. She was shaped like a broomstick, tall and thin, which made for knee cramps and back pain aboard the puny, fourteen-foot trawler. On especially long days like this one, when they left the house before dawn and worked in the bay until suppertime, she felt like a sardine in a tin.

"Ten more minutes," her mom said. "Then we reel everything in."

"But we haven't tagged a single shark!" Fidelia said.

"We haven't done our final fin count for the university. And we still don't know who's been eating the halibut—"

"Fidelia," her mother said, as tenderly as she could through the radio. "We've knocked on their door. All we can do now is wait."

Fidelia pulled a wrinkly issue of *Adventures in Science Engineering* from her bag. "I know," she grumbled.

"Plus, think of all the data we *did* gather this summer," Ida said. "Two new subspecies of red seaweed! The crab migration! The puffin dives! Remember?"

As if Fidelia could forget. All the beautiful things she'd seen in the last three months wove together in a tapestry in her mind—the vivid purple of marine ferns in the seabeds of Bleu Island, where they spent a blissful three days diving off cliffs into clear water. The scarlet of thorny oyster shells in the eastern lagoons—an unplanned detour on their way back from Canquillas. The shocking yellow of a ribbon eel's tail from their week in the tropics. The dusty white of glaciers up north.

And the shades of home, of Arborley Bay—the olive green of the algae covering the rocks on the shore; the soft pink of the stingrays; the dappled brown wings of Arborley ducks as they waddled along the docks. Yes, it had been quite the busy summer.

"If you're worried about our grant renewal," her mother said, "don't be. We've had a spectacular year."

"It's not that," Fidelia said. Dr. and Dr. Quail's contributions to the scientific community more than guaranteed a long industrious future of study. The university would approve any funding they required, for any project they wanted to undertake.

She watched the blue water break white against the boat. "It's our last day together," she said. "Us and them. I just wanted it to be special."

"I know they're your favorite," her mother said, and even with fifty feet of seawater between them, Fidelia could feel her mother's beaming approval.

Yes, sharks were Fidelia's favorites.

Their bodies—marvels of evolutionary design. Some the glorious, elongated silhouette with perfectly cut fins and glossed skin. Some the flattened, ornate, ray-like carpets of the seafloor, masters of disguise. Some only the size of a human finger, but with eyes large and dark as blackberries. A variation for every ecosystem.

Their grace—the way they cruised through the water, stoic and effortless.

Their danger.

Sometimes in bed, when the clouds blew over the face

of the moon and the light in her room was muted, Fidelia would remember the first time she'd seen a great white shark breach the surface to feed on a sea lion. From the hidden depths came the shark, launching its thousand-pound body up and out of the water in a flash, with the still-wriggling sea lion powerless in its jaws. Then it disappeared as quickly as it arrived, the only evidence of the attack a smear of oily blood, crimson against the wake.

Fidelia would think of that moment and grin, and shiver, and pull her bedsheets up over her head, grateful to be a clumsy, clomping land animal.

How could sharks not be her favorite?

The radio crackled.

"Come in." Fidelia switched the radio on and off. "Come in, Mom and Dad. Do you copy?"

Hum, hum, click. The *Egg's* reception always got spotty past descents of fifty feet.

Fidelia took her seat and flipped through her gazette, *Adventures in Science Engineering*—the premiere publication for scientific advancements and inventions. She scanned the pages advertising helmet vales and hemp ropes. "New! New! New!" boasted an ad. "Double-barreled flank tube allows for collection and transport of two specimens at once!"

She rolled her eyes.

Fidelia had made her own double-barreled flank tube . . . when she was six. The flank tubes she was currently experimenting with had multiple interchangeable compartments, with space for a dozen samples at a time. *Adventures in Science Engineering,* the periodical was called—and yet, Fidelia was always an adventure ahead.

The water was flat, steady, empty. Where were those sharks?

She tucked the gazette in her bag and opened her observation book—a simple red leather notebook that went everywhere with her. Her parents had wisely taught her, "Always be armed with something to write with," and she followed this philosophy like it was law.

Uncapping her pen, she jotted down:

September 30
First day of autumn storms. Last day of shark season. Starting tomorrow, they'll swim to warmer waters until springtime. I won't see them for months. I hate winter. I always miss my sharks—Bluetail, Gumbo, Prudence, Spotty . . . even Bluntnose, the old grouch.

The end of summer on Arborley Island meant nautilus shells washing among the pebbles of Stony Beach. Sea

sponges in the cold-water reefs turning blue. The arriv
firefly squids in moonlit October evenings.

But it also meant the Undertow.

And, of course, the end of summer meant the end of
sharks.

The sleek sharks left Arborley Sea in big-fanged fleets,
chasing their last bites of rubbery cod before escaping to the
tropics for winter's cold stretch. The final day of shark season was as celebrated in the Quail family as any other holiday, albeit a bittersweet one. The end of summer was always
a good-bye.

This year alone Fidelia had seen a hundred sharks at
least—jumping makos, beady-eyed lemons, twitchy blues,
matronly nurses scrounging the bay floor for shellfish.
They'd even glimpsed a whale shark, that rare leviathan, a
gentle giant passing serenely through a red cloud of krill.

Eleven years of studying sharks with her parents, and
the sight of these creatures still made her gooey. Scared and
quiet and fizzing with joy, right under her ribs.

In her observation book, she wrote:

> *Some shark's been gobbling all the halibut. The fisher-*
> *men have complained about holes being chewed through*
> *their nets, all their halibut chomped to bones. Our locals*

here just eat cod and mussels—so we must have an out-of-towner. Mom was hoping we'd get a glimpse of the visitor before the Undertow hits, but here it is, the eleventh hour, and not a fin in sight.

Something burst from the sea depths—a common white surf clam, sent up from the *Egg.* Fidelia reached down with her forever-long arms, plucked the clam from the water, and held it in a stream of sunlight.

The clam yawned its shell open. Inside, right on its fat pink tongue, was a scroll of paper. Fidelia giggled at the soggy cartoon her father had scribbled, depicting all three Quails devouring a tureen of soup. "Shipwreck Stew at the Book and Bottle for dinner?" was written beneath the picture.

This was the standard Quail-to-Quail message delivery system—inserting notes into clams—and it was a symbiotic win-win. Just like the birds that eat ticks off rhinos, or the bees that pollinate flowers, the clam brought the message from sea bottom to surface, and so Fidelia let it photosynthesize the algae that grew on its tongue before she dropped it back into the steely blue fathoms.

Fidelia laid the cartoon flat on the railing to dry. Shipwreck Stew, yum. Her tummy rumbled.

Or was that thunder?

If the Undertow was close enough to hear, it was definitely time to dock, sharks or no sharks.

"*Platypus* to *Egg*, come in. The clouds are growling at us. We better head to shore. Do you copy?" She held the radio receiver with one hand and grabbed the mop with the other, cleaning a few splatters of fish blood from the deck of the trawler.

The radio fizzled. "Fidel—" (*static, click*) "*Platypus*—" (*click, click, static*) "go ahead and dock her—" (*hum, static, hum*) "meet us at the Book and Bottle—" (*hum, static, click*). With a pop, the speaker dissolved into silence. Fidelia turned the radio off—the system probably needed to cool down. Not a problem. She had brought the *Platypus* to harbor alone dozens of time.

Shrimp, garlic, cubes of buttery lobster, a few cockles in clear broth with bay leaves and saffron . . . A nice hot bowl of Shipwreck Stew would be a fair consolation for her long, fruitless—sharkless—day.

No. Not fruitless. That wouldn't be fair to the hagfish they'd found, tying itself into knots. Or to the translucent ghost crabs, patrolling the seafloor. Or to the kaleidoscope of seaweed clippings Dr. Quail had collected for his samples.

But the sharks were the big hitters, and they hadn't bothered to show up.

Yes, Shipwreck Stew to drown her sorrows in and a couple of baguettes. That's what she needed. Maybe even a trip to her favorite sweets shop, BonBon Voyage, for a choco-glomp and a plum-milk float.

Mmm, chocolate . . .

More seagulls came. They plopped their ragged-feathered selves in the chum and plucked out chunks of rotting fish to gulp down their beaks.

"Shoo! Shoo!" Fidelia waved her arms. "Get out of here, you sea rats." Two gulls bobbed their heads, peering at her, but she wasn't threatening enough for them to abandon their stolen meal.

She went back to mopping. Behind the wall of dark clouds, the sun shifted, pulsing its peachy-white rays across the water. The *Platypus* held still. Everything was quiet.

Too quiet.

The seagulls were beelining it back to the island, leaving ripple rings in the water. Suddenly the mackerel line spun out and cast itself to maximum length, the spool of rope smoking with the speed.

Fidelia dropped the mop with a clatter.

The Hydro-Scanner pinged, red needle bouncing.

She glanced at the water and squealed. Shipwreck Stew would have to wait.

Fish, the Hydro-Scanner announced. Big fish.

Shark.

A dark blue shadow cruised along the side of the *Platypus*. The mackerel line tugged down into the sea, then snapped clean off.

The triangular fin of a shark sliced through the water. Fidelia reached for her Track-Gaff—a one-motion, trigger-and-release tagging pole that sank tags into even the slipperiest of sharks. She loaded a tag into its chamber and held it over the water.

"Oh, my sea stars!" she whispered. This definitely wasn't one of their regulars. He was twenty feet long at least—when the creature aligned himself with the *Platypus*, his nose jutted out past the propellers.

Fidelia's chest bristled, a thousand itty-bitty stingrays swimming and flapping their wings, all at once. She had hoped this day would be special—now it was quickly rivaling the most exciting day of her life.

The shark made another rotation around the boat. A jagged scar wrapped around his dorsal fin, a constellation of pink-white tissue. The sight made her burn with rage. She had seen these battle scars on loads of creatures. Cause of injury? Barbed fishing lines. They were illegal here in Arborley, but the law didn't extend to other parts of the world. Greedy industrial fishermen spread these death traps around the tropical seas as if the sharks were monsters, deserving only of slaughter. They were lucky this beast got untangled; he was big enough to take any standard-size fishing boat down with him, if he was angry enough.

He swam back and forth, too far out for Fidelia to nab with the Track-Gaff. She took her binoculars out of her bag—just a refashioned pair of Ida Quail's old copper opera glasses, but they gave Fidelia the perfect close-up view.

The shark's skin faded from a polished, pearly black on top to a dappled gray underbelly. She studied his jawline, his pectoral fins, counted his gills (five of them, standard for sharks in the Lamniformes order). His wide, sweeping tail curved like a sickle—this creature was built for speed and power. His teeth were long thick triangles, so she knew he ate seals and dolphins and other critters with plenty of fat.

"Hey!" she cried suddenly. "You're the one who's been eating all the halibut!" How many dozens of fish did it take to satisfy a shark this size? No wonder there'd been such a dip in the halibut population this year.

Less halibut in the bay had led to an increase in sculpin (halibut's dietary staple), which led to a decrease in sea grass (*sculpin*'s dietary staple). Such was the way of the sea—a delicate ecosystem, every pairing of predator and prey carefully balanced. To lose one or the other meant the whole biological orchestra jangled out of tune.

Fidelia tapped her chin as she thought. She knew the records of documented sharks backward and forward, knew all two hundred species by sight, silhouette, and scientific name. But she'd never read about a shark like this.

"You are gorgeous," she said to the mystery shark. "The question is, what are you, exactly? You have mako teeth, and a great white's tail. But you're too big to be a hybrid."

She pictured the Drs. Quail's view—fifty feet beneath the surface, the *Egg* puttering among the clawed reefs, and the shark looming above them, ragged teeth poking from his snout like crooked rows of ivory headstones, his creamy belly glowing in the darkness.

Fidelia put her binoculars back in her bag and snapped the radio on.

"Mom, Dad, come in! Are you seeing this?" Her hands were shaking.

"Seeing what?" Her mother's reply was calm. "We just dipped down to pick some mermaid's wineglass, and—"

"Starboard side!" Fidelia burst. "Quick!"

"All right, we're moving!" Arthur Quail grunted as he cranked the *Egg*'s helm. Sometimes salt water gummed the wheel—a quirk of the submarine Fidelia was still working out.

The shark busied himself with the mackerel Fidelia had offered, nonchalantly chewing until it was shredded to fleshy ribbons.

"Do you see him?" Fidelia impatiently transmitted.

A moment of static, and then—"We see him! We see him!" Ida Quail was so giddy, the radio couldn't transfer the highest pitches of her squeals.

"What a monster," Arthur Quail said. "A beautiful, beautiful monster."

"It's him! Our halibut thief—it's got to be," Fidelia said. "Did you see his teeth?"

"How could we miss them?" her father said. "They're as big as my good jam knife!"

"So, what are we looking at here? A hybrid? Or is this just an oversize great white, trolling the world for spare halibut?" Fidelia waited for Ida's expertise, but there was only silence. "Mom? Are you there?"

"I think," Ida said, each word reverent, "we're looking at a new species."

A new species. Fidelia's goose bumps were the size of mosquito bites. "I can't believe it! It's been ages since we found a new species—"

"We?" her mother echoed through the radio. "Oh, no. No, darling. This is your discovery."

The *Platypus* bobbed. Fidelia was stunned, the radio clenched in one hand. "But—"

"Your mother's right," Arthur piped in. "You know the rule. He who spots it, gots it. Or she, as the case may be— and that's you."

A new species . . . Her own discovery . . . If she tagged this shark, the Track-Gaff would be splashed on the next cover of *Adventures in Science Engineering*. She'd patent all her gadgets, and then every wonder in the ocean would be explored with a Fidelia Quail invention.

Maybe she'd even win a Gilded Iguana.

The shark cut through the water like a razor blade— still too far out to tag, but he was circling closer, getting curious.

A Gilded Iguana . . . It was the most prestigious award a biologist could win, an honor bestowed only on those who discovered something great. Someone who left a mark.

Her parents each had one, both of them displayed on a shelf in their parlor—the first things Fidelia saw every morning on her way down to breakfast.

If I tag him, I get to name him, she thought, her head light with glee. Ida had an entire collection of mollusks named for her favorite candies. Arthur once thought he was clever when he gave a trumpet-shaped plant its nom de plume: tootweed.

Now, at least, it would be Fidelia's turn.

The shark rotated again, zipping past the length of the *Platypus*—just a casual swim for the two-ton beast.

What should she name him?

Carcharhinus arborleyan? Roughly translated, it meant "sharp-toothed Arborley shark."

No, his official title for the books should use her own name. That way there would be no doubt that she was the one who discovered him.

Lamnidae fidelius? "Fidelia's fish of prey?"

She'd pin down an official name in time. For now, he needed a nickname.

The white foam splashed against the shark's mottled, grizzled skin as he cruised around the trawler, mouth gaping, those gargantuan teeth just bright-white blurs in the water.

Grizzle.

"That's what I'll call you, until I can think of something better," she said. "Grizzle." The name suited him. He gave her a sharky grin and rolled past, her reflection gleaming in his round black eye, her pointy features furrowed in concentration.

"Did you tag him?" Ida asked on the radio.

Fidelia tightened her grip on the Track-Gaff. "Not yet." Not yet, no—but she was ready to sink the tag into his fin. Ready to make her mark.

"He's all yours." The radio blared Ida's final, supportive words before the whole system dissolved into fuzzy static again: "Go get him."

All mine.

Fidelia set her jaw, squinting past the sun's mirrored rays and into the water.

The *Platypus* leveled in the chop. Grizzle flipped around and barreled toward her. She leaned over, determination flushing through her like a fever. This was her chance.

Just a little closer.

A burst of wind shook the *Platypus* just as Fidelia clicked. The tag missed the fin and sank into the watery blue.

"Son of a squid!" she exploded, then regrouped with a

deep breath. No worries—she had plenty of tags with her. She reloaded her Track-Gaff and waited.

Come on, Grizzle. Come on back.

Another salty breeze blasted her cheeks like a smack from an open palm. The afternoon's peaceful, sorbet-colored clouds were completely gone; the sky had darkened to charcoal. Seawater swirled around the *Platypus,* tossing it like a bathtub toy.

Then someone turned on the rain.

Fidelia tried to plant her boots on the slippery deck, but the *Platypus* was just a cradle, violently rocked in the waves. She grasped the railing, the trawler whipping her to and fro like a rag doll.

It was here.

The Undertow was a shift in the ocean's current, a result of the hot summer air leaving the island and colliding with the incoming cold weather front. Its chaos had earned itself a catchphrase—"During the Undertow, anything can happen." Whirlpools appeared out of nowhere and tore ships to splinters. Schools of cod flopped onto fishing boats, surrendering without a fight. Forests of kelp uprooted themselves from the seafloor and floundered ashore.

Anything could happen, yes. But the Undertow's specialty was destruction.

The wind screamed. Grizzle, spooked by the madness, dove down.

"Wait, Grizzle!" Fidelia managed to stay upright, her beanpole shadow spearing the last of the shark before he slapped his tail into the stern of the *Platypus,* then disappeared.

She hesitated, raindrops freckling her glasses. She should warn her parents that the storm was here, close enough to feel. And she needed to get the *Platypus* into the harbor before the Undertow turned it into driftwood. But she hadn't put a tag in Grizzle's fin.

It was September 30 — the massive shark would likely be migrating to the tropics tonight with the rest of his fishy cohorts, to spend the winter where it was nice and warm. If she didn't tag him now, right now, he might be lost forever, free game for someone else to discover. A lesser scientist. Or, even worse, just a person. A citizen.

She pictured a third Gilded Iguana on the shelf between her parents' awards — hers a particularly shiny gold, especially when the sun crept through the garden window and hit the letters on the plaque: *Fidelia Aurora Quail, Scientist.*

She had to tag that shark.

Even as the storm wailed around her, she opened the cooler and roped another mackerel, her mind whirring at top speed.

Should she break out the diving suit?

The suit was standard, professionally made diving equipment—a canvas suit lined with rubber, which clamped into a twelve-bolt helmet—and all three Quails hated using it. The so-called watertight seal was unreliable—every other dive, their helmets came up sloshing with seawater. Corselets, the pieces that connected the helmet to the suit, rusted and broke constantly.

And it was the most advanced diving technology available.

Inflating the canvas suit took a good twenty minutes, which she didn't have. But maybe she could skip the inflation and just head underwater with a saggy suit? If Grizzle wouldn't come up to her, she would swim down to him.

She fiddled with the door to the hatch.

If only the Water-Eater was ready, she thought.

But before she could get the diving helmet and begin improvising, a wave curled over her, tall enough to cast the entire *Platypus* in shade.

"Here we go," she muttered, and held on to the rail tightly as the water succumbed to gravity and fell.

Hair, glasses, dress, stockings, boots—all soaked. Miraculously, the boat managed to stay afloat, but a spray of seawater burst through the slats of the *Platypus*'s port side.

A leak!

Forget the diving suit—the whole boat was about to head underwater.

She radioed the *Egg* between tidal-wave splashes—no answer, just static.

Submarines, for the most part, fared just fine in ocean storms. So she wasn't worried about her parents. They would be safe.

But, a voice in her mind nagged, *they're in a submarine built by an eleven-year-old. A child's contraption, the patent office would call it.*

Again, she called the *Egg*. Again, static.

Her parents were probably already on the dock—shivering and worrying and wondering where their brainy daughter was.

She could feel the *Platypus* grow heavier and heavier as it filled with water. Grizzle's tail must have split a hole clear through the wood.

Just then, all the bait lines went slack. For a moment, the sea leveled. The waves had blended the chum like a milk shake—now it sank straight down, the blood diluted, fish guts reduced to pinkish-brown grains. The nibbled mackerel's head floated, a single silver eye staring up at the storm.

The *Platypus* was leaking, yes—but even worse, Grizzle was gone. Her chance was gone.

With blistered hands and a scowl that would startle a stonefish, she flipped on the *Platypus*'s propellers and prepped the vessel for transport.

The back of the trawler dragged below the surface as she flashed to shore, a trail of icy white foam behind her. Her adrenaline dissipated from her body in waves, leaving her exhausted and aching—she hadn't eaten in hours. She'd bring in the boat and get dinner with her parents. She'd regroup, make a new Track-Gaff in the workshop. Tomorrow morning, if the skies had improved, she'd tar the split boards on the *Platypus*, and together the three Quails would sail back out to find the shark, and she'd slip a tag in his fin.

Her first discovery.

She snorted at her own gumption—or at her desperation. Did she really think Grizzle would stick around for the first chill of winter? Did she really think the storm would cooperate for one more day of open-water fieldwork?

But then again, in the Undertow, anything could happen.

Fidelia managed to steer the *Platypus* into the harbor just as the engine sputtered a briny burp and gave out. She looked for a familiar flash of aqua-blue metal near the Quails' regular spot on the dock, but the *Egg* was nowhere to be seen.

Arborley was a ghost town. Usually, Friday evenings brought a traffic jam of ships, each one impatient to unload its exotic cargo—crate after crate of raw cocoa beans, freshly harvested from the tropics.

But tonight the port was dead. Skiffs slumped in their moorings like snoozing dogs; the boardwalk's everyday stench of fried shrimp was a faint memory. No rowdy sailors exchanging tall tales while their crews tied off along the dock, no children poking at the strange things in the tide pools of Stony Beach. No dogs barking joyfully, just to bark.

Again, the culprit was the Undertow. Only a dimwit would dare stay near the water when it hit. Even now, the black swirling clouds whistled in the bay, gathering steam as they galloped toward the shore.

Fidelia quickly tied off the half-sunken *Platypus,* then glanced around the eerily empty port. No sign of her father's pointy black beard. No sound of her mother's happy, goose-like laugh.

They should be here by now.

She ran up onto the bridge.

The port narrowed into a canal that flowed through the island as its main road for transportation. The water streamed along the high street, past the shops, past the gabled houses, which all had small white wooden docks in lieu of front porches. Above the mouth of the canal was an arching stone bridge, the highest point in the bay. From here, she could see the entire harbor.

No *Egg.*

Her heart thumped. The Undertow was getting closer. She could hear the growl of its thunder, feel the air around her practically seize up in anticipation of the incoming chaos.

They weren't still out on the water, were they?

She pulled out her binoculars and scanned everything—the boardwalk, the beach, the chandler's warehouse, the gate to the shipyard. The sky dimmed even darker; the wind howled even louder. Fidelia wrapped her arms around her thin frame, scooting along the stones of the bridge slowly, carefully, to keep from being blown over.

On the boardwalk, rowdy laughter surged from the Book and Bottle. Fidelia watched the wooden sign flap in the wind, the amber glow of the pub's windows shining like beacons.

Maybe she should go inside and wait. Maybe if she ordered three bowls of Shipwreck Stew, her parents would appear. Summoned by shellfish.

She opened the door, and the warm air inside the pub sent prickles along her chilled skin. One more look back at the beach, and when she saw nothing, she slipped inside the pub, the wind slamming the door shut behind her.

Come on, Mom and Dad, where are you? she thought. *Nice hot soup at the Book and Bottle, if only you'll walk through the door.*

Every sea dog who came through Arborley Island considered the Book and Bottle to be a home on dry land. Always a fire burning in the hearth. Always room for another seat at the bar. Always a fiddle or two filling the lulls between conversations. Always a better fish story than yours.

Always, always more ale.

Inside, the pub was gritty but cozy. Stale cigarette smoke

hung in the air, thick as a curtain. The cedar beams in the ceiling crissed and crossed like the staves of a woven basket. Chandeliers flickered their primitive candlelight, providing just enough illumination to see if your mug was empty.

Fidelia took a table near the window. The docks might have been deserted, but the Book and Bottle was busier than a reef during a feeding frenzy; at least two dozen sailors teetered on stools around her, drinks in hand.

"Fernalia!" a sailor slurred, and shook her hand with his own, sticky from ale. It was Ratface, the whiskered, windburned captain of a cocoa ship called the *Anemone*. "Join us for a drink!"

"I'm only eleven," Fidelia reminded him.

"Then let's get you some milk." He belched, pounding the counter. "Barkeep! Some milk for Quail and refills all around, on me!" The pub erupted in cheers.

Fidelia ignored the drunken buffoons and took out her observation book. Her hands were desperate to stay busy. She loosely sketched an outline of Grizzle's body—huge and barreling, but compact as a bullet as it shot through the water.

Five gills or seven? She closed her eyes, picturing the sleek shark. Five. All athletic breeds of sharks had five gills, and Grizzle was certainly athletic.

"Where are Ida and Art?" Ratface asked. "Out counting the hairs on a walrus's belly?"

Before Fidelia could respond, a group of sailors crashed into the pub. A woman limped between them—Captain Beagle, of the *Honey Fox*, a gash on her forehead streaming with blood.

"Get her a chair, mates!" someone said.

"And a clean rag! She's dripping on the hardwood," someone else said.

"Blimey, Beagle." Ratface guffawed between sips of ale. "Did the Undertow crack your melon?"

Captain Beagle let her shipmates plop her down on a stool and drained a whole mug before answering breathlessly. "Not the Undertow. . . . Pirates."

The whole pub seemed to wince.

"Pirates." Ratface wiped the foam from his top lip and snarled. "Those bold bastards. As if the Undertow isn't deadly enough."

Fidelia sat up taller, her ears alert. Something inside her opened, a chasm of panic deepening. Already the Undertow loomed in the bay, but now pirates, within striking distance? *Just walk through the door,* she bade her parents silently. *Hurry, hurry, so I know you're safe.*

Like the sharks that fed on the cod around Arborley,

pirates preyed on the cargo ships that sailed to and from port. They pilfered cocoa beans, tropical fruits, and expensive sailing supplies like rope and canvas. Occasionally they took a whole ship at gunpoint, and the poor sailors were left to drown or swim for shore—if they were lucky. Better than being taken captive.

Ida Quail had a run-in with pirates once, when she was crossing over from the mainland, returning home after a symposium on marine mammals. The pirates let her go once they realized that the *Platypus* had nothing to steal except empty mermaid purses and red algae specimens.

"We were heading home after our last run." Captain Beagle flinched as she pressed a cloth full of ice to her forehead. "They hit us just before the rain came. They took it all—every last bean." Most of the sailors were too drunk to stir sugar into coffee, but they reacted to every part of the captain's story as if it had been their own captain, their own ship, their own mates.

Fidelia only half listened. Through the window, her eyes roved the beach, the docks, the water, over and over, scanning like sonar . . . *Mom and Dad, please! Where the devil ray are you?*

"One of their cannons blew through the rigging. Sent the boom right into my noggin." Captain Beagle gestured to the wound on her forehead, which was finally beginning to clot.

"Where are they now?" Another sailor frowned, his hand finding the pistol at his belt. "Should we sail out and meet them? Give them a warm Arborley welcome?"

"Don't bother," Captain Beagle said. "The horizon's blacker than a coal chute. Let the Undertow take care of them."

"It'll eat their ship for dinner," someone else piped in.

Fidelia bounced her legs up and down beneath the table, a little nervous soft-shoe. The *Egg*'s helm was still gummy—why hadn't she fixed it this morning? How could she be so careless, to let her parents take the submarine when there were still so many kinks to work out? All confidence in her machinery drained out of her.

Ratface was trying very hard to look at something out the window. His whole face squinted like a raisin—because of the distance or because of his drunkenness, Fidelia didn't know and didn't care . . . until he said, "Say, Quail. Isn't that your submersible doohickey out in the water?"

Fidelia pushed back her chair so fast, it tipped over. "Where?" She scrambled to the window, forehead pressed against the glass.

There was the *Egg*, stranded in the shallows of Stony Beach, waves lapping at the aqua-blue metal.

"Mom!" she cried, and everyone in the Book and Bottle stopped talking. "Dad!" She bolted out the door, down the boardwalk, and across the bridge.

Back outside, the elements seemed to conspire against her. Wind shrieked in her ear; rain blew sideways, tilting her as she ran. The closer she came, the tighter her gut clenched with the sickening wrongness of it all — the *Egg*, stuck on the shore like a beached whale, porthole window crookedly facing the sky.

She crunched over the pebbles of Stony Beach, the storm throwing sand against her cheeks. When she finally hit the cold water, her breath deserted her.

The *Egg* was barely recognizable as a submarine. It was folded in on itself, dented into a twisted metal mess. The aqua paint was scratched away in long lines, as if a gruesome creature had dragged its claws across the exterior — or as if the *Egg* had been tossed mercilessly against the rocks and coral of the seabed. Wrenched from its hinges, the hatch door lay useless in the incoming tide.

The rain fell harder, but she waded closer. The *Egg*'s cabin was a shambles. Files were emptied of their contents, which were strewn all over Stony Beach like a soggy paper-work snowstorm. Drips of seawater clung to the keypad of command buttons. The dull sound of static still echoed from the radio, the receiver swinging on its wire.

"Mom," Fidelia whispered, trembling. "Dad."

"You there! Girl!" A constable in a black trench coat and galoshes flashed the orange lights of his patrol boat from the canal. "Quail, is that you? What the blazes are you doing? Get inside!"

"My parents!" she wailed.

"Are you mad?" the constable said. "It's the Undertow! Now hustle!"

"Not until I find Mom and Dad!" She charged into the water, nostrils flaring, eyes stinging with tears. Her mind jumped from thought to thought like frogs on lily pads: What happened to the *Egg*? Where were they? Swimming back to shore or being swept farther and farther out to sea . . . ?

The constable brought his boat out of the canal, where the submarine lay. "They were in this thing? Didn't they know the storm was coming?"

Fidelia stood there, cold water biting her calves. "It was tagging day." The words barely seeped out of her—suddenly her voice was missing, too. She had been the one who insisted they stay out longer than they should have. "How close is the storm?" Ida had asked, trusting Fidelia's eyes, Fidelia's judgment.

And Fidelia had pushed, pushed to the very edge of the storm's mercy. . . .

Was this her fault?

Black waves reached like hands, farther and farther up the shore. The constable pointed at the town. "You can't be out here."

Fidelia's feet didn't budge. "I have to find them!" Was she the only one who thought they should be charging into the sea, Undertow be damned? Searching every reef, every ripple?

The constable sighed. "We'll do everything we can, Quail. There's nothing else for you to do but wait somewhere safe."

But Fidelia refused, and finally the constable motioned for someone to come and forcibly remove her—another constable, perhaps? Or one of the sailors from the Book and Bottle? Fidelia never saw whose arms linked under hers, dragging her across the shingle beach to the bridge as she kicked for freedom, shrieking the entire way.

The arms placed her on the edge of the bridge, legs dangling over the canal, and left her alone, rain soaking her to the bones. There she sat, and she watched.

Watched more constables surround the *Egg* in the distance, like a swarm of flies investigating a bloated carcass. Watched the water rush higher and higher up the beach.

She wasn't sure how long she was there—the sounds of the storm drowned everything else out. It was just the rush of the canal, and the crash of waves against the rocks, and the roar of the Undertow . . .

"Fidelia?" A soft voice somehow cut through the pollution of noise. "I'm here to collect you." Ida Quail's sister, younger by ten years, stood on the bridge under a pale blue umbrella.

If Fidelia was a broomstick, Aunt Julia was a feather duster—wispy, somber, with frail-looking limbs. Fidelia had always thought her aunt looked like she'd escaped from an oil painting—too delicate for reality. She, like Fidelia, was bespectacled, but while Fidelia's glasses were square and bold, Aunt Julia's were subtle, round peach frames.

Fidelia's throat tightened. "Mom and Dad . . ." But she couldn't say it. If she didn't say it, maybe it wasn't real.

A lock of Aunt Julia's hair blew free from its chignon; she caught it and immediately tucked it back into place.

"Oh, Fidelia, darling." She pulled her niece off the edge of the bridge and into a hug.

"We have to—Why isn't anyone—?" Fidelia stammered frantically against Aunt Julia's collarbone.

As if in response, a deafening gust of wind pushed across the bridge, nearly strong enough to carry Aunt Julia away. Fidelia sobbed. She wouldn't be convincing anyone to rally a search party; even the constables were scrambling back to the boardwalk, their trench coats blowing behind them like great rubbery wings.

"Shh." Aunt Julia patted Fidelia's head. "Nothing to do now but get out of the storm. Let's go dry off and we'll wait—"

"Wait for what?" Fidelia pushed herself free from Aunt Julia's embrace. "For Mom and Dad to wash onto shore like horseshoe crabs?"

Aunt Julia blanched at the image, but Fidelia couldn't bring herself to care. "We should be scouring the beach! We should be searching every rock and reef in the bay!" Her aunt gently took her elbow and guided her down the bridge and into a waiting canal boat.

She slouched on the back bench while the paddler pushed the boat down the canal. Her teeth chattered. "They're okay," she said, mostly to herself. "They're marine biologists, right? They're probably fine, aren't they?" The words came out in circles, overlapping themselves like ripples in a puddle.

Aunt Julia's chin trembled. "I suppose—anything is possible."

Fidelia's mind turned over the details of the situation, hunting for a crack, a burst of light, an answer.

Fact: Dr. and Dr. Quail had last been seen approximately one hour ago, in the southeast quadrant of Arborley Bay.

Fact: Dr. and Dr. Quail were navigating the submarine—powered by an electric motor and propellers.

Fact: Fidelia had refilled the *Egg*'s gas tank this morning.

So where were they?

Did they escape out the hatch with snorkels? Were they treading water? Were they clinging to the cliffs on the other side of the island?

Last year the Quails had published a topographical map of Arborley Sea. They'd charted every dip, every ridge, every detail of the seafloor around Arborley Island—but maybe they had missed a cave for their map. Yes, an underwater cave, one of those rare ones that kept a pocket of oxygen beneath the ocean . . . And the Quails could be hiding inside, waiting for someone to track them down and rescue them.

But even as Fidelia finished the hypothesis in her mind, the unlikeliness of it—the futility of such thoughts—overwhelmed her, smothering her like a swell at high tide, and her thoughts trickled into silence.

So there was truly nothing she could do.

Fidelia curled her toes inside her boots. Her fingers squeezed the skin on her forearms. Every part of her clutched to anything available, anything that could ground her. Secure her.

Tears filled her eyes. As the canal boat floated into the city, the shape of the *Egg* blurred in the distance, an aqua speck on the beach. Her poor crushed submarine—months of work had gone into its creation, all undone in a single evening.

And the other things she had lost tonight . . .

The last thing Fidelia saw before the canal angled away from the sea was a twilight wave, barreling and sparkling before it was crushed by the darkness of the Undertow. Somewhere in the water, Grizzle lurked, untagged, untraceable.

Lost forever.

When the *Mother Dog* sailed, it didn't just cut through the water—the sea humbly parted itself for the flagship of the Queen's Own Navy.

The forty-gun frigate proudly protected Her Majesty's coasts from any crime or tomfoolery. It was top of the line, built from live oak and scrubbed to godliness—the finest vessel in the nine seas. The masts were sanded so smooth, one would think they had never met a storm. Gold writing on the stern spelled its name in flowery script.

The commander of its voyages wiped a white-gloved finger along the rail. *Not a speck of dust or brine,* he gloated. *Not on my ship.*

Admiral Percy J. Bridgewater's head was the shape and color of an oversize beet, with a hay-bristle mustache and two tiny rodent's eyes that were always roaming, always judging, behind a pair of small round spectacles. Silver piping ran along the seams of all the naval officers' cobalt-blue uniforms; Admiral Bridgewater's own silver piping was stretched to capacity around his massive girth. Forty years he had served in the Queen's Own Navy, and he bore those years proudly—crow's feet earned in the second civil war, frown lines along his jowls from the takeover at Jolitrou . . . And the deepest crease in his face, a wrinkle in the center of his forehead . . . The last ten years had carved that particular beauty into his skin. A full accounting of his records as admiral, right in his flesh.

The *Mother Dog* was finishing its three-week inspection of the cocoa route. So far, two pirate ships had been impeded, the wicked thieves clapped in irons below in the *Mother Dog's* dark, drippy hold. The pirates' boodle—sea chests heaping with gold medallions, precious jewels, and pearls—was carefully stashed in the admiral's quarters. All of it would be returned to Her Majesty—after a private accounting by Admiral Bridgewater, of course.

A nice, clean sweep—Admiral Bridgewater should have been satisfied. Any day when pirates were removed from the bounding main should be a good day. But those weren't the right pirates.

The faded green of land finally unfolded across the horizon, and the naval officers exhaled with relief when they thought their commander wasn't looking. But the admiral missed nothing. They would be permitted a week of shore leave, and then it would be back aboard the *Mother Dog* for another voyage. Shore leave was the only antidote for the difficult life of a navy man—a chance to experience hot showers, shoe shines, delicious stove-cooked meals chased by cream-filled desserts, the pleasurable company of a fashionable young lady at the opera.

Admiral Bridgewater found no need for it. While his officers gallivanted around the port like half-starved animals released from their cages, he stayed locked in his office on the flagship, poring over maps and sea charts by flickering lamplight.

Soon, he vowed. *Soon I'll have him.*

"Veer west when we come in range of the harbor," he ordered a lieutenant whose name he didn't know and never would. "It's tax day for the *Miranda.*"

The *Miranda,* a tidy little sloop with faded sails, waited at anchor just offshore, placid ripples sparkling blue around its waterline.

Admiral Bridgewater sneered at the puny *Miranda,* at its sea-warped beams, its wrinkled canvas. His officers angled the *Mother Dog* until it was parallel to the lesser vessel, close enough that the admiral could smell the earthy tropical dirt still clinging to the cargo of cocoa beans aboard the sloop.

"Ahoy, Admiral!" The scraggly captain of the *Miranda* waved his greasy cap. "Lovely day we're having, wouldn't you say? The boys were thinking we'd come ashore and find spring blossoms, not autumn leaves—"

"Small talk is for small people," Admiral Bridgewater cut in. "Do you have my payment?"

The captain swallowed. "We have . . . most of it, Admiral."

"Most?"

The captain held up a bulging jute bag to show the admiral—half the usual payment. "We'll have the rest to you by the first week of March—"

"March?" Admiral Bridgewater frowned. "That's six months from now. A trip to the tropics is a week's sail, at most."

"But—the Undertow!" The captain looked around at his men for backup. "It's due to strike any day!"

Admiral Bridgewater pulled off his white glove and examined his fingernails. "Yes, I suppose the weaker seamen of the world can't be expected to brave a little rain and wind. Very well," he said with a sigh. "Officer, write down that the *Miranda* now owes us three hundred blue notes."

"Three hundred?" the captain sputtered. "But—but that's double the usual amount!"

"A lesson in punctuality," Admiral Bridgewater said. "Lest you think I will ever tolerate this again."

The captain glowered, but motioned for his boatswain to toss a grapple hook with rope pulleys—it easily caught onto the *Mother Dog*'s railing. He hung the jute bag of cash on the rope and the naval officers began hauling it over.

"May I remind you," Admiral Bridgewater said, "that my royally bestowed task is to catch pirates and bring them to the gallows. Nothing more. Your personal protection in open waters is none of my concern . . . unless you pay to make it my concern."

The jute bag now dangled above the water, between the two ships.

"If you provide half the cost, I can guarantee only half the safety," Admiral Bridgewater continued.

The jute bag was nearly to the *Mother Dog*—just a few more feet.

"And pirates," Admiral Bridgewater said, "the rotten, blackened souls, lurk in every stretch of the nine seas, waiting until your guard is down—"

A porthole on the *Miranda* suddenly flew open. A

black-haired man poked out of the hold, a lit tallow candle in his hand.

"Merrick!" A fleck of spit flew from Admiral Bridgewater's mouth and landed on his impeccably clean railing. "I should have known you didn't really hang in San Sebastian! That corpse didn't stink half as bad as yours would have!" Behind him, the crew scrambled, preparing the guns.

"How'd he get in there?" The captain of the *Miranda* cried, his men around him as bewildered as he was.

"My dear Bilgewater!" Merrick saluted from the porthole, the candle's flame illuminating the laughter in his steel-blue eyes. "Still robbing the good sailors of the cocoa route, are we? And to think—you call *me* the pirate!"

"Surrender now, you dung-munching varmint, and I'll make sure none of your body parts are left for the krill," Admiral Bridgewater said.

Merrick reached for the rope between the ships with one hand, steadying the jute bag.

Admiral Bridgewater narrowed his eyes. "You're not a pirate. You're a devil. A dead one, at that. Shoot him," he commanded.

The *Mother Dog*'s swivel guns were aimed and fired.

Grapeshot peppered the side of the *Miranda,* narrowly missing Merrick, who ducked back into the hold.

"Hey!" the captain of the *Miranda* shouted. "That's my ship! Take it easy!"

Merrick popped back out the porthole like a gopher and grinned. He lifted his candle, higher and higher, until the orange flame kissed the rope where the jute bag dangled.

"Put that fire out!" Admiral Bridgewater shrieked. "Now, I command!"

But the fire danced along the rope until it reached the jute bag, which was not full of money at all, but full of explosives.

The noise was terrific; the flash of white light and rich blue smoke was even better. As the string of blasts filled the air, the officers and crew of the *Mother Dog* and the sailors on the *Miranda* threw themselves onto their decks, ears plugged, protecting themselves from the onslaught.

Admiral Bridgewater himself dove onto his hot water bottle of a stomach, his nose pressed against the very boards on which his boots had just walked. Bits of debris from the firecrackers nailed him on the head; his rage was now well past the boiling point. "Get him!" he ordered. "Take down the whole ship if you have to!"

The naval officers and crewmen staggered to their feet, blinded by the bright flash of the fireworks, and gunners stumbled toward their stations. Admiral Bridgewater watched them with his top lip curled—a deck full of flopping, foolish minnows, and he the only shark.

He'd shoot the pirate himself.

Seizing the railing, he pulled himself up, then reloaded a swivel gun and aimed it right between Merrick's eyes.

But Merrick blew him a kiss and jumped ship, diving into the waves. The admiral's shot hit the railing of the *Miranda,* sending splinters of wood flying.

"Blast!" Admiral Bridgewater said.

The white foam from Merrick's splash dissipated, shifting back to blue.

"He's got to come up for air sometime," said a lieutenant by way of reassurance. "We'll get him then."

Admiral Bridgewater waited, squinting at the water with his piggy little eyes, fantasizing about the scoundrel's eventual surrender—emerging from the sea half-drowned, staring into the endless black tunnels of the *Mother Dog*'s guns.

Any second now.

Instead of a soggy pirate gasping for air, an entire ship flew out from behind the *Miranda.* A sloop of war, embodying speed and nimbleness—Merrick the Monstrous's beloved seacraft. If it were an animal, it would be something muscular, compact: a sleek fish, fast and fanged—and it made a lumbering elephant out of the *Mother Dog*.

Merrick was already climbing a line that dangled from the stern of the ship, reeling himself onto the deck like a marlin winding its own fishing rod.

Admiral Bridgewater could barely get the words out. "Get him! Get him now!"

The *Mother Dog*'s guns fired, but the lithe sloop of war rode the waves like a bucking stallion, and so the shots sank deep into the ship's boards instead of landing in the pirate's rib cage.

The admiral aimed at Merrick's quartermaster, who rolled an eight-pounder into the ship's cannon and chased it with powder. His shot just missed one of her tattooed fore-arms, but she chortled and fired back with her flintlock, dinging the railing right in front of Admiral Bridgewater's belt buckle.

"Your aim's gotten worse, old man!" she called. "Did our little fireworks show leave you cross-eyed? Or did you come out of your mother that way?" She fired again, and this time her shot would have hit the admiral square in the forehead, if he hadn't lurched sideways.

Cannons exploded; the *Mother Dog*'s twelve-pound balls crunched the pirates' wooden spars, sending splinters flying. Merrick's crew fired their own cast-iron howitzers and took out the naval ship's mainsail.

"Surrender!" Admiral Bridgewater said. "The *Jewel*'s no match for the *Mother Dog*!"

Merrick took up the helm, shaking away the excess seawater from his hair. "No, Bridgewater—your little peanut brain is no match for mine!" The pirates' ship cut across the water, making for open sea while the *Mother Dog* moved slower than a fat, expectant goose.

"Fire at will!" Admiral Bridgewater screeched. "Fire, fire! Blast it all, don't let them get away!"

Gunners reloaded and aimed the cannons, but by the time they fired, it was too late. The pirates were out of range.

"Get this sorry lumberyard moving!" The admiral was absolutely steaming. "What are you waiting for?"

There was a sickening crunch.

"He's poured molten lead into the rudder housing, Admiral! We'll only go in circles."

"And look, sir. His squibs did some damage to our mainsail." Above them, the *Mother Dog*'s once perfectly crisp main canvas was now tattered as widow's lace.

"Admiral!" An officer ran across the deck, holding one of the liberated sea chests under his arm. "They're all empty, sir! He's taken the treasure—I don't know how he did it—"

"No one knows how the devil does his work," Admiral Bridgewater muttered, "only that he must be stopped."

By now the *Jewel* was a fly on the horizon. The admiral could have wrung his own neck for failing to squash it when he had the chance.

"Chip the rudder free," came his order, short and clipped. "Get my flagship back to port. Row it in if you have to."

"What about the pirate, sir?" an officer dared to press.

Admiral Bridgewater stared past the *Miranda* at the water. "Merrick never keeps his head in the sand for too long. He's too brash. He'll poke out when he's bored, and we'll be ready for him."

It is tempting to mourn the loss of gills as the human species evolved from amphibian water-dwellers to bipedal locomotives. Gills would have allowed us to reside in the glorious sea as equals to such wonders as the mimicking octopus (see fig. 1) or the gulper eel (see fig. 3). Instead, we may celebrate the depths of human passion and innovation, which push us to find new ways to join in the grand dance, even as we're landlocked.

—*Exploring an Underwater Fairyland* by Dr. and Dr. Quail

Fidelia creaked open her eyes. A smell had pulled her out of sleep, one so pungent her tongue felt coated.

She rolled onto her stomach, and her pillow meowed.

Aunt Julia's fat orange cat grumpily repositioned himself into a fuzzy doughnut. He had been made to share his sofa with her, so she gave him an apologetic scratch behind his ears as she blinked the sleep out of her eyes.

Her observation book was on the windowsill, the pen capped. She hadn't opened it in six weeks.

She stretched, her long arms nearly grazing the loft's low ceiling when she stood. Out a tiny round window, everything was blurred without her glasses on, but she knew what she would have seen — the harbor, a miniaturized version of itself in the distance. If this were a warm-weathered day, ships would be casting off, heading to the tropics for a haul of cocoa beans. The sun would be shining through the leaves of the poplars. Arborley's port would be bustling—a healthy, balanced, thriving ecosystem.

But as long as the Undertow still prowled in the bay, it would remain cold and rainy, the sky dark. An island in hibernation.

She slipped into a sage green crepe dress and a pair of thick gray stockings and laced up her boots. Her glasses were folded on the table; she put them on as she walked. A last glance out the window, and the gray-blue ocean came into focus. Once upon a time, she would have stayed at the windowsill, nose glued to the glass, enchanted by the waves, marveling at how the sea changed with every second. The tide bringing in new molecules of water by the gallons, the old water washing away. Always something new to see in the ocean. Something new to love.

This time, she didn't stare. She saw, she blinked, and she moved along.

The acrid smell got stronger when she passed through the kitchen. A pot of lumpy green soup bubbled on Aunt Julia's single-burner stove, a large enough batch to last for several of their future meals. Aunt Julia was nothing if not a well-organized, red-blooded planner.

Unlike Fidelia's mother, Ida, Aunt Julia's big sister, who'd had room in her brain for the entire sea jellies phylum but never remembered to stock the pantry or make a meal plan. She'd work until sundown, then burst into the kitchen with mad, hungry eyes and holler, "I'm starving! Arthur, are you going to magically make some dinner appear, or shall we get Shipwreck Stew again?"

Fidelia had forgotten how Shipwreck Stew tasted. She'd forgotten how all good food tasted—Aunt Julia's cuisine was best consumed with nose plugged and breathing stifled.

As she marched down the stairs, she finger-combed her ratty hair. Aunt Julia made Fidelia scrub her head with a violet-scented hair tonic every night, but Fidelia still stank like fish guts. As if it had permeated her very soul.

Arborley Library was a three-story building made of white marble bricks, the largest, cleanest building on the island—and it was filled to the brim with books.

Here, Aunt Julia was librarian supreme. She ordered books and assisted patrons. She shelved. She reshelved. She cataloged, repaired, and circulated—a massive task for a single person. Occasionally she attended big-city library conferences on the mainland—well, she used to. Aunt Julia's trips to conferences had halted now that Fidelia had come to live with her.

The vast collection was housed floor-to-ceiling in the bottom three levels, but books also trickled up the stairs into the loft, which was Aunt Julia's living space. It was teeny, but tidy. Books stacked up to the chair rails along the walls, books scattered across the kitchen table, books stacked next to the coffee and dried herring in the pantry. The loft was cramped enough without these literary intrusions, but to Aunt Julia, they were welcome trespassers.

For Fidelia, the loft served as a reminder of how different life at sea — life with her parents — had been. A life that felt like a hundred years ago. Aunt Julia was patient, but she frowned when Fidelia accidentally dribbled her milk onto a book, or forgot to ask to be excused from a meal, or talked too much about dolphins.

There was no one on the third floor of the library (periodicals, biographies). Fidelia went down another flight of stairs.

Every morning when she woke, she helped Aunt Julia with library duties until dinnertime, and then the two of them usually spent the evening in silence, reading. She hadn't put so much as a toe in the ocean since that night. She hadn't even left the library.

Except for the funeral.

Fidelia liked organizing the catalog cards best — drawer after drawer of entries to be sorted, alphabetized, and filed according to Aunt Julia's stringent system. Time flew past when she was at the catalog cabinet. It kept her mind occupied. Distracted.

No Aunt Julia on the second floor (atlases, maps, general nonfiction).

A man made eye contact with Fidelia—one of the chandlers, from the warehouse near the harbor. Someone from her old life. Could she duck behind a bookcase? No, he had already spotted her. He waved as the gap between them closed.

"Fidelia . . ." he said.

She pressed her lips together, her eyes finding a scuff on the hardwood floor.

"It's sure been quiet around the boardwalk," he said.

Fidelia rubbed the toe of her boot along the scuff. The scuff only got bigger.

"We—well, we miss seeing you around, kid." The man rubbed the back of his neck. "Nothing's been the same since—"

"I'm sorry," Fidelia cut in. "I need to find my aunt Julia."

"Of course," he said. "Just wanted to—"

But she didn't stick around to hear what he wanted. She ran down the last stairway two steps at a time.

All of Arborley wanted to talk to her, it seemed. Tell her

how sorry they were, reminisce about her parents—reminding her over and over again that they were gone and never coming back.

Here in the library, she was safe. Here, she didn't have to talk about it—or think about that awful night.

On that night, just as the blackest hours began splintering into a deep tangerine sunrise, there had been a knock on the door. The knock Fidelia had been dreading.

Fidelia heard only snippets of the conversation between the constable and Aunt Julia: "Dragged the bay and recovered the bodies . . . Next of kin . . . Death certificates will be issued. . . . Absolute tragedy . . ."

Then Aunt Julia had shut the door and held on to Fidelia, and the two of them had collapsed as one, wrung-out and raw-faced, crying too hard to sleep.

Fidelia finally found Aunt Julia on the main level (sciences, histories, medical texts). The librarian was halfway up a ladder, stocking encyclopedias onto a polished bookshelf with loud thumps. Her Oxford heels pointed straight out to both sides, like a ballerina in first position.

"There you are," Aunt Julia said without turning around. "Did you sleep all right?"

"Fine." A lie—for weeks, her nights had been the same. Endless tossing, dreamless sleep, except for two faces with dark hair and identical black glasses, floating in a suspended sea of fog.

"You slept through breakfast." *Thump, thump.* "There's turtle soup in the loft."

"I'm not hungry." Another lie. But if the smell of that soup was any indication of its taste, she'd rather deal with the groans of an empty stomach.

"Fidelia, darling . . ." *Thump, thump.* "We need to discuss something. Something important." Aunt Julia spoke so softly, as if someone had used a damper pedal on her vocal cords. "It's about your parents' estate."

Fidelia waited. Was that her heart that thumped, or an encyclopedia landing on the shelf?

"I just received a letter," Aunt Julia explained. "Your parents left you a respectable sum of money, which will be yours when you come of age. The house will be turned over to the bank and auctioned off to new owners, but all the things inside the house . . ." She paused, swallowing. "Their collection has been left to the university."

Fidelia's jaw tightened. To the university? "But . . . but . . ." she stammered.

"Your parents funded their studies with research grants," Aunt Julia said. "So legally, all their findings, all the equipment—everything belongs to the school. The university is sending someone tomorrow to collect it. They've asked that we make sure everything is packed and ready for pickup."

Fidelia tried to picture it—the Quail family home without any microscopes, without sea stars scattered across the dining table. The garden shed without its mishmash of fishing nets and spare spools of line. It would look empty, lifeless. It would look *normal.*

"We'll walk over this afternoon," Aunt Julia said. "After we've finished sorting the returns."

Her father's set of rocks covered in mustard lichen, proudly displayed in the foyer. Her mother's assemblage of molted lobster shells, lined up like antique suits of armor next to the tea tins on a shelf in the kitchen. Things that had been in the house since Fidelia was brought home as a baby.

"Are you all right?" Aunt Julia stepped down the ladder's rungs. "Fidelia?"

Fidelia scrunched her toes inside her boots to keep from crying. She pointed to a gap on the shelf. "You're missing a volume."

Aunt Julia blinked at the sudden switch of topics. "It's been lost for months." She turned back to the shelf. "A library runs on efficiency, you know. All books must be returned on time, to their proper homes on the shelves . . ."

Fidelia wasn't listening. She had picked up Aunt Julia's clipboard to see the title of the missing book, just in case she'd shelved it in the wrong section—

Exploring an Underwater Fairyland by Dr. and Dr. Quail.

"I'm in the mood for a nice fruit pie for dinner," Aunt Julia continued, oblivious of the fact that to her niece, the earth had stopped spinning. "Perhaps after we're finished at the house, we'll stop by the vendor for some lemons."

Fidelia reached out and ran her fingers along the names on the clipboard.

Something inside her pulsed, threatening to crackle.

Aunt Julia plucked the clipboard from Fidelia's hands like a seagull plucking a fish from the water. "I need to reorder some things for the catalog," she said. "And we need to get some food in you." Gently, she took Fidelia's shoulder and tried to steer her away.

"I'm not hungry," Fidelia said again, and this time it was the truth; all the soup in the world wouldn't make this cold stone in her belly go away.

But Aunt Julia guided her niece toward the stairs, and Fidelia climbed them listlessly.

* * *

At the kitchen table, Aunt Julia placed a bowl of turtle soup and a platter of honey biscuits in front of Fidelia. "Eat," she implored.

Fidelia bit down on a honey biscuit and immediately regretted it; the thing was harder than a mollusk shell. She stirred the sickly green soup, her spoon clinking the side of the bowl.

After a moment, Aunt Julia said, "There's something else I wanted to bring up. I wondered . . . I wondered how you might feel about a change."

Fidelia watched the steam rise from the soup in curlicues. "A change?"

"A move." Her aunt dabbed at her mouth with a napkin. "To the mainland."

Fidelia's heart fell, anchoring itself in her stomach. She opened her mouth, then closed it again, like a landed fish, but no words came out.

"We can come back to Arborley to visit, of course —"

"But . . . But Arborley is home," Fidelia said. Hot tears filled her eyes, fogging her glasses — how could Aunt Julia even talk about moving away?

Aunt Julia gripped the edge of the table with both hands. "Don't you see their faces everywhere?" she whispered, and Fidelia's throat tightened. "In every shop window? Every cup of tea, every book? I see them every-where I look. . . ." She gazed at Fidelia, and Fidelia finished the thought for her: *I see them in you, Fidelia. In my own niece. It hurts to even look at you.*

How do you think I *feel?* Fidelia wanted to cry out. *I look down at my hands and they're my dad's hands—long-fingered, knobbly-knuckled. I touch my hair and it's my mother's, and she's twisting it back in one of her braids. I'm a Quail. It hurts to even* be *me.*

"Think about it," Aunt Julia said. "You could go to a new school and make friends—friends your own age," she said. "It's not natural for a young lady to be friends with sail-ors and ship brokers and . . . and *barkeeps.*"

"What about the library?" Fidelia asked.

"I've already secured a position at a library on the main-land. You can still help me with the daily tasks," she added quickly, as if this were Fidelia's concern.

Fidelia had been to the mainland enough times. The architecture was impressive enough, she supposed—a sky-line that was glorious to see silhouetted from the ocean as one approached the port. But that was where her affections stopped. On the mainland, roads didn't end in shorelines—they didn't end at all, but kept winding farther and farther around one another in a confusing web. No canals, no shipyards, no seafood. Towns were surrounded by more towns, rooftops as far as the eye could see.

She'd be landlocked. A fish, drowning on the sand.

"Fidelia . . . we need a new start," Aunt Julia said. "To get away from all these — these memories." She waved her hand as she said this, as if Fidelia could so easily wipe her mind clean of her parents, her old life. Like erasing a chalkboard.

"But what about our work?" Fidelia said. "All our research is here, in Arborley."

Aunt Julia took the bowls to the sink and scrubbed them clean. "There is no more work. The collection is going to the university, remember?"

"It was my work, too," Fidelia challenged, and for the first time since that horrible night, she let herself think of Grizzle. His long, torpedo body; his eyes, black buttons; the five gills slit into his rubbery skin; his jagged smile. A shark still waiting to be tagged, and tracked, and named. Her spine tingled.

"Ida and Arthur were trained, accredited scientists." Aunt Julia's mouth was a long, serious line. "You are just a girl."

Fidelia squeezed her fists into tight little balls so she wouldn't explode.

Just a girl, whose gadgets rivaled anything you'd find

in *Adventures in Science Engineering*. Just a girl, who had dissected her first guppy when she was two. Just a girl, who six weeks ago discovered a new species of shark. If she gave up now, she'd always be a footnote to the late Dr. and Dr. Quail.

"Listen," Aunt Julia said carefully. "You can still continue your research from the mainland, if you like. Science isn't only about field studies, after all. We'll order some new science books for the catalog—"

"No! No more books! Stop trying to make everything better with books!" Fidelia pushed away from the table, her chair falling back with a clatter. The fat cat meowed in protest.

Fidelia loved books—of course she did. But there were some things a book couldn't give her. The smell of the sea, salt burning in her nose. The chill of spray on her cheeks. The sound of whale pods harmonizing as they floated, shifting continents in the watery blue.

"Can't you see I'm trying to keep you safe?" Aunt Julia burst out. "To lose Ida and Arthur is bad enough. To lose you—" Her voice broke. She sank into a kitchen chair, covering her face with her hands, and wept.

Fidelia held her breath until her own tears ebbed and the lump in her throat melted. "I don't want a new life," she said. "I want my old one."

Aunt Julia wiped her damp cheeks with her wrists. "Well, it's gone."

Fidelia walked to the windowsill. Her observation book was still there, still closed. She touched it—a layer of dust came off with her fingers.

Ashes to ashes, and dust to dust . . . The minister's words from the funeral came into Fidelia's mind uninvited. She remembered all the people who had come to lay the Quails to rest—scholars and amateur biologists, bird-watching hobbyists, and the sailors . . .

The sailors. Their heads had looked so tiny without their nautical caps—oily hair smoothed back in respect, sea-battered faces twisted in grief when they trailed past the caskets.

Sailors who had taught Fidelia how to spit-shine her boots, sailors who slipped fragrant oranges into her hands on her birthday. Surrogate aunts and uncles, all of them.

And she'd been avoiding them, hiding in the library like a moray in a reef, because she knew if she looked in a sailor's eyes, she'd feel that sudden coldness at both her sides without her parents there—without Arthur cracking his salty jokes, Ida laughing like a happy goose.

Without the two of them, did Arborley even feel like home?

"I think," Fidelia said, "I'll go to the house and start packing." She tucked her observation book and binoculars into her bag, a habit as old as she was.

"I'll come with you," Aunt Julia said. "Let me grab my umbrella."

"No." Fidelia slipped her bag over her shoulders, right in its place—crossing her body like a banner.

"You're upset—"

"I want to go by myself." She let Aunt Julia look at her face. "Please."

"Be home for dinner," Aunt Julia finally said.

Then Fidelia turned and ran down all three flights of stairs, and when she pushed open the library doors, the scent of the ocean hit her like a riptide, sudden and violent. She swallowed the sea air, a frigid shock to her lungs. Her quarrel with Aunt Julia faded to a hidden alcove in her mind as she headed through the silent town, braced for the storm.

Fidelia walked down the cobbled street past the ink emporium, past the chemists' shops, past the drapers. An elaborate new sea chart was displayed in the window of the lithographers' shop. Fidelia crossed the street; it couldn't even tempt her.

She scampered right past the road that would have led her to the boardwalk, her neck cemented forward. The last thing she wanted was to bump into anyone who might try to talk to her.

The sound of the Book and Bottle's laughter and fiddles dwindled as Fidelia went the opposite direction, down Hemlock Avenue. Then it was as quiet as open water.

Evidence of the Undertow's spiteful winds were everywhere. The poplars lining the canal were blown back, angled like pens scrawling on paper. Windows and doors were still bolted shut; every shrub was a hen with ruffled feathers. She glanced down just as rain started plink-plinking the surface of the canal, shattering the water's mirror image of the gray cotton-down sky.

She turned the conversation with Aunt Julia over and over in her head like a found coin. Could Fidelia really thrive in a new habitat? Could she live without the sea surrounding her on all sides? Without the native star-apple trees that grew in the green spaces between buildings? Without the promise of tide pools mere minutes from her front door?

Her boots clomped easily through the puddles in the street. They were grade A, rubber-soled black flenser boots, staples in all three Quails' wardrobes. "You'll never know when you'll need to chase a specimen through a bog," her mother had said, and wisely so. Last year, Fidelia and her mother were tracking a marmalade frog, and the critter had led them through a mile of swampland before settling on a stump. The Quails had kept up just fine — thanks to the boots.

Oh, Mom. Fidelia swallowed away the hurt that swelled like a wave inside her, and tried to ready herself as she turned down Oleander Road.

The shingle-style canal houses were tall and narrow, with thick white wooden trim like frosting on gingerbread houses and yards full of tangled ivy. Every house's door was painted a different color — robin's egg blue, daffodil yellow, grass green.

She stopped in front of a house with drawn curtains, its door the color of a goldfish. A signpost above the mailbox said *Quail* in bold lettering. Before she could lose her nerve, she charged up the front stoop, honeysuckle taking over the terra-cotta brick stairs. She found the hidden key to the front door beneath the loose shingle under the bay window, held her breath, and went inside.

It wasn't as hard as she thought it would be, to see the home she'd shared with her loving parents. But then again, things weren't as dramatically different as she'd expected them to be. The parlor was freezing, only ash in the fireplace. Her mother's tea set was still arranged on its cart in the bay window, the stack of her favorite ginger cookies as stale as stones.

A thin layer of grime coated everything, including her parents' Gilded Iguanas — but not even the dust could reduce the awards to mere trinkets. The weak noon sunlight poured through a crack in the kitchen curtains, hitting the Gilded Iguanas like a flashlight. Right there, right between them — that's where she would have put her own award. And she would've put one of Grizzle's massive teeth on the shelf next to it.

Grizzle . . . The shark cruised through the shallows of her mind, and her shoulders sank.

All the things she'd lost—Grizzle, her parents, her home, and now Arborley itself—stacked themselves on her back, the load unbearable. Maybe it was a good thing that her parents' collection had been left to the university. Less things, less burdens, less tangible memories. The house itself would be gone, too—sold to new people. Maybe even to a nice fishing family, someone who would love the five-minute walk to Stony Beach as much as the Quails had.

Maybe Aunt Julia was right. Maybe it was time to migrate somewhere new, away from Arborley. To rebuild.

She ran a finger along the brim of her father's favorite boater hat, still on the chaise lounge where he always tossed it as he came through the front door. Ida would pretend to shake hands with the hat rack and say, "Arthur, dear, may I introduce the two of you?"

Fidelia closed her eyes. She didn't believe in ghosts; she was only interested in things that could be observed, measured, collected. But this house was haunted in a different way. Haunted by memories: Ida Quail's voice chirping in the hallway upstairs; Arthur Quail banging around in the garden shed, getting the equipment ready for an early-morning field study.

There was a sound above her, in her parents' bedroom. What was that?

Another sound—someone was walking upstairs.

Fidelia grabbed a whale bone, held it up as a weapon.

Her parents' bedroom door squeaked.

She stopped breathing. Could it be—? Was there a chance—?

"No," she whispered, and repeated it in her mind, like a chant.

No. No. Her parents had drowned. The constables had recovered the bodies. There had been a *funeral.*

No. It couldn't possibly be. . . .

Footsteps started down the stairs. She tightened her grip on the whale bone.

During the Undertow, anything could happen.

"Mom?" she called weakly. "Dad?"

She took a step forward—and a steel-strong hand clapped over her mouth from behind.

Fidelia screamed, but the hand trapped all sound. She threw kicks. Punched. Hacked with her arms to no avail. She was lifted like a sack full of freshly caught cod and thrown over the person's shoulders.

Fidelia's captor carried her upstairs, her boots bumping

against the banister as she thrashed like a gator caught on a line.

She was dropped unceremoniously in the armchair in her parents' bedroom. Many a night had been spent in this chair, on her mother's lap, her mom murmuring a lullaby to soothe Fidelia out of a nightmare. Now two strong arms pinned her there, more terrifying than any bad dream.

"Keep her there," a man growled from a corner of the room. It was so dark that Fidelia could make out only his silhouette; the shutters blocked what little late-November light there was. "Tie her up, if you have to."

She'd been in bad binds before. There was the time she got her hair caught in the snap of a wolffish. Or the time she'd accidentally ingested a poisonous water lily. But she wasn't out in the wilderness now, dealing with plants and animals—these were people. And she had no idea how to handle them.

"Yes, Captain," said the man holding Fidelia in a deep, molasses-dipped voice.

Captain.

Fidelia knew every captain who came through Arborley's port. She racked her brain, trying to match a face to that gravelly voice. . . .

"Get a fire—" the captain started, then burst into dry coughs.

A woman said, "Captain, are you—?"

"I'm fine," the captain grunted. "Just get a fire lit."

A match struck, and suddenly a golden light filled the room, the hungry flames devouring the logs in the grate.

Fidelia blinked, her eyes adjusting.

A woman crouched on the Quails' rug, tying a rope around Fidelia's ankles. She wore a pair of rolled-up men's knickers and a billowing blouse. A red scarf wrapped across her hairline, keeping her white-blond hair out of her eyes. Her face was hard and tanned, cheeks weathered by wind and sun, and her brawny forearms were covered in blue-black ink: rows of solid lines wrapped around her wrists like bracelets, and a swallow, flying across her left hand.

"Nice boots," the woman said with genuine admiration. "Rubber?"

Fidelia didn't answer; she was trying to place the woman's accent.

The man who'd carried Fidelia up the stairs now came around the front of the chair and lashed her wrists together with a length of that same itchy rope. He was tall, dark-skinned, and broad, with biceps as big as grapefruits. His bald head reflected the firelight, and his thick eyebrows knitted themselves together like one fuzzy caterpillar as he worked. A tiny canary jewel was pierced into his nose—a common fashion in the southeastern islands.

"What do you want?" Her words came out sounding stronger than she felt. "Why are you tying me up?"

They ignored her, knotting their ropes. The man went to the Quails' dresser and opened a drawer.

"You won't find anything valuable in there." Despite her fear, a curl of scorching rage flickered in Fidelia's chest—how dare these strangers come into this house? How dare they touch the Quails' things? "Unless you're interested in shark sperm samples."

"You hear that, Charlie? She fancies you a cat burglar." The woman snickered.

The man slammed the drawer shut and glared at Fidelia. "Give me your scarf," he said to the woman. "Let's gag her now and save us all a headache."

"Enough." From the shadowy corner of the room, the captain spoke. "Where are they?"

His voice . . . quiet and steady, but tight as a plucked wire. It sent chills along Fidelia's skin, scurrying like shore crabs along the sand. "Who?" she said, trembling.

"The unsinkable Dr. and Dr. Quail—where are they?" the captain said, every syllable crackling.

"They're . . . They're . . ." Fidelia stammered. "Gone."

"Gone where?" the captain said. "On holiday? Moved? Retired?"

The captain stepped forward, and a blaze of the firelight caught the profile of his face.

Skin so pale it was almost lavender, but wind-burned and rough. One black sideburn curving along a sharp jaw and a scraggly black beard. One silver hoop earring, half a stern mouth, and one blue eye, burning like a moonstone.

The other half of his face remained concealed in the darkness.

"Speak, girl!" he commanded.

Fidelia started, even in her bindings. "They're . . . they're dead." A stone dropped into her stomach. There. He'd made her say it.

The news seemed to physically wound him—he bowed his head, shrinking back into the darkness.

"How?" he said softly. "How did it happen?"

"The Undertow," Fidelia whispered, then frowned. "I don't understand. Did you know them?" He must have; why else would he care that they were gone?

The captain exhaled a gust of air. "I knew *of* them— let's put it that way. And they knew of me."

He knew *of* them? "Well, I'm their daughter," she said.

"If they knew *of* you, they certainly never bothered to mention it." She strained against her ropes. "My parents might be gone, but this is still my house." At least for the moment. "I demand you get out."

"Their daughter," he mused. "Interesting. And judging by the way you stink like a dried-out porpoise at low tide, I'm guessing you share their unusual passions?"

Fidelia raised her chin. "And you stink like . . ." She sniffed, her well-trained nose picking up a mixture of gunpowder and salt, ocean brine stuck in wedges of wood, a crate of limes. The smell of a harbor. The smell of a sailor. A captain.

He turned to her, the rest of his face illuminated by the hearth, and Fidelia gasped.

The captain had one brilliant, frighteningly blue eye, which seemed too rich to be natural—vivid as a sapphire. But his left eye . . . Fidelia wondered how an eyeball could cling to a skull like that while still respecting the laws of gravity. The iris was carbon black, an endless mine shaft. Scarlet liquid held the iris aloft, a black dot awash in a stormy sea of blood.

"Not the most beautiful shade of red, is it?" he said. "But we all make our little sacrifices for the Queen's Own Navy."

"You're in the navy?" Fidelia said.

"Was," he corrected. "I served three years." He fingered the scarred skin around his eye. "This was courtesy of an artillery ricochet. At least I was left with my head, which is more than most of the naval commanders can say."

He took a seat across from Fidelia in her father's favorite reading chair. There was an unnatural calmness about him, as if he were in command of every molecule in his body.

Quite the opposite of Fidelia, whose pulse hammered with warning shots: *danger, danger, danger . . .*

"If you're going to kill me," she said, "do it fast."

"Kill you?" The captain raised his eyebrows. "You seem like a smart girl: If I wanted you dead, why would I tie you up?"

Fidelia immediately thought of the dozens of poor creatures she'd seen on fishing lines, twisted up, left to slowly die, gills flapping desperately. Was she heading for a similar fate? "Then what is happening?"

"To be straightforward," he said, "I'm here for a Quail. I came for your parents, but since they are . . ."

Fidelia braced herself for the word.

". . . unavailable, I'll be taking you." His black eye was a tunnel; she felt like she could fall right into it and be lost forever.

"You're kidnapping me?" Fidelia flexed against her ropes.

"Call it what you—" He broke off, coughing. "You're coming with us."

"Who are you?" she whimpered. "Why are you doing this?"

The captain pointed to his own chest. "Merrick the Monstrous. Terror of the nine seas. Pleased to make your acquaintance."

Suddenly, Fidelia's insides tangled like vines. "You're a pirate."

Merrick's smile was crooked, his gold-capped teeth gleaming. "I'm not just *a* pirate, Quail. I'm *the* pirate."

"Pirates," Fidelia whispered. Her entire body flooded with adrenaline; if it weren't for the ropes binding her to the chair, she'd be running back to the library. Oh, why hadn't she stayed on the couch with the cat?

"But you said you hurt your eye in the navy," she said.

"It's a naval injury, one way or another," Merrick said. "I served three years as an officer before I decided on a career change. All pirates have seedy backgrounds. Mine is easily the seediest."

"Cheapshot Charlie," the woman said, gesturing to the bald man, "and I'm Bloody Elle, since you asked. At your service." She bowed so deeply and dramatically, Fidelia knew it was meant to mock her.

Cheapshot Charlie pressed his lips together and exhaled through his nose. He folded his arms, his muscles straining against his tunic. "Do you understand who you're dealing with, shrimp?" He pointed at his captain. "Merrick the Monstrous, wanted in thirty nations for robbery, burglary, arson, murder, jail breaking, and piracy."

Jail breaking? "You were in prison?" Only the most notorious, most dangerous of criminals were sent to the naval prison — a windowless iron barge that floated a mile off the mainland's arctic coast, its own tiny island.

"Only long enough for a good rest," Merrick said. "Then I left." He spoke of the prison as if it were a cozy inn — one that he could simply check out of when he was finished with his stay.

"But how?" Each prisoner on the barge was fitted with a heavy vest, a wearable anchor of sorts, secured with chains. Even if someone managed to ditch his or her cell and get past the guards and the dogs, to jump ship was to sink to the bottom of the sea and drown miserably.

Merrick didn't bother to answer. Instead, he walked to the washstand on the left side of the bed — her father's side. The porcelain basin was still full of water, a clean folded towel and a shaving kit laid out and ready.

A sour taste filled Fidelia's mouth as she watched this pirate use her father's bristly brush to load his face with shaving cream, then run her father's blade along his jaw to clear away his patchy mustache and beard. Only his two sideburns remained, and Merrick slicked those and the rest of his black sea-devil hair down with Dr. Quail's greasy pomade.

Fidelia blinked. The spicy, woodsy smell of pomade hit her nose — her father's scent.

"Much better," Bloody Elle appraised after inspecting her captain. "You look like yourself again."

"I could use a good dip in turpentine." Merrick scratched his head. "Damned prison gave me nits, I think."

"I don't understand," Fidelia said. "You're Merrick the Monstrous. If you can do all that — escape from prison and elude the navy — then . . ." She paused. He didn't look much older than Aunt Julia. But he had already carved out a name and a reputation for himself — and a monstrous one at that.

Merrick finished her sentence for her: "What could I possibly want with you?"

Before he could elaborate, he coughed, a string of violent hacks that made Fidelia's throat tighten in sympathy.

Bloody Elle rushed to his side, holding out a canteen.

But Merrick waved her away. "It won't make a difference," he snapped, "and you know it."

He collapsed in the armchair, panting. He coughed once more, just a tickle, then straightened, locking Fidelia's gaze with his clashing eyes. "A treasure of mine fell into the sea," he said, "and you're going to get it back."

Sunken treasure.

Electricity jolted her nerves.

She tried to remember how it used to feel to be gently swallowed by the sea, to sink down into the water until the world was upside down, brighter, filtered blue . . . The underwater fairyland, her parents called it, and that's how it felt now—as if her old life had been a fairy tale, far away. A passage from a book.

Merrick was demanding that she dive into a dream.

"There's more," the captain said. "I don't know where it is."

She gaped at him. For eleven years, she had studied the ocean and its inhabitants with her parents. Dr. and Dr. Quail had done it on their own for a decade before Fidelia came around. And the three of them had seen only a speck of the ocean's secrets. "There are nine seas," she finally said, stunned. "How could you possibly expect me to find—?"

"Don't be an idiot," Merrick barked. "I know the general vicinity. But the seafloors have all shifted. Everything down there—it's moved. Different." He picked a ball of lint from the wool of his threadbare peacoat. "The Undertow wreaks havocs on the tides. Sweeps sand and shells and lord knows what else over my treasure."

"I don't know what you expect from me," Fidelia said. "My parents were Dr. and Dr. Quail. They were brilliant. "They doubled the list of known marine species in just five years. They saved the great northern narwhal from over-fishing. They knew everything about the sea, and—"

"And they're gone," Merrick finished. "And you are what's left behind." He dashed his hand like a blur into his boot and produced a sleek, silver knife. The firelight glinted off the blade—a warning, a hint. "Surely some of their expertise rubbed off on you."

Fidelia stared at the knife. "What if it didn't?" She kept still, concentrating on keeping her hands from fidgeting beneath the ropes.

Merrick darkened. "Don't test me, girl," he said. "You're getting my treasure if I have to hog-tie you and throw you into the water myself."

He angled his knife so the light hit Fidelia's eyes. "But if you cooperate, I'll have you home safe within a week." He sliced through her restraints.

Home. Fidelia watched the fire flicker in the hearth— the hearth that no longer belonged to her. Nothing in this house belonged to her.

No, Fidelia didn't have a home. Not anymore.

She stood shakily, the ropes falling to the floor in coils.

"Smart girl," Merrick said. "I'd hate to see you lose one of those hands." He inspected a silver pocket watch and growled. "Now, we have a hell of a trip ahead of us. A week's sail southbound, along the cocoa route, and we're going to do it in half that time."

"Wait, we're leaving *now?*" Never mind Merrick's absurd delusion that they'd be able to pinpoint their exact moment of arrival; traveling by sea was a notoriously slippery thing, since there were so many factors—crosswinds, and traffic on the routes, and unpredictable ship maintenance. He was ignoring the most important—the most dangerous—factor of all. "What about the Undertow?"

"We'll see if the remaining Quail can make it through the storm a second time. What is it you say here? In the Undertow, anything can happen?"

The cruelty of his comments chilled Fidelia to her marrow. "But why—?"

"Because the navy begins their winter patrols next week." Merrick's blue eye seared a hole in her. "Because the faster I can be rid of you, the better. And because," he finished with particularly lethal poison, "some things you have to do now. Right now, and hope to the stars it isn't too late."

Fidelia swallowed, adjusted her glasses, and nodded.

"Now, when the navy finds me—"

"When?" Fidelia cut in, her mind still churning like high tide.

"When," he repeated. "They'll hang me. This time, they'll stay and make sure I die." His good eye burned in the firelight. "If you give me any trouble, any at all—you'll swim back home. Whole or in pieces. Do you understand?"

For some reason, a memory flashed into Fidelia's mind—a beached marlin she'd found with her parents, struggling for breath in the sand. It flopped pathetically, trying to swim back out to deeper water, but it was pale, malnourished, one fin mangled and twisted and useless. Its cerulean scales flaked off every time it fluttered across the shore; the sight of its naked white flesh beneath its failing chain-mail armor made Fidelia intensely uncomfortable, itchy all over.

Fidelia's mother, ever the tender-hearted zoologist, had rushed over and gently placed her arms beneath the marlin's twitching body—only to receive an ungrateful chomp on the thumb.

"We're trying to help you!" Fidelia had scolded the fish.

Ida had pulled her daughter back, wrapping the hem of her dress around her bleeding digit. "He's asking for space," she had said. "We need to respect his wishes."

"But he'll die!" Fidelia had cried.

Ida had nodded. "He's going to die no matter what we do. That makes him extremely dangerous. He's got nothing to lose."

Merrick the Monstrous spoke like a man with nothing to lose.

"What about supplies?" Merrick turned to his comrades.

Bloody Elle started to open her knapsack, then paused. "Now, Captain," she said slowly, "I know this isn't your first choice in grub—"

"We found the crate unattended in the harbor," Cheapshot Charlie cut in. Both pirates were nervous, Fidelia realized: Bloody Elle traced her finger along the thickest of her bracelet tattoos, and Cheapshot Charlie's eyebrows pushed so far down on his forehead, they cast a shadow over his eyes.

"There isn't a spare bit of bread or salted meat on the island," Cheapshot Charlie said, unapologetic. "The Undertow's got everyone on lockdown."

"And there won't be any ships to loot, either," Bloody Elle added.

Without a word, Merrick took the knapsack from her hands and peered inside.

"It was all we could find, Captain," Cheapshot Charlie said.

Merrick tipped the knapsack upside down, and an avalanche of sweets fell onto the floor: kaleidorainbow figs, crack-o-mallow bars, choco-glomps. A logo was emblazoned across every bright-yellow wrapper: a hot-pink ship with mint-colored flags curling like ribbons sailing on a whipped-cream sea beneath the words *BonBon Voyage Sweets Shop.*

Fidelia's heart panged at the sight. BonBon Voyage was her favorite sweets shop. The heavenly cotton candy–scented wonderland was located right next to the Book and Bottle on the boardwalk, so most nights after field studies, Dr. and Dr. Quail had let Fidelia pick a green note's worth of sweets (usually as many apple crantruffles as she could fit in her pockets). The smell of the sweets hit Fidelia like a sugary wall—she still hadn't eaten breakfast.

Merrick, however, glared at the pile of candy with this good eye as if sweets were his sworn enemies. He nudged a choco-glomp with his boot, his breathing slow and deliberate.

"Captain?" Bloody Elle pressed.

"Pack them up," Merrick's orders came. "Put out the

fire. Then we leave." He stalked to the Quails' bedroom window and pulled back the curtain with a scarred finger.

The two pirates knelt down and shoveled the candy back into the knapsack. Cheapshot Charlie unwrapped a striped, sprinkled bar and took a bite. "Mmm," he said.

"I haven't had one of these in ages." Bloody Elle grabbed a sweet, practically drooling.

Fidelia's stomach lurched with hunger. Or maybe that was a knot of fear and uncertainty snarling inside her as she pondered the enormous task ahead of her: a dive, possibly hundreds of feet down, to locate a lost treasure, buried by algae and sand and time. And if she didn't do it—or couldn't—Merrick the Monstrous would no doubt add her to his list of victims.

If they even survived the journey.

"We're all clear." Merrick let the curtain fall, turning away from the window. "Time to go."

The pirates slung their knapsacks over their shoulders. Cheapshot Charlie snuffed out the fire in the hearth; Bloody Elle scarfed down one more kaleidorainbow fig and threw the wrapper onto the rug.

Fidelia stared at the wrapper—part of her wanted to shout at the pirate for the careless littering. But it didn't really matter, did it? It wasn't her parents' bedroom anymore. It wasn't her house anymore.

When she didn't move, Merrick seized her arm to *make* her move. "Wait," she said. "I'm supposed to just swim down to the bottom of the sea and fetch your treasure?"

"You're a Quail," Merrick said. "Isn't that your second nature?"

"We use equipment for our research," Fidelia pointed out. "For a dive that deep, my parents would use a diving suit." *Or the* Egg, she thought with a pang.

A growl like an annoyed jaguar came from Merrick's throat. "You have one, I assume?"

"Down in the garden shed," Fidelia said.

She pictured the department heads from the university showing up tomorrow morning to gather the Quails' collection and finding their expensive diving suit gone. More than a fair trade, she decided, considering they were taking away everything else. All the tangible, touchable memorabilia of the Quails' adventures would be locked away in a cold university laboratory, to be squinted at beneath microscopes. Or in a display, stowed behind glass. She hated that. The house should be allowed to stay just like it was forever — a museum dedicated to the two greatest scientists to ever live.

Rain pelted Fidelia as she led the pirates through the yard. She didn't stop to prepare herself as she hurled open the garden shed door, and before she could think, or breathe, there it was—the salvaged fragments of the *Egg*.

All she could do was stare at the smashed submarine. Her invention. Her creation. She had been so certain it would be safe in an ocean storm, but the Undertow had squashed it like a sea snail. Her parents had always trusted her inventions, and it had cost them their lives.

She turned away from the pirates so they wouldn't see her blurry eyes and took a few steps into the shed. A hole in the roof dripped raindrops onto her head.

"Get what you need," Merrick said. "Clock's ticking."

Fidelia tiptoed around a pile of mismatched fins, past the rusty diving bell (an antiquated relic of marine biology equipment the Quails kept around as a sort of joke), past life jackets, past dragnets . . .

But where was the diving suit? It should have been here, in the back left corner of the shed. But all she saw was an old broken helmet, barnacles still crusted on the visor. Fidelia nudged it with her foot; a refugee spider scurried away into the shadows.

"It's gone!"

"Well, where'd it go?" Merrick said.

Fidelia thought. "The university. They must have come early." But why didn't they take the rest of their equipment? Clear out the house? Typical academics. They made sure to grab their costly diving suit first, and left the true prizes behind: the unicorn fish skeleton, the bramble shark skin, all the photographs . . .

She cursed, then looked at Merrick helplessly, who shrugged. "Now what am I supposed to do?" she said.

"You're the inventor," Merrick said. "Make a new suit on the way."

Fidelia shook her head. "I don't have the right tools—I'd need a bolt of canvas, and a pump, and . . ." She stared at the pirate captain. "How did you know I was an inventor?"

"I know all about how you Quails conducted your research," Merrick said. "Your Hydro-Scanner, and your Air-Spinners, and your submersible there." He jutted his chin toward the ruined *Egg*.

Fidelia's mouth fell open.

The Air-Spinners were Fidelia's early attempts at replacing regular old fins with foot propellers, thus reducing the amount of energy used by a diver. A brilliant concept but an utter failure in execution; the Air-Spinners weren't flexible enough to be steered.

"How do you know about—?" Fidelia started, then answered her own question. Air-Spinners were her special project at least four years ago, right around the time the Quails were working on their manuscript. "You read their book. You read *Exploring an Underwater Fairyland.*"

Merrick wrapped his peacoat tighter around his chest. "It passed the time on the crossing to Molvania." His brilliant blue eye burned past the lenses of her glasses, right into her. "Now quit stalling. You're fetching my treasure. I don't care if you have to grow your own set of gills."

Gills.

Fidelia's skin prickled. "Gills," she repeated, and straightened.

Cheapshot Charlie lunged for her, but she sidestepped his grip. "She's wasting time, Captain. Let's go."

Fidelia ignored him. She walked to the back of the leaky shed, where a dinged-up farm table served as her old workstation. Bolts and screwdrivers littered the surface, along with sketches of half-baked ideas on blueprint paper.

Her hands ran along the sides of a dusty cocoa-bean crate. She lifted the box and turned toward Merrick.

"A box of toys for the long trip?" Merrick said, and Fidelia swallowed hard so her cheeks wouldn't burn. *Nothing more than a toy for bored schoolgirls who like to play at science,* the patent office had said of the Hydro-Scanner, one of her most successful inventions. What would they say now, about this box of junk? A hodgepodge of misplaced ambition? A waste of scrap metal?

"My own set of gills," Fidelia said, rattling the contents of the crate. "At least, that's what it was supposed to be."

The Water-Eater—an invention she'd worked on for almost a year. It was her pet project, the one that kept her up most nights, turning it over and over in her mind. . . . It was also the project that she could never get right. Every few weeks she had what seemed like a breakthrough, which only ever lasted a day before she threw it back into the crate, disgusted and discouraged. It had been sitting in the shed for months, put away in its crate—in its grave, where it couldn't taunt her. Where she could forget about it.

Merrick looked down into the crate, and Fidelia held her breath. "Doesn't look like much," he said of the strange little mask, its failed filtration system broken down into its basic parts, the loose screws rolling around the bottom of the box rebelliously.

"Well, it's not finished yet." Hot defensiveness curled in Fidelia's chest, its flames momentarily melting the chill of her fear.

"And you think you can finish it before your big dive."

99 ↝

Merrick didn't ask this, but it still sounded like an inquiry. And it sounded like he already had the answer.

Fidelia crumpled, staring at the crate.

If she couldn't get the Water-Eater right when her parents were here—bringing her toast with tomato jam during late-night work sessions, lending an ear when she needed to talk through the mechanics—how could she possibly get the Water-Eater right without them?

"Captain," Cheapshot Charlie said, his teeth gritted. "We need to go."

"One minute," Merrick said. "She has sixty more seconds, and then we leave."

Fidelia's thoughts raced, her body drumming with panic. She set down the crate and took her observation book from her bag, flipping through it—maybe a solution would jump out among her scribbled notes and slapdash diagrams.

"Quail," Merrick said.

"I need more time!" Fidelia cried.

"You're out of time!" Cheapshot Charlie shrouded her in shadow. "Grab your box of junk and start walking."

Fidelia picked up the crate, her arms shaking. "I can't—I can't do this without them." Before she could stop it, a tear streaked down her face.

How could she ever have believed this could work?

She was just a girl, orphaned and lost, treading water alone.

"You have to." Merrick's voice rolled like thunder, vibrating Fidelia's ear as he leaned over her. "Now get your head on straight and think."

Fidelia walked past the pirates and back into the shed. She tuned out Cheapshot Charlie's impatient glare and Bloody Elle's pacing and ducked her head into the cockpit of the submarine. *Right here,* she thought — *this is where Mom and Dad were, right when it happened. What were they thinking, as the water rose higher and higher?* She bit her bottom lip, trying to focus through the slow ache of her sadness. *If only I could speak to them one more time. Hear their voices. Pick their brilliant brains —*

"Wait!"

She opened a compartment in the *Egg* — yes, her parents' observation books were still there, wrapped in oil-skin. Her mother's small plum notebook, bound closed with a strip of leather; her father's square black notebook, with his square bold print.

Fidelia flipped through her mother's observation book, and entries jumped out at her — notes on the reanimation of starfish limbs, notes on rubber eels, notes on the sleeping habits of carpet sharks. Dr. Quail's hen-scratch handwriting was difficult enough to read when curled up in a cozy reading nook, but the leaking raindrops soaked the ink, making the letters run like black teardrops.

She scanned her mom's recap of the day a sea otter sneezed on her dad, sending him toppling down a riverbank—one of the funniest days of Fidelia's life, and now she had to bite the inside of her cheek to keep from toppling into despair.

"I don't know what Mom and Dad would do," she told Merrick, each word wobbling, "but I think I can find out."

Merrick the Monstrous leaned close, his bloodred eye inches from her glasses. "I hope so," he said, "or you'll be closer to the fishes than you ever wanted."

8

The autumn morning stayed overcast and wet as the unlikely group walked along the main canal. Fat raindrops fell in a gray curtain. That, combined with the Undertow's ever-looming presence in the bay, meant Arborley's streets were empty of people. Merrick nevertheless pulled the collar of his peacoat up as high as it would go, tucking his face out of sight. A turtle retreating into its shell.

He was short, Fidelia realized—not much taller than she was, a detail she hadn't noticed until his two comrades left his sides to flank her instead, hustling her along.

An intersection came up—Arborley's high street, cutting in front of them. If they turned left, they'd walk right past the library. Fidelia could see it now—the white-bricked back of the building, the flat roof, the loft window, round as a porthole. Her pulse spiked. What was her aunt doing right now? Finishing the encyclopedias? Working the circulation desk? Still expecting Fidelia to trudge back home from the Quails' old house for dinner in just a few hours?

Fidelia would be long gone by then.

If she could steer the pirates within range of the library, she could yell. Aunt Julia kept the library bone quiet — maybe Aunt Julia would hear her and run outside, and then Fidelia would be out of this mess. She could go back to the sofa, and the cat, and the books. *And the mainland,* she reminded herself, and grimly pressed her lips together. A new life on dry land, but a safe one.

She veered to the edge of the curb casually, trying not to give away the fact that her heart had leapfrogged into her throat. "You know, the library will have information on indigenous diving techniques," she said. Merrick and the other pirates stared at her as if her nose had just turned into a sea cucumber.

"It would probably be good to have a book or two — just as a backup —"

"Books." Merrick spat the word out like it was moldy. "Enough books." He gripped her arm roughly. "You stay close. We wouldn't want you wandering off."

Look out the window! Fidelia shouted mental messages at Aunt Julia as the library slipped farther and farther away. *Come outside! Now, before it's too late!*

Merrick strong-armed her down a side street and an alleyway—a shortcut to the harbor that bypassed the high street and the Book and Bottle.

Fidelia could smell it before she could see it.

A sniff of brine. Of wet rocks.

There it was—the stretch of dappled gray and brown pebbles, white foam lining the shore like antique lace, and the ocean. Fog collected in the bay, so she could barely make out the sea beneath it—slate blue, shimmering, beautiful and terrifying in its infiniteness.

As Merrick corralled her along the boardwalk, dread collected under her rib cage like beach trash. Yes, the ocean had once felt more like home than her actual home. But now all she could think about was how, in these very waters, her parents had—

"Quit your stomping." Merrick's fingers dug into the softness of her forearm. "You're making more noise than a three-legged man."

This would all be easier, Fidelia thought, *if it was a normal day.* Not only would the pirates have a devil of a time snatching her in front of a crowd, but if the harbor was humming with the usual business of the cocoa trade, if the sky was clear blue, it would feel more like greeting a comfortable old friend than this silent, still implosion of unbearable memories.

But everything was exactly as it had been on the day she'd lost them. Rows of ships floated, stiff as a line of coffins awaiting their eternal occupants. The earthy smell of cocoa beans was ghostly faint, carried by the rancid, low-tide breeze.

With every vessel they walked past, Fidelia thought of all the sailors who ran it. A carrack with shining turquoise banners—the *Puck,* Captain Beagle's cargo ship. An old caravel called the *Spanker,* which Ida Quail called antique and charming and Arthur Quail called dowdy. The *Anemone,* Ratface's clipper—the lazy mermaid carved into its bowsprit in desperate need of a good polish.

All these sailors—sea dogs and rascals, every one of them, but at the Quails' funeral, their faces hooked down into frowns so sharp, they could've fished with them.

Would that be the last time she'd ever see them?

Merrick stopped at the gate of the chandler's warehouse—a roofed yard filled with shipping supplies. "Open it," he commanded his comrades. "Grab a dory."

"A dory?" Fidelia echoed, and her blood turned to ice. Did the pirates think they could paddle a dory in the Undertow? "We can't take a dory all the way to the tropics!"

"You think I would be so stupid?" Merrick said, his grip

on Fidelia's arm still concrete strong. "I've gutted men for lesser insults."

Cheapshot Charlie jimmied open the lock, and he and Bloody Elle dashed into the warehouse, past bottles of linseed oil, past the buckets of pitch for waterproofing wooden crates, past gleaming new hatchets and lanterns, past brooms and mops. Back in the far corner of the warehouse, a row of white dories leaned against the fence, their long noses pointed up at the sky.

Cheapshot Charlie lifted one of the boats with his massive arms and Bloody Elle carried the oars.

"Nice and easy," Merrick muttered as the two pirates slunk down an aisle. If the dory knocked against even one of these shelves, they'd all fall over in a domino effect—loud enough to bring someone running to investigate, Undertow or no. Fidelia held her breath, hoping one of them would trip or stumble. But the pirates managed to safely sneak the dory out of the warehouse without a sound.

Merrick tugged Fidelia's arm until she was forced to follow. "This way." He led her away from the warehouse, away from the boardwalk, and to the beach.

To the beach.

Cheapshot Charlie carried the dory to the shallows and

threw it on the water with a slap. Instantly the tide tried to pull the boat away from land, out to open water.

Out where the Undertow could tear it to driftwood.

Fidelia froze. "You said we weren't going out in a dory—"

"I said no such thing. Now move." Merrick dragged her forward, her feet making parallel tracks in the pebbles.

Fidelia's boots dipped into the icy water for the first time since—

"No!" her voice was strangled. She locked her knees and skidded to a stop, the toes of her boots sliding beneath a mound of pebbles and sea foam. She couldn't do it— couldn't go back in the water.

"Get in the boat." Merrick clenched her arm above the elbow. His blue eye seared into her with a simmering, subterranean fury.

But just as Fidelia was about to submerge her boot in the water, drown her last hope, Merrick coughed so violently, he bent over, dropping his grip on Fidelia.

Her chance to run.

She took it.

She twisted out of his reach and sprinted back toward the boardwalk.

"Charlie, Elle!" Merrick barked between coughs. "She's running for it!"

Pebbles crunched under Fidelia's boots. Her legs were on fire. It had been weeks since she'd stretched them like this—they were achingly out of practice.

Away, away she ran, the sound of crashing waves fading with every step. Which was she running from harder: Merrick and his mates, or the water?

A gunshot.

The pebbles beneath Fidelia's feet flew into the air.

Behind her, Merrick stood at the bow of the dory like a king riding atop a fur-lined litter, loading his pistol while Cheapshot Charlie and Bloody Elle kept the boat parallel to the shore. "Either we take you with your toes, or without!" he hollered.

Fidelia didn't stop. *Let him shoot,* she thought. *He'll wake up the whole hibernating island with that noise—and then they'll have him.*

"You'll also be missing these," Merrick said.

Fidelia looked back.

The pirate captain held her parents' observation books, one in each hand, open so the pages fluttered in the sea breeze.

Fidelia's stomach flip-flopped. She stumbled to a halt. Their notes. Their research. Their journals, their random thoughts—every moment her parents had deemed worthy of capturing. All of it was there, in Merrick's hands. He must have stolen them out of her bag, knowing they'd make the perfect hostages.

"They come with me," Merrick continued, "and I guarantee I won't be as careful with them as you are." He dangled them over the side of the dory, letting the spray dampen the pages. "Anything could happen to them, fragile little things. What if they go for a dive of their own—?"

"Stop!" Fidelia shouted, almost roared. She pivoted in the pebbles and ran back to the water's edge. Losing her parents' books, their words, her only link to them—she'd sail straight through the heart of the Undertow to keep that from happening.

She waded in the frigid water up to her ankles. Then to her thighs. Then to her waist.

The dory had drifted far enough out that she'd have to swim for it. Her lungs seized—from the cold, yes, and also from the gasping fear that suddenly paralyzed her muscles.

"It's a shock you haven't grown gills," Ida Quail used to say every time Fidelia emerged from the sea, sopping and smiling.

Six weeks since she lost them. Six weeks since she'd last taken to the water.

Oh, Mom, she thought now. *Would you even recognize me now, this timid girl I've become? A landlubber? A coward?*

Summoning every bit of courage she could find, she swam, limbs sweeping through the water as if she were embracing it—or clawing and kicking at it, more accurately. A baby wave gently swept over her head; under the water, she panicked and scrambled for air. Had she already forgotten how to bob with the tide? Or hold her breath?

The cold water seeped into her airways, a salty flood through her nasal passage. Just as she opened her mouth in a frantic, underwater gasp, a huge hand grabbed her collar and hauled her up into the dory. Sputtering, she pulled off her glasses, blinking away seawater, and as soon as the world came back into focus, grabbed her parents' observation books from Merrick.

"You keep threatening to hurt me or kill me if I don't do what you want," she said flatly, her teeth chattering. "Well, the Undertow will turn this entire boat into matches." She shivered, her nerves raw. "We won't even make it out of the bay. Nobody sails in the Undertow. Not even my parents would have risked this. Please. This treasure of yours can wait until spring. It's not worth your life, is it? And Cheapshot Charlie's, and Bloody Elle's?" *And my life?* she added silently.

"The Undertow should be the least of your worries."

Merrick pulled the silver pocket watch from his peacoat and checked the time. Then his good eye brightened, finding something behind her.

Fidelia arched herself around in the dory. Emerging from the swirling fog, anchored to the last shoal before Arborley Bay deepened into true, wild ocean, was the ugliest, sorriest ship Fidelia had ever seen.

It was a monster of a ship, an old sloop of war built at least a generation ago, with dark masts jutting crookedly like the ribs of a beast. Ribbons of paint peeled off the beams, and an emerald slime coated the hull at the waterline.

"That's your ship?" Fidelia didn't bother masking the mockery in her voice. "Does it even sail?"

"Better than any on the water." Merrick spoke as though it were a lover, not a ship.

"Captain," Bloody Elle said softly—carefully, Fidelia noticed. "Look at her bulge."

They all tilted their heads, peering at the port side, which curved far more than was desirable. Water damage, Fidelia diagnosed, the wood warped far beyond repair.

Merrick pressed his lips tightly together.

The pirates rowed their captain and their captive to the side of the ship, and the closer they got, the worse the ship looked: grime along her boards, ropes fraying, a tattered

red flag hanging on a mast. A red flag—the mark of a ruthless pirate.

"Can she make it, Captain?" Bloody Elle asked.

"Of course she can," Merrick said.

But Fidelia couldn't hold back a scoff—this was Merrick's grand vessel? The ship that would carry them along the cocoa route to the treasure? By her guess, it wouldn't make it out of the bay. "We just left an entire harbor of ships. Good ships," she said. "If we turn around now—"

"I don't sail on any ship but the *Jewel*." Merrick's tone was clear—this topic was doornail-dead, buried and finished. He seized a frayed rope and pulled himself onto the deck of the ship.

The *Jewel* . . . What a perfect name for the flagship of a pirate treasure-thirsty enough to kidnap a girl and send her overboard for his gold.

But misshapen boards and faded sails aside, the *Jewel* embodied speed and nimbleness. Fidelia could easily picture this ship in a previous life, darting through shoals and outrunning the gigantic pinks and galleons of the Queen's Own Navy.

With Bloody Elle and Cheapshot Charlie on her tail, she followed Merrick up and into the *Jewel*, landing on the deck just in time to see Merrick touch a brine-wrinkled railing.

"Look at her wood," he whispered. "So far gone."

"Does she have one last trip in her?" Bloody Elle asked as she climbed aboard the ship.

Merrick coughed—or was he clearing his throat of some sentimentality congesting there? "Let's get her out to sea, mates, and find out."

Fidelia settled herself onto a bench in the lower deck, the lull and sway of the ship rocking her into a trance. She gave in, closing her eyes. It had already been a long day—the longest since September 30—and it was barely afternoon.

"Are you sure she's the right girl?" Cheapshot Charlie's voice could barely be heard above the din of the sails flapping. "She's panicked at water like a cat."

"Maybe so," Merrick said, "but she's the one we want."

The *Jewel* got her bearings, her cream linens catching the wind. By the time the pirates brought the ship out of the bay, Fidelia was fast asleep, glasses askew on her nose, the bag with her parents' observation books in it clutched tightly against her chest, a life preserver to aid against this great mess she'd found herself drowning in.

Two Years Earlier

It was a crisp, blue morning, the kind that should exist only in paintings. There wasn't a swell on the sea as the *Jewel* sailed, sunshine gleaming off the polished wood, her hold full of spoils from the latest raid: chests brimming with strung rubies, crates of fresh cocoa beans, gold doubloons.

A rolltop desk in the captain's quarters was plastered in nautical maps — charts of detailed cliff lines, charts of water depths, charts of territories, charts of unknown seas . . . The papers overlapped and bubbled — mirroring what the inside of Merrick's brain must have looked like.

On top of the charts were letters. They'd been read and reread so many times, the delicate stationery had started to tear at the creases.

Merrick picked one up and traced its salutation with his rough fingers.

My dearest love . . .

A knock came at the door.

"Come," he said gruffly, and hid the bundle of letters beneath the maps.

His quartermaster came into the office.

"Are we there?" Merrick asked.

"Nearly," Bloody Elle said. "A knot or two away."

"Tell the crew to unload everything from the hold but the beans. We'll give those to Taj next time we hit the bodega." He strolled to his drink cart and uncorked a bottle of rich chocolate rum. "And put Charlie on first watch—"

"A thousand pardons, Captain," Bloody Elle interrupted, "but you should see this."

Merrick scowled, smoothed the maps on his desk, and followed her out to the deck.

The *Jewel* slowed as it came into a stretch of turquoise water. An island with moon-white beaches and a jagged green palm-tree skyline sat peacefully on the horizon, just a mile away—a paradise, but not the *Jewel*'s intended destination.

Merrick's crew hopped out of his way as he stomped across the boards. This was supposed to be a quick stop in the tropics; whoever was responsible for holding him up would be at the receiving end of his full wrath.

He spotted it immediately, the reason for all the fuss: the gaff-rigged sails of a schooner, moored in the water not fifty feet from where the *Jewel* now cruised. A crimson flag billowed from its mast, a black silhouette of a bear on all fours prowling across the fabric.

Pirates—and because of their ursine epigraph, Merrick knew exactly which ones.

Cheapshot Charlie came up behind Merrick, his eyebrows furrowed into a line. "Should we open fire?"

"That won't be necessary," Merrick said. "Pull up beside her."

As the *Jewel* neared the bobbing schooner, Merrick could see its crew. They were the olive-skinned pirates of the eastern mainland, patterned scarves tying back their twisted, sea-gnarled hair.

A bearded man stood at the helm—their captain, judging by the way his tunic hung, its fine Molvanian thread shimmering gold. He gaped as the *Jewel* moved closer, as though he couldn't believe what he was seeing.

As though he had tunneled through an abandoned mountain mine and stepped into a dragon's lair.

And here comes the dragon, Merrick thought.

"Hello, there!" He waved jovially with his free hand. The other still clutched his pistol.

One of the pirates crossed herself and muttered a prayer.

"Fine afternoon, isn't it?" Merrick said. "These tropical seas are like stained glass; such pleasant sailing."

The other pirates still said nothing.

"How strange it is, to see unfamiliar faces along this stretch," Merrick continued. "And the *Rasculat* is such a long way from Molvania! Are you here for the fine fishing?"

The *Jewel's* crew tittered behind their captain, hands finding their various guns and blades. Merrick the Monstrous was frightening enough when he brooded or raged, but when he was polite, when the adder pretended to be a friendly garden snake who wanted only to slither up your arm and ride on your shoulder like a pet . . . that's when he was most dangerous.

That's when he struck.

"Captain," Bloody Elle called from the lower deck. She hauled a soggy, sputtering pirate up from the side of the *Jewel* and over the railing. "He was in the water!"

"Please," the half-drowned man cried, the sea dripping off him as Bloody Elle dropped him onto the deck like a trout. "I was only checking our hull for barnacles." The pirate pulled off his soaked paisley headscarf and wrung it between two nervous hands.

"Tell me," Merrick said quietly, trusting the breeze to carry his words. "How in the world did you manage to find it?" He fiddled with his silver hoop earring, his entire face the epitome of boredom. "You Molvanians don't usually loot this far south, do you?"

"N-no," the pirate admitted, "but we keep a cache on one of these island: food barrels and coin and rum, for emergencies. The navy's pulling some sort of blockade— Bridgewater's got thirty galleons parked between here and the cocoa route—so we took the long way round, and . . ."

"And you found the cave," Merrick finished.

"We weren't looking for it, I swear! Someone spotted a glint in the waves. As if the sun itself was shining from under the water. Captain sent me down to investigate, and I—I saw it." He dipped his head back, the seawater on his forehead glistening like pearls. "None of the reef fish would swim past the opening. I knew right away what it was—I've heard the story so many times." The pirate didn't have to recount the story. Every sailor alive knew it by heart and by gut: a cave filled with treasure. More treasure than a man could spend in a lifetime, more treasure than a man can conjure up in his mind. A gemstone for every grain of sand on the beach. A gold coin for every star in the sky . . .

"Well." Merrick broke the pirate from his spell. "You found it. Most sailors don't get this far. I hope you feel lucky."

Still trembling on his knees, the pirate refused to look at Merrick.

"As if heaven itself directed your sails." Merrick suddenly cracked into a smile. "So go get it."

The pirate whipped his head up, alert.

"Get the treasure," Merrick said. "I won't stop you."

A sound rose from the pirate's chest—part whimper, part sob. "No," he started, "no, I don't want—"

Merrick scratched his chin with his pistol. "You know the stories, which means you know what guards my treasure."

"Yes," the pirate whispered.

Merrick closed the gap between him and the pathetic, quivering pirate. "Perhaps you thought those parts of the legend were an elaborate lie? Exaggerations of my cruelty?"

"No!" the pirate cried. "No, I—"

"Because let me assure you." Merrick touched the barrel of his pistol to the man's temple, gently; it could have been the wind, tickling his face. "I am as monstrous as they say."

The *Rasculat*'s captain and crew tensed, their weapons ready.

The poor pirate clenched his eyes shut. "I—I thought it would be worth the risk."

"And now?" Merrick said, twisting the gun's barrel, leaving a rut in the man's skin. "Now what do you think?"

"Now," the pirate said, and finally peered up, right into Merrick's eyes, "I wish we had taken our chances with Bridgewater."

Merrick's blue eyes burned. "Too late." He yanked the pirate up to a standing position and pushed him to the railing, the pistol still digging into the man's temple. "You wanted to see the great treasure of Merrick the Monstrous, so go see it."

The captain of the *Rasculat* finally spoke: "Please, *pra-lipe*. We did not mean—We'll sail away now and never speak of what we have—"

Merrick cocked the pistol—a deafening click. "You're going to swim into the cave," he told the pirate shaking at the railing, "and you're going to get the biggest jewel you can find. You're going to bring it back up here. If he surfaces without it," he ordered his crew, "shoot him on sight. Turn him into shark bait."

A wail escaped from the pirate, guttural and saliva-choked, a horrible noise to come from a feared robber of the sea. He protested, and begged, and tried to bargain, but

Merrick motioned impatiently and Bloody Elle lifted the man with one arm and tossed him into the sea.

Minutes of ghostly quiet followed. Both vessels floated, waiting, the captain of the *Rasculat* frozen. The white foam from the pirate's dive faded, and the ocean calmed itself back into turquoise glass.

One of the *Rasculat*'s pirates bravely called, "He has a family, you know. Two boys, ten and six. The six-year-old lost an arm last year in a fire—"

"Then pray they grow up to be smarter than he" was Merrick's response.

Bubbles finally trickled up, those of a man desperate for air, and the pirate kicked through the surface gasping, a pale-pink diamond the size of a melon under one arm.

"What have I done?" he cried, swallowing air with loud gulps. "What will become of my family?"

The captain of the *Rasculat* motioned for his men to reel the pirate back into their schooner.

Merrick waited until the man stopped his cries. "You're going to take that diamond to the first market you find, and you're going to sell it. Sell it and buy everything you've ever wanted. Retire from the pirate's life. Spoil those two sons of yours, and buy your wife the most expensive dress she can find." The wind once again brought his words right to the pirate's ears. "And then buy yourself a headstone."

The *Rasculat* left first, speeding away from this nightmare as quickly as they could. Then the whole episode was nothing more than fading ripples on the sea.

The *Jewel*'s crew dropped their recent plunder down into the cave—the finest of precious stones, rare obsidian blades, and yes, enough gold coins to create their own constellations. Down, down, sinking down . . . Straight down through the water and into the mouth of the cave. They worked fast, knowing their captain would punish anyone who couldn't make up for the squandered time with the *Rasculat*.

When the hold was empty of its riches, Bloody Elle turned to Merrick for his orders.

"Chart a course for the market," he said after a moment.

Bloody Elle raised her eyebrows. "Someone is expecting you," she reminded him.

He swung his pocket watch by its chain, as if it were a yo-yo. As if time itself were nothing but a plaything. "Yes," he said. "But I don't want to show up empty-handed."

She frowned. "We just raided half a dozen cocoa ships and a luxury cruiser. Wasn't there anything—?"

"No," he cut in. "There wasn't. Nothing worthy. We'll stop by the stalls before we head to the grotto."

Bloody Elle started to leave, then turned back and lifted her finger, rubbing the embroidered collar of his greatcoat—tiny spots of blood smeared across the white stitching, remnants of an earlier skirmish. "You might want to get cleaned up before your big date."

To witness the ocean's many-pronged ecosystem is to watch the great saga of survival unfold. Consider the seabirds who roost in colonies on perilously rocky cliffs, or the brave clownfish who make a home of venomous anemones, or the polar bear cubs who learn to paddle through the icy waters of the north. . . .

This parade of mortal struggle is enough to make one ask: How can life endure such inhospitable conditions? How can life go on with the bleak shadow of death constantly lurking, fangs sharpened, teeth glistening with hunger?

To which we say, joyfully: What other choice is there but to thrive?

—*Exploring an Underwater Fairyland* by Dr. and Dr. Quail

9

The sound of Bloody Elle landing loudly on the deck woke Fidelia with a start.

"Morning, sunshine," the pirate said, reeling a rope around her wrist and elbow. She wound it into a tidy bunch, then tossed it onto a pile of fat wooden pulleys, all of them splintered.

"Morning?" Fidelia sat up on the bench and glanced at the sky, then sank back in relief when she saw the thin blue light of midday. Arborley Island was barely out of sight, then—a recent memory on the horizon.

No sign of the Undertow. Not yet—the clouds were wispy now, thin and clear as ice—but Fidelia knew better than to believe a calm sky at this time of year.

"How long was I asleep?" she asked, and checked her bag. All three observation books were safely tucked inside: her mother's, her father's, hers.

"We're about twenty knots from Arborley," Bloody Elle called from halfway up the mainmast. "And you snored through all of them."

Fidelia stood, and immediately felt her legs quaver. Her mouth pooled with hot saliva, her stomach pitched, her head spun . . .

"Oh, cobbers, you're green as a bog." Bloody Elle dropped back down onto the deck and guided Fidelia back to the bench. "Lost your sea legs, have you?"

Fidelia defiantly rose back to her feet. "No, I haven't, I just . . ." She closed her mouth quickly—her digestive system was threatening to reverse itself. "I just . . . need a minute."

"Breathe through your nose." Bloody Elle pointed over the railing. "The head's that way."

Sucking in cool, salty air slowly, Fidelia waited for the world to stop spinning and tried to forget what Bloody Elle had said about losing her sea legs. *Just a minor adjustment,* she thought. *A few more minutes, and I'll be right as rain.*

A seasick Quail—it was as ridiculous as a shark swimming backward.

But the whirlpool in her belly couldn't be blamed on the ship: the *Jewel* met every swell with the confidence of a racehorse—head-on, galloping, smoothing out the bumps for its passengers. Impressive for such a raggedy ship.

No, this was all Fidelia. She was woefully out of practice for life at sea, drooling and strung out, her eyes dead-fish glassy.

Bloody Elle offered Fidelia a blackjack of water and a bit of dried ginger root.

"Ginger root . . . is for landlubbers," Fidelia muttered, her stomach still pitching, but she took it and held it to her nose, inhaling. Almost instantly her tummy calmed its storm, and she was able to breathe without gagging on the briny air.

Bloody Elle refastened a splitting line, her fingers quick with the rope. Her sleeves were pushed up, showing her tattoos: those thick black lines around her wrists, and that swallow flying across her left hand.

"What do they mean?" Fidelia asked. "Your tattoos?"

Bloody Elle wrapped the rope around itself, tying a complicated knot. "Have you ever been to Canquillas?"

"Just the lagoons," Fidelia said. The teardrop-shaped country jutted out from the mainland north of Her Majesty's Sovereignty. Its coasts were rich with weaver fish and beds of sea urchins; Fidelia had driven the *Platypus* along the continental shelf many times while Dr. and Dr. Quail dove for samples.

"Well, in Canquillas we have a saying." Bloody Elle

finished the knot and secured its loose ends. *"No essa suetro problemita."*

"And what does that mean?"

"'Mind your own business.'" Bloody Elle snapped her fingers at Cheapshot Charlie, and pointed to the mast—he immediately climbed the mast to check the rest of the lines. A branch of leaves, dried to crunchiness, fell to the deck. Fidelia looked up and frowned.

"Where has this ship been?" she wondered aloud.

"Pretty much everywhere," Bloody Elle said with a smack of pride. "A snow cave up north. Inside another big ship. We hid her in a forest once. Hence the leaves."

Fidelia squinted at the mizzenmast—fuzzy green fibers coated the beam. "Did you hide her near a lake?"

"Not near a lake, *in* a lake," Bloody Elle said. "How'd you know?"

"Pine mold," Fidelia said, pointing to the mizzenmast. "Did you say you sank this? A whole ship? How?"

"Sealed off her chambers with clay and piled her with sandbags. Captain's idea." Bloody Elle glanced across the deck at Merrick, who was checking a winch near the stern. "He wasn't sure if we'd ever see the *Jewel* again, or if she'd be rotting at the lake bottom until kingdom come."

Fidelia stared at the wrinkled, patched sails, the lines

crossing at all angles. "But I don't understand. Why hide a ship at all?"

"The navy wants the *Jewel* as much as they want Merrick the Monstrous. She's a trophy to the admiral. A symbol." Bloody Elle peeled away a splinter from the railing. "Like those hunters who skin a lion to make a rug."

"But why not let them have it? Why not take another ship?" Fidelia asked. "You're pirates, aren't you?"

"Because this is my ship." Merrick suddenly stood a foot away from Fidelia, her glasses reflected in the liquid of his black-and-red eye. "And I don't sail without her."

His peacoat was off, draped over the railing—how shockingly small he looked, without his layer of heavy wool. A pirate captain should be strong, shouldn't he? At least strong enough to scale a mast or man the pump. Merrick didn't seem steady enough to stay upright in the wind.

"Elle, are we gossiping over tea, or are we sailing a ship?"

Bloody Elle hardened her face at once and gave her full attention to the mizzenmast.

Fidelia thought about the sailors who docked in Arborley, the ones she'd known for years. Every captain had his own set of superstitions. Ratface never allowed bananas on the *Anemone,* for fear of bad luck. Stinky Jane, boatswain of the *Tinderbox,* never changed her socks between voyages, which made her awful company during the Undertow. Perhaps the *Jewel* was Merrick's own unique superstition — not a single voyage without his lucky ship.

She unfolded her legs and tested their strength — this time, they let her stay standing. She took a few cautious steps across the deck, watching Cheapshot Charlie billow out the canvas sails with his thick arms, Bloody Elle testing a half-rotted pulley, and Merrick . . . Merrick was doing twenty tasks at once. He plugged oakum in the seam between two planks, straightened a line of empty barrels, and consulted the ship's compass.

"Where is everyone?" Fidelia asked.

"Everyone who?" Merrick said.

"The rest of the crew," Fidelia said.

Merrick checked a line in silence.

"How can you possibly man a ship without any men —?"

"Tell me." Merrick yanked the line, his hands white-knuckled — skeleton's hands. "Did your parents actually enjoy your incessant questions?"

Fidelia blinked. She had expected the physical dangers that came with pirates — gunfights, mutiny, scurvy — but less so any emotional rocks they would throw. She jutted out her chin and recited, defensively, "'Knowledge is a vessel deeper than the sea. A fool splashes in a pond and thinks he has the answers, but a wise man knows that the only way to reach its depths is to ask questions.'"

"A quote from a beloved Dr. Quail?" Merrick asked with a sneer.

"No." Fidelia folded her arms. "From my aunt Julia."

He stopped cold, staring out at the water. "Another one of your scientists?"

She shook her head. "A librarian." She was surprised at how fiercely the sadness struck her as she thought of her sweet aunt. Sadness and guilt; Aunt Julia had been trying so hard to make a new life for her. A life of comfort and safety—and this morning, Fidelia had snapped at her for it.

Where was Aunt Julia at this very moment? Fidelia wondered. On the library steps, waiting for Fidelia to come home for dinner? Was she out on the streets of Arborley, searching for Fidelia in the dark? Had she already called the constables? Aunt Julia would be all alone tonight—with another missing Quail to mourn.

Fidelia closed her eyes and wished she was back in the loft, seated at Aunt Julia's little green table. She'd even choke down a bowl of that vile turtle soup as an apology for their spat. *You probably think I'm gone forever,* she messaged her aunt telepathically. *But I promise I'll find a way home.*

Home. Fidelia still didn't know where that really was.

"I have a question for *you,* Dr. Quail." Merrick's mocking broke clean through Fidelia's thoughts. "Have you figured out how you'll get to the bottom of the sea?"

Fidelia adjusted her glasses. "No."

He pointed to a bench below a group of shrouds— where he could keep a close eye on her, she noticed. "Then get to work."

10

FROM THE JOURNAL OF DR. ARTHUR QUAIL

May 11

Today Ida's studying the migration of the pink crabs on Crabmoore Shore. We've been waiting here for six hours; the only critters we've seen so far are dozens of oysters, a few limpets in a tide pool, and the molted shells of black-tailed shrimp. Fidelia's trying to be patient, but it isn't easy for a young girl. "The crabs will come when they're ready," Ida keeps reassuring us, but then she taps her own foot when she thinks we're not looking.

Sometimes this is how it feels—like nature waits until we're not looking.

Fidelia's eyes blurred as she scanned the scene her father had doodled in his observation book—a crab waving its pincer in greeting, the back of Fidelia charging into the water with her dress sashes untied and streaming, Ida looking back at Arthur, a smile in the corner of her mouth.

Slam! Cheapshot Charlie plunked the crate with the Water-Eater in it on the bench next to Fidelia, all the contents rattling. "Get to work."

"I am working," Fidelia retorted, and defiantly ran her eyes over the same sentence in her father's observation book, again and again, until Cheapshot Charlie left her alone.

She pulled the busted-up pieces of her invention out of the crate and set it on the bench next to her. Flipping through her own observation book, she found her original blueprints for the Water-Eater, all her initial notes, and the sections that had been scrubbed out, scribbled over, and rearranged altogether. Even though she hadn't looked at these plans for weeks, they were seared into her brain.

This was her last chance to get it right. If she couldn't figure it out, it would be the end of her. Merrick had promised that.

The Water-Eater, as it existed in her daydreams and sketches, was a small rubber mouthpiece attached to a long, cylindrical device, which stretched out to both sides like a handlebar mustache. The device was covered in rubber scales, each of which allowed seawater to seep through small holes and enter the filtration chamber. The chamber separated the water molecules from the air molecules, leaving free, clean oxygen to flow into the wearer's mouth.

In theory.

In reality, however, she had never been able to successfully filter enough oxygen — after a few small gulps, her test runs always ended with the whole system flooding.

She opened her observation book to a clean page, then uncapped her pen and made an inventory of all the pieces she had.

Mouthpiece. Hollow cylinder. Scales. Filtration system. Oxygen chamber. Hoses. Small tool kit (screwdriver, wedge, hammer, worm gear, and a handful of bolts and screws). And that was it. No raw materials, so she couldn't start over from scratch. No way to plug up the holes in her filtration chamber, no way to extend the cylinders so more water could flow into the system, no way to adjust the angles.

No way and no time.

She closed her eyes, searching through the caverns of her brain for an answer. A fix. Even a starting place. But all she could see was the *Egg*, smashed on the shore of Stony Beach. An invention she'd had such confidence in — she would have bet money that it would survive the Undertow. But she'd been so wrong.

How could she believe the Water-Eater would be any different?

"Hungry?" Bloody Elle interrupted Fidelia's stream of thoughts and offered her a choco-glomp. Fidelia munched it down gratefully.

"How's it coming?" the pirate asked.

Fidelia didn't answer, but Bloody Elle seemed to read Fidelia's thoughts. "You'll figure it out," the pirate said. "Your folks were fish people, weren't they?"

"They studied fish, yes," Fidelia said. "Fish people" made it sound like she'd descended from some *ichthyo-sapiens* hybrid — Ida and Arthur Quail with gills and fins and scales.

She waited for Bloody Elle to leave, but Bloody Elle pulled out another choco-glomp and unwrapped it for Fidelia. Fidelia ate it, feeling some of her melancholy dissipate as her body took to the sugar.

Her parents, the fish people . . .

Fidelia opened her mother's observation book, turning pages until she found a diagram of angelfish's gills. She studied her mother's pen marks, the way the ink pooled at the tops of her loopy *L*'s . . . How she wished Ida were here now, on the other side of the bench, saying calmly, "Pull it apart in your mind. Stand on the other side. Now stand on your head. What does it look like now?"

Mom. Fidelia's eyes stung with tears.

Bloody Elle pointed at a picture of a shark on the opposite page, its tail stretching longer than the paper would allow. "That's one scary-looking beast."

"It's a thresher. See its tail?" Fidelia dragged her fingers along her mother's drawing. "They crack them like whips and stun their prey. We saw one once. . . ."

She stopped talking, letting her mind play the memory—she and her mother in the *Egg,* Ida at the helm while Fidelia gawked out the porthole at the shark. "Six feet of fish, six feet of tail," Ida had said of the thresher shark, and Fidelia hadn't believed her until she saw for herself. So many animals sounded too fantastic to be true, like fairy-tale beasts—horns, and giant eyes, and hundreds of legs, and scales every color of the rainbow . . .

"There are different kinds of sharks?" Bloody Elle said. "I just watch for the big sharp teeth and start swimming."

"There are three hundred species." Fidelia flipped a few pages and found a goblin shark: a rare pink shark with a rusty-nail smile and a long, flattened spike for a snout. A funny unicorn, seven-year-old Fidelia had called it. A living fossil, Ida had called it, and had been too goo-goo and starry-eyed to sleep that night.

"Wow," Bloody Elle said. "I'd hate to run into one of those while taking a dip."

"You think this one is a monster," Fidelia said, "you should have seen this one." She showed Bloody Elle her own observation book, the slapdash sketch of Grizzle she'd made while waiting for her parents at the Book and Bottle that night.

Talk about mythological creatures—was Grizzle truly that massive? She hadn't really let herself think of him; it was too easy for her mind to wander from the shark to her parents. *Did that really happen?* she wondered again, for the thousandth time since that night. Was Grizzle a real shark, a shark she had baited and tried to tag, or just a fabrication that had grown, ripple by ripple?

Her parents, lost. Did that really happen?

"He's wide as a lifeboat." Bloody Elle was still balking over Grizzle. "So this is one of the famous Quail discoveries?"

Not yet. That's what she would have said six weeks ago. Before everything in her world upended.

"No," she said quietly, and closed her observation book.

Bloody Elle watched Fidelia, and looked like she was about to say something when her belly gurgled. "Whoops."

She slapped it. "Time to fill the pit." She rustled through her knapsack for another sweet from BonBon Voyage Sweets Shop — a kaleidorainbow fig.

Fidelia was starving, too — but when Bloody Elle tried to pass her a crack-o-mallow bar, she refused.

"Please, no." Her stomach felt wrenched inside out. "I can't possibly eat any more candy." She searched around her pathetically, as if one of the masts might suddenly sprout apples. Her eyes found the sandpit, a cast-iron cook pot dangling from a tripod above a pile of forsaken coals on the main deck.

Mmm, fresh seafood. A couple of scallops, grilled on the coals. Blackened cod. Some boiled sea lettuce . . . Her mouth watered. "Does the *Jewel* have a fishing pole?"

"But we already have the fish." An unfamiliar voice boomed across the ship.

The hatch to the hold was flipped open, and a group of strangers clumped on the quarterdeck, each holding a pair of antique revolvers, silver with ivory inlays, one in each hand. Except for a woman with maroon lips and a ribbon with a rose around her neck — she held two curved daggers, which she twirled expertly.

Fidelia stayed where she was on the bench — barely moving, barely blinking.

"You have no need for your pistols," a large olive-skinned man with a dark ponytail said to Merrick, who stood at the helm, his gun aimed calmly at the intruders. "So you can drop them."

Cheapshot Charlie and Bloody Elle waited for their captain's orders, their own guns steady. Merrick didn't move, except his top lip, which curled ever so slightly, ever so dangerously.

"Shall we convince you to obey?" the man said, his accent heavy. A throng of clicks; the strangers readied their own guns to fire.

"We have been in the dark, drippy hold for many hours," the man went on. "We're tired, and impatient, and I'm sure a few of us are anxious to test our guns. Make sure they still fire."

With a poisonous glare, Merrick dropped his pistol to the floor, and motioned for his two mates to do the same.

Fidelia's heart clenched with sickening fear—what happened now? Merrick's crew was bad enough, but at least they needed her for something. These others . . . What if they didn't see her as valuable, but as fish food?

"I thought stowaways were supposed to stay hidden during their stolen ride," Merrick said. "Even rats know better than to do their scurrying in daylight."

Stowaways . . . Even Fidelia knew this was an insulting word to just sling around. Back on Arborley Island, whenever stowaways were caught, they were flogged or jailed—or worse. Most stowaways didn't make it past a ship's crew, who were always eager to punish anyone who took a ride without pulling his weight.

"Stowaways?" The barrel-chested man with the ponytail and thistly black beard smiled. "Now, *pralipe,* you've lost an eye since we last met, yes. But do you truly not recognize us?"

Fidelia held her breath. The strangers' faces radiated hunger, she now realized—not for food, but for something else. Something crueler, bloodier.

"You and the *Jewel* may look like you've sailed to hell and back," the man hissed, "but I know it's you."

Merrick said nothing, only twitched his fingers ever so slightly. The man pursed his lips. "Well, *pralipes,* I suppose we can't expect Merrick the Monstrous to remember every person he's pillaged."

The man spat at Merrick's feet and shifted his revolvers so they reflected the last gasps of sunset's gleam. "I am Niccu, captain of the *Rasculat.* Two years ago, you took something of ours."

Merrick's black-and-red eye pulsed in its socket like a

man-of-war. "So you've come to avenge some chest of gold," he said, as if he were already bored of these intruders. As if this had happened many times before. "Go ahead, search every beam—you'll be sorely disappointed in our offerings."

"No. Not gold," Niccu whispered. "A cousin." With a sudden burst, he leaped forward and shoved his guns into Merrick's neck, pressing hard enough into the cords and veins to leave an indentation. Fidelia opened her mouth to yelp, but no noise came out.

"A cousin," Niccu repeated, his eyes shining. "And now we finally make the monster pay."

Bloody Elle and Cheapshot Charlie strained, but the other strangers' guns stayed locked and aimed at their foreheads. Fidelia's heart thudded against her ribs. She closed her eyes, bracing herself for the blast of Merrick's death.

Niccu clenched his teeth, his finger itching the trigger.

Then Merrick coughed.

He coughed, and coughed, and coughed.

And instead of shooting, Niccu stared at the pirate captain, and tipped his head back, and laughed.

As Niccu laughed, a hearty, beefy sound, the sun tucked itself behind the horizon, sending long, mast-shaped shadows across the *Jewel*'s deck in black stripes.

"Don't tell me," he said over the din of Merrick's hacking. "Could it be?"

Merrick caught his breath and spat at the feet of the other pirate, returning the gesture.

Niccu ogled the bloody spit as if it were a rare ten-legged octopus. "Merrick the Monstrous," he marveled, "finally undone by his own cave of wonders."

"It's only a chest cold," Merrick said.

"You wish it were so, don't you?" Niccu said. "But the cough of the red daisies is unmistakable." Niccu hooted, then lowered his guns from Merrick's jawline. "Luca," he directed one of his comrades. "Bind the pirates. Tie Monstrous to the mainmast."

A brawny man with arms almost as big as Cheapshot Charlie's immediately grabbed a rope, but Bloody Elle dashed forward, scooped up her pistol, and shot at Niccu, narrowly missing his head. One of Niccu's men backhanded her with his revolver, sending the *Jewel*'s quartermaster tumbling to the floorboards, her hair splaying like white lightning against the darkening sky.

Cheapshot Charlie bellowed and punched at two of the other pirates, who grabbed his thick arms and clung to them like seaweed. He lifted them both without effort and threw them across the deck, then stormed across the ship to his own gun.

Fidelia rushed to help Bloody Elle to her feet, but Niccu caught her. His arm wrapped around her neck, and her blood froze as he placed his revolver to her temple. "Now, now, little *bebelus*," he said in a cooing, mocking tone, the barrel of his weapon cold against her skin. "You stay here with me."

"Let her go," Merrick stopped coughing long enough to say.

Bloody Elle picked up her gun and aimed it at Niccu, massaging her jaw with her other hand. Cheapshot Charlie, too, aimed his pistol at Niccu.

"Toss your guns down," Niccu said, his dark eyes flashing, "or I blow her head off."

Fidelia stopped breathing.

"I order you to release her." Merrick set his sapphire eye burning on the other pirate captain. "Now."

"You're in no state to be giving orders." Niccu twisted the gun deeper into Fidelia's skull—deep enough to leave a mark. She swallowed a yelp. "Tell your crew to drop their weapons."

With a wave from their captain, Cheapshot Charlie and Bloody Elle surrendered their weapons once again. Merrick was lashed to the mast, the fat ropes stacking around his middle like a crocodile's armored belly. Cheapshot Charlie and Bloody Elle both struggled, but eventually their wrists and ankles were bound, and both of them were secured to a barrel on the main deck.

"What about the *bebelus*?" A bristly man in a purple headscarf pointed at Fidelia with his pair of guns. Her stomach clenched.

With the *Jewel*'s crew secured, the other pirates now stalked around Fidelia like wolves, pivoting their revolvers so they were all aimed right at her sweat-slicked forehead. The woman with the daggers homed her glare in on Fidelia especially, her eyes cold, mineral green flames, the fat of her pupils reflecting the twilight like a wild animal's.

Niccu, too, circled her, assessing. "You're puny for a pirate."

"I'm not a pirate," she said. "I live in Arborley. Merrick kidnapped me for—" Fidelia stopped. If they learned that Merrick was using her to retrieve his sunken treasure, they might not let her go. She stared at the six revolvers still aimed in her direction, her mind scrambling to come up with a lie. Six bottomless holes, six black tunnels . . .

"For a ransom," Merrick finished from the shadows.

Fidelia watched Niccu's face and hoped to the sea stars that he believed Merrick.

The stowaway pirates exchanged a few words in a foreign tongue, and gradually—and grudgingly, it seemed—they holstered their weapons. When Niccu looked back at Fidelia, he flashed a large white smile.

"Please, *pralipe*," he said, and gestured to the freshly caught fish hanging from his belt. "We would like you to share our vittles."

Fidelia nearly drooled—she was still so hungry. All she'd had to eat the entire day was candy from BonBon Voyage Sweets Shop. But her gut also told her to keep her distance. She had no idea who these new pirates were, only that they were bold enough to sneak onto the *Jewel* and challenge the notorious Merrick the Monstrous.

"Why?" she asked slowly, cautiously.

Niccu spread his arms wide. "Any enemy of Merrick's

is a friend of the *Rasculat*." He dropped his arms and scrutinized her with slivered eyelids. "Unless you are not an enemy of Merrick's, in which case . . ."

Ida Quail always said, "Always approach new critters with a tiptoe, in case what you thought were paws turn out to be claws."

In the end, Fidelia's hunger persuaded her to take their fish—although she decided she would wait until they ate theirs before she took a bite herself. Just in case they tried to get rid of her by poisoning her dinner.

The pirates scattered themselves around the cook pot, starting a fire in the sand. Fidelia took a seat on the far end of the bench, sneaking a glimpse at Merrick. He seemed a million miles away, staring at the embers with his signature glower.

As two of the pirates cleaned the fish and skewered the meat onto kebabs, they spoke to each other in their native language, their tongues rolling and flicking out sentences.

"That is my brother Hanzi"—Niccu suddenly leaned toward Fidelia and pointed to the fellow in the purple headscarf—"my brother Luca"—the strongman with the beetle-black eyes—"and Drinka, our sister." Drinka jutted her chin out in Fidelia's direction—more a threat than a greeting.

Fidelia nodded politely, her nerves still prickling. A sea breeze ruffled the sails, highlighting the silence.

"Shall I teach you some manners, *bebelus*?" Luca touched a finger to his gun. "We gave you our names. Aren't you going to give us yours in return?"

"Please." Niccu put his hand on Luca's back. "Let us not be rude." He turned to Fidelia. "Forgive us. Your name is yours to keep."

When Niccu passed Fidelia her share of the food, she muttered a thank-you and ate it slowly, her head down.

"The *Rasculat* makes berth in Molvania." Merrick broke through the silence. "You're a long way from home."

Niccu glowered at him. "I'd have sailed much farther to avenge Yanko."

"Didn't think there were any of you left," Merrick continued from the mast. "Rumor had it the navy caught up to the *Rasculat* and sold her off to beanies."

"We are all that remains," Niccu said, sadness coating his voice. "Our beloved *Rasculat* was sunk on the Molvanian shelf not three months ago."

"Bridgewater surprised us at the gulf with sixty galleons." Luca broke his kebab stick in half and threw it at the fire. "He slaughtered us. No mercy."

"The navy's supposed to run on due process," Drinka said, her cheeks blooming red. "Not extermination orders."

"Bridgewater is his own process," Merrick said.

"His cannons took the ship right down, as if it was made of straw," Niccu said. "He'd have sunk us, too, if we hadn't made it to the coast alive."

How quickly things had shifted, Fidelia pondered as she chewed the most delicious-tasting cod of her life. Moments ago, it was Merrick the Monstrous who had held her imprisoned; now he was the captive on his own ship. Such was the life of pirates, she guessed — kings of the food chain one minute, their necks between the teeth of bigger, stronger beasts the next.

And apparently for both the pirate crews, this Bridgewater was the beast above them in the chain.

Fidelia gratefully finished her kebab. Only then did she notice that Merrick was watching her from across the flames. She held back a shiver.

The moon, a wheat-colored sickle, rose higher above the water. Night cloaked the ship in darkness. The fire in the sandpit striped the two groups of pirates in golden light and shadows as the *Rasculat* captain and crew licked salt from their fingernails, smacking their lips for the last morsels of flavor before tossing their skewers into the flames.

"So," Niccu said to Fidelia, "you are captive here. Shanghaied?" He twirled his beard between his grimy fingers. "You want to barter for rescue?"

Fidelia focused on the toes of her boots, the dull light of the moon flashing off the rubber. "No, I—"

She was cut off by an eruption of coughs. Merrick braced himself against the mast, coughing so violently, red spittle flew from his lips, painting the deck. Fidelia's own chest tightened at the sight.

The cough of the red daisies, Niccu had called it earlier, and Merrick hadn't wasted a second before he denied it.

"What are the red daisies?" she asked, and immediately felt the air on the deck thicken, dense as soup.

Niccu took a pipe from his pocket and filled it with cropweed.

"From the stories, *pralipe.* Stories of a turquoise sea that gleams against the sky like liquid gemstones. Stories of an underwater cave, with enough air to breathe for a day and a night, deep beneath the waves." Drawing a dramatic breath, he finished, "Stories of treasure." He puffed his pipe, emitting a chalky smoke ring.

Merrick tilted his head back against the mast, mismatched eyes to the stars.

Fidelia, on the other hand, felt her pulse suddenly spike.

Treasure.

12

"There isn't a sailor alive who doesn't wonder if the stories are true." Niccu held his pipe aloft, silhouetting it in the firelight. "But few are brave enough to seek it, and those who are have no idea where to find it."

He reached into Bloody Elle's knapsack and found a stack of crack-o-mallow bars, which he passed around for Fidelia and the *Rasculat* sailors to unwrap and nibble.

"The man who owns this treasure is the most feared pirate to ever sail the nine seas," Niccu continued. "His name alone is the stuff of legend."

Fidelia stole a glance across the fire, but Merrick was now concentrating very hard on the dark sea.

"Now, there has never been a treasure of this size, *pralipe*," Niccu said. "Mountains of gold, the stories say. Stockpiles of jewels. Riches that would make the queen sick with jealousy." He puffed on his pipe. "But even if the stories were true, few sea dogs would dive down into the cave. Even if the stars guided them right to it."

"Why not?" Fidelia nudged her crack-o-mallow nearer to the flames in the sandpit until it got nice and gooey.

Niccu exhaled smoke through pursed lips. "The red daisies," he said.

Hanzi crossed himself.

"An odd breed, they are," Niccu said. "They grow on the walls of the cave, clinging like ivy —"

Fidelia shook her head. "Daisies need sunlight to grow."

"These daisies do not." Niccu spoke with such certainty.

"But . . ." But if the red daisies were real, she would have heard of them. She was the daughter of a Gilded Iguana–winning marine botanist. She would have known the red daisies' scientific name, their bud count, their native habitat. They would have been sketched in her father's observation book.

"It's only a story, *pralipe*," Niccu continued. "Anything is possible in a story. Now, the red daisies are beautiful flowers, they say. Beautiful and deadly. But it is not the touch of the petals that kill you, no." He took a drag from his pipe. "They have a lethal pollen. One inhale, and it is the beginning of the end for you."

Everyone seemed to stop breathing at the same time. Fidelia's eyes danced over to Merrick.

"How does it happen?" she asked. Another one of her incessant questions, perhaps—but she had to know. "In the stories, I mean?"

Niccu grimaced, as if even speaking of this delicate subject caused him pain. "It is not a pleasant death, *pralipe*. The pollen breeds in your very lungs. You stagger for oxygen. A horrible persistent buzz infects your body until you can barely take ten steps without collapsing into coughs."

Beyond the flames, Cheapshot Charlie squirmed under his ropes.

"Next is the purpling of the joints. The capillaries slowly burst and eject their liquid into the muscles. Painful, so very painful, to experience. Your skin becomes mottled with purple flecks."

Fidelia tried to remember how Merrick's arms had looked earlier that day, when he'd removed his peacoat— were there noticeable lines on his skin? Bulging veins? But she couldn't think of anything but that dead, red eye of his.

"Finally," Niccu said, his voice barely audible above the rustling of the *Jewel*'s tattered red flag, "your lungs deflate like burst balloons. You die, gasping for air, reaching for your last breath, but you never find it—"

Merrick suddenly burst into coughs, blasting noise up into the stars. Fidelia's ears rang from the shift—the near-silence to the harrowing noise of Merrick's lungs, straining for air.

She knew the story was real—of course it was, and Merrick was the dangerous, legendary pirate who owned the underwater cave full of riches. Merrick the Monstrous—Niccu had said it himself: the pirate's name alone was legendary.

But the red daisies couldn't be real. Arthur Quail wouldn't have been able to keep such a morbid specimen out of his discourses. He would have been the only person to ever hunt for the legendary cave not for its treasure of gold and gemstones, but for its bounty of peculiar marine bot-any. Fidelia's breath snagged in her throat as she thought of her brilliant, good-hearted father.

But if the red daisies were just a fiction, just a story . . . What about Merrick's cough? Despite what he said, despite how he growled when he said it—this was no simple chest cold eating away at him from the inside.

Niccu put his pipe out, smacked it against the bench to empty it of cropweed residue, and walked to the mainmast, where Merrick coughed, still bound.

"I've dreamed of this very moment for two years," Niccu

said. He reached forward and grabbed Merrick's throat with both hands. "You sent Yanko down into your cave. You sent him to his death," the *Rasculat* captain said through bared teeth.

Cheapshot Charlie and Bloody Elle thrashed in their bindings like fish in a net. But to no avail—they had to watch their captain gasp for breath, his face reddening, Niccu's hands tightening around his neck.

"I held Yanko every night as his lungs slowly choked him," Niccu went on. "Everyone could hear him, every night, his cough echoing across the whole ship. Like hearing a ghost before the man had died."

Merrick still coughed, Niccu holding his head in place against the mast. "Every night he asked me—begged me—to put him out of his misery," Niccu said. "And one night, he coughed so long and so hard, I nearly went mad from the sound of it. And this time, when he asked, I obeyed." Niccu's voice softened. "Can you imagine? Putting a bullet into your own cousin, just to ease his noise."

Fidelia held her own breath, her pulse hammering; behind her, the pirates of the *Rasculat* stood and readied their guns.

"Then do it," Merrick sputtered, his lips coated in red spittle. Fidelia closed her eyes, too terrified to watch.

But Niccu released Merrick's throat and rubbed his slick hands on his tunic. He smoothed his thicket of curls back into a tighter ponytail.

"The reign of Merrick the Monstrous comes to a fiery close at last," Niccu announced to the *Jewel,* looking right at its captain as he spoke. A bead of sweat dribbled down the *Rasculat* captain's forehead. "But just because you are going to rot away into obscurity doesn't mean your treasure has to."

Niccu squatted down to meet Merrick's eye level. "You will go back into your cave and you will bring up every piece of your treasure," he said. "Every jewel, every gemstone. Do this, and I will kill you before the pollen does."

Fidelia shivered. What Niccu was offering—it was an act of mercy, really.

But Merrick lifted his head, utter blankness on his face—not a whiff of gratitude or desire for this potentially charitable act. "How generous of you to offer," he said, "but I intend to end on my own terms."

"*Rasculat*s." Niccu stood and clapped his hands. "It is nearly *miezul*. We have a long way to sail tomorrow—first to Glassport for supplies, and then to the tropics." He pointed at Hanzi. "Take first watch—" and then, pointing at Fidelia, he said, "and you." He gestured to the hammock beneath the shrouds. "You stay right there. If you move from that spot, I'll tie you to the hull and scrub the ocean floor with you."

She should feel some relief, she realized. Merrick was finally tied up, so she was free from his captivity. Free from the crux of the Water-Eater, all of that. But what would the Molvanian pirates do with her once they'd gotten Merrick's treasure? Would they sail her back to Arborley? Would they simply let her go?

Hanzi extinguished the flames in the pit with a kick of sand and stood next to the mast like a naval officer—chest out, hands on his guns, nose alert and in the air. He glared at Fidelia, who quickly flopped into the hammock and pulled her legs up.

The ship looked eerie in the cold moonlight, without the amber glow of the fire—the shredded sails silver as cobwebs, the shadows from the masts stretching long and black like tentacles across the deck. Fidelia tried to bundle herself with the pathetically thin blanket that stank of mildew.

But her thoughts spiraled. Red daisies, creeping up a dark cavern wall. Merrick gasping for breath, his single blue eye wide and bulging. Her parents' faces pressed against the *Egg*'s porthole window as the submarine circled in the Undertow like a whirlpool in a bathtub drain.

The smoke from the dead fire wound its last curlicues up between the lines, then vanished against the pitch black of night. Across the deck, the Molvanian pirates were motionless. They'd forgone hammocks or cots, and instead strewn themselves onto the floorboards like a pile of slumbering sea lions.

Fidelia tossed from side to side, but exhausted as she was, she couldn't get comfortable. A ship used to be calming to her, a rocking cradle to lull her to sleep. Now her insides shifted with the *Jewel* as she tried to keep everything level.

After counting imaginary dolphins leaping out of the water in majestic arcs, she gave up and left the hammock.

"Hey," Hanzi warned, raising his guns for leverage. "Get back in bed."

She scanned the deck for an excuse to walk near Merrick and spotted the blackjack of water next to his mast. "I just need a drink," Fidelia said.

"I don't care if your throat is the Nesmian Desert," Hanzi said. "You stay in your hammock."

Fidelia thought. "You know, if your captain decides to take me back to Arborley for a ransom," she said, borrowing Merrick's earlier fabrication, "my parents will want to know how I was treated." It made her stomach a bit uneasy, using her parents for this lie, but she kept going. "They won't be in much of a mood to negotiate if they find out you deprived me of basic necessities. So are you sure your captain wouldn't want you to let me wet my whistle? Maybe we should wake him."

A mild threat—but it worked. Hanzi's upper lip twitched in annoyance, but he motioned to the blackjack, muttering something in Molvanian as she crossed the deck.

"Bad dream?" Merrick said while Fidelia sipped from the blackjack.

Fidelia didn't hesitate. "Is it true?"

Merrick stared out at the sea. "Parts of it."

"Which parts?" she asked. "The treasure? The cave?" She didn't ask about Niccu's cousin, whether Merrick had truly sent him to his death. She didn't need to.

"Buzzing, buzzing, with the questions," he hissed. "You're worse than a damn mosquito."

One more question: "The red daisies?"

Instead of answering, he coughed—and that was enough for Fidelia.

"Then . . . you're dying," she whispered, as if it were a secret. But they all knew it, didn't they? Cheapshot Charlie and Bloody Elle did, with their sideways glances and their tight, strained sighs—they had entire conversations with their eyes every time their captain coughed. Niccu knew it—he pegged the very cause of Merrick's condition the second he heard it.

"We're all dying," Merrick said.

"Not as fast as you are." A chill inched down her spine. "That treasure . . ." She found it difficult to breathe—is this what it felt like, when the red daisies took their horrible effect on a pair of lungs? Drowning in air? "You tried to get the treasure out yourself," she hypothesized. "Didn't you?"

He finally used that bright blue eye to look at her, to pierce her. "Go away."

"I don't understand," she went on. "You, of all people . . . You knew how dangerous that cave was. Why would you go in that cave without a diving helmet, or a mask?"

Anger flamed in her chest. How could Merrick treat life this way? Like an angelfish, beauty of the sea, swimming right into a tiger shark's mouth, willingly dying useless and alone.

"Enough," he said.

"You're dying for gold?" She couldn't wrap her mind around it. "For jewels?"

"I said enough!" He spoke so sharply, Hanzi finally noticed.

"You, *bebelus!*" the Molvanian barked at Fidelia. "Get away from him. Back to your spot, or I wake Niccu."

Fidelia obeyed.

Back in the hammock, Fidelia lay flat on her back, peeking at the stars.

We're all dying . . . Merrick's words flitted through her mind like damselflies above a pond.

What would it be like? To know your own countdown had started? To know, every day, that the end was coming, soon enough to measure?

She thought of her parents in their final moments. At what point had they known it was their time?

She pressed her face into the smelly blanket. She would give anything—all the treasure in Merrick's cave and then some—if she could redo that last day. She would have done everything different. She would have docked the *Platypus* before the Undertow hit. She would have chained her parents to the boardwalk if she'd known the field study would end with body bags. If she'd known it was their last day—

She flipped over onto her stomach. These were Merrick's final days, and what was he doing with them?

Chasing after a treasure—no, now he was bound to his own mast, and his great treasure, source of all the legends, would go to someone else.

Irony was a cruel mistress. "Merrick the Monstrous, finally undone by his own cave of wonders," Niccu had said.

Her repulsion for Merrick bubbled up like seasickness.

Tired as she was, it was a long time until she fell asleep.

Two Years Earlier

Molvania's market was exceptionally busy that day. Merrick stepped off the dock and into the wet market, strolling through five different conversations conducted in five different languages. People haggled for their own versions of the best prices, shouts of excitement, and anger, and frustration, and delight, and a thousand other emotions all bending at once through the bodega—the spectrum of commerce. It was loud enough to drown the thoughts in a man's own mind, but Merrick was quiet as he wove through the stalls.

The sun was a fiery golden ball hanging low in the sky like a pendant. Cheapshot Charlie and Bloody Elle flanked their captain as he moved through the bazaar, twin pillars with sharp eyes scanning the crowd for a flash of silver buttons or the royal blue of naval uniforms.

The paisley maroon headscarf of a Molvanian coast-guardsman? Not a threat. But any sighting of a thatched-hay mustache or a head reminiscent of a beet? Make for the ship at once.

Tacked to the bricks of a hash house was a poster—a perfect charcoal sketch of Merrick, smirking at the viewer as if he knew something they didn't.

Merrick the Monstrous, the poster read. *Wanted for robbery, burglary, arson, murder, jail breaking, and piracy. Extremely dangerous. Ten thousand blue notes for capture, dead or alive.*

"Ten thousand blue notes." Bloody Elle whistled. "Imagine what we could buy with that kind of bread."

"Do you two want to turn me in? Split the cash?" Merrick said. An obvious joke—ten thousand blue notes, as impressive a sum as it was, would be mere pocket change to them.

They walked away, leaving the poster where it was.

He wandered past baskets of dried shark fins, wooden crates filled with live crabs, florists' booths with fresh orchid branches, spice merchants with displays of exotic cinnamon sticks, cardamom, cloves . . .

At every stall Merrick would do the same thing: stop, scan, then leave, scowling.

"This place will be swarming with officers by sundown," Cheapshot Charlie reminded his captain.

"We're not leaving until I find something," Merrick said.

"The admiral knows you're here—"

"The admiral can choke on a barnacle." But Merrick did pick up his pace. If he didn't find something here, today, at this wet market, he'd be returning empty-handed. He wouldn't do that again. Not this time.

He'd brought her things before: mother-of-pearl earrings, emerald necklaces, a belt made of hand-woven alpaca. Each time he'd present something to her, and she'd just stare at him with those soft eyes, gray as doves, as flint, as the sky after an ocean storm. She didn't even have to say anything—those eyes said it all.

Thank you, but I'm not interested in things you've stolen. Thank you, but I don't want trinkets. Not something you picked up from a beanie ship. Not something you wrenched from a dying duke's hands.

No, she didn't want any of his spoils.

But still. For years he had searched for the perfect thing to give her. Something to remind her that their love was, to him, as tangible as the gold he plundered. Something for her to hold when she couldn't hold him. Something that told her that he saw into the very heart of her, just as she saw him.

For years he had searched, and come up empty-handed.

And oh, how a pirate hated to search for treasure and come up empty-handed.

He stopped at a jeweler's booth. The owner watched Merrick with suspicious eyes, smoking a glass *shisha* with long, lazy drags.

"What about this, Captain?" Cheapshot Charlie held up a milky-white comb, inlaid with abalone shell.

"No," Merrick said as soon as he looked. "She doesn't wear things in her hair."

"Well, cobbers, I don't know the first thing to look for." Bloody Elle skimmed the booth and found a diamond-encrusted tiara, shiny enough to put the sun out of work. "This?"

Merrick scoffed. "You just picked up the flashiest thing he has."

"Don't mind her," Cheapshot Charlie drawled. "She doesn't know the first thing about picking out jewelry."

Bloody Elle glared at him but didn't argue.

"The merchandise is for buying, not looking," the jeweler said.

"How can we buy it if we don't look at it?" Merrick asked calmly, examining a ring.

"If you won't buy," the jeweler said, "then we're closed."

"Closed?" Merrick repeated. "In the middle of the afternoon?"

"Closed to you," the jeweler snapped. "Now, go. Other customers want to buy."

Merrick pulled a wad of blue notes from the breast pocket of his embroidered overcoat. "Here," he said, peeling off a note and tossing it at the jeweler. "That should buy us the freedom to browse without you whining."

The jeweler hesitated, then took the money. "Ten minutes," he said, greedily fondling the bill while Merrick ran his eyes over every piece in the booth.

Merrick.

He could hear her voice in his head now—a small voice, but powerful. Like the northern wind.

I don't want your spoils.

A set of opal cuff links.

I don't want your stolen gold, or rubies, or diamonds.

A peacock-shaped locket, with garnets for the bird's glistening eyes.

I only want you.

There. He spotted it, tucked in the back corner of the booth like the jeweler was ashamed of it.

A pewter brooch, with a frilled edge. No gloss or shine to it. Just metal.

"A fine brooch," the jeweler immediately boasted, "worn by the duchess of Molvania for her wedding—"

"Save it," Bloody Elle snapped. "Captain, are you sure? It's so . . . gray."

Gray, like a pair of eyes. The color of storms.

"How much?" Merrick asked.

"Twenty thousand green notes," the jeweler said, testing the waters.

"Like hell it is!" Cheapshot Charlie's jaw clenched. "I should pull out your beard, hair by hair, for thinking you could swindle us."

"Fine. A thousand green notes," the jeweler said, and puffed his *shisha,* "and I'll be glad to be rid of it. It cheapens the rest of my wares."

Merrick reached for his wad of notes, then stopped. This was money he'd acquired through work. Through piracy. Either he'd pilfered this cash directly from cocoa ships or he'd sold the things he'd stolen. He had quite the stockpile of money on him, and on his ship, and even more hidden away in a secret location, but—

I only want you, she'd said.

That's what he wanted to give her. A part of himself.

His hand bypassed the money and found the only honest thing he had: a silver pocket watch, the one his father had given him when he was a boy. He held it out without a word.

The jeweler lifted it to the sky, as if he expected it to be transparent. He checked its gears, then gave a short nod. The trade was accepted.

He gave Merrick a little box, and Merrick carefully cradled the brooch in the layers of crushed velvet.

"That box is probably worth more than the brooch," the jeweler said, his *shisha* clacking against his teeth, "so don't be surprised when your lady is insulted and throws the whole thing in your face for thinking she has such poor taste!"

When the smoke in his booth finally cleared, the three strangers were gone. The jeweler reached his arms into the air, stretching his back, and rolled his head around his neck socket—and the crowd parted, just for an instant, long enough for the jeweler to see the poster glued to the hash house wall.

That face . . . That crooked smile, the fire dancing behind the eyes.

"Him!" he shouted to the shopkeepers around him. "The pirate from the posters! He was here, in my booth!"

"What a fool!" they shouted back. "Ten thousand blue notes to kill him, and you let him walk free?"

The wet market suddenly burst into a frenzy of yells—it was always loud, yes, but with this news that profitable pirates were roaming wild, the clamor was unmatchable.

The Molvanian coast guard blew their horns. Booths closed their canvas flaps. Beefy mercenaries with tattooed faces dashed to their schooners, readying their curved scimitars and salivating for their handsome rewards as they paddled out of port.

But it was too late. The pirates had already slipped away to their ship, and as the sunset painted the horizon in rosy stripes, Merrick took the helm and guided the *Jewel* into open waters, the weight of his pocket watch replaced by the heft of a pewter brooch in a velvet-lined box.

Something from him.

The ocean, like any jungle, has its monsters—its tigers and its bears. Of course, the supreme king of these underwater beasts is the shark, and he should be treated with utmost respect. Entering the ocean means trespassing into his kingdom—and he can be a fiercely protective monarch.

—*Exploring an Underwater Fairyland* by Dr. and Dr. Quail

"Fidelia!" Dr. Ida Quail's voice carried through the rain-
forest like a bird's call.

Fidelia was crouching on the pad of a giant water lily
(*Victoria amazonica*), collecting algae samples with a cotton
swab. She paused, a catfish splashing her as it crept up the
riverbank.

Her mother repeated the cry. "Fidelia! Come quick!"

The hairs on the back of Fidelia's neck stood at attention. She jumped onto shore and cruised through the green
undergrowth until she reached the tree house.

The tree house was about twenty feet up, the perfect
height for the Quails' research hub in the jungle: too high
for most carnivorous prowlers, too low for pesky mon-
keys—or so they thought. Fidelia hurried up the bamboo
ladder, her gut knotted in terror. Mom sounded like she was
in trouble.

Her imagination whizzed with the dreadful possibilities: Had Dr. Quail been cornered by a jaguar? Did she get scraped up by a patch of walking palm trees? Had a foul-tempered anaconda slithered into the tree house? There were countless other things that could go wrong during a field study; so far, the Quails had been lucky.

But what if today was the day their luck had finally run out?

Ida Quail was in the tree house, hunched over with her back to the door—limbs still intact, still breathing, as far as Fidelia could tell.

She approached her mother cautiously. "Mom? What's wrong?"

Her mother giggled and spun around. She held a baby three-toed sloth, which had its arms wrapped around her neck like a human infant. The sloth was wearing Fidelia's spare glasses, the awful horn-rimmed ones she only kept around as a backup. "She won't take them off!" Dr. Quail said.

Fidelia tickled the lethargic sloth under the chin. "She can keep them. They look better on her, anyway." She placed a sunbonnet on the critter's head, and the sloth dreamily leaned its head back, modeling it.

"Fidelia?" Dr. Arthur Quail jogged up the ladder, a sliver of suma root in his hand. "Ah, there you are. Let me see that arm." A cloud of mosquitoes hovered around Dr. Quail's chin. His blood-sucking companions were determined to penetrate his wiry goatee but were ultimately unsuccessful, thanks to a newly concocted mosquito repellent, made from vine juice and figs.

She extended her arm. A bite from a rat snake crossed her wrist. "It's not that bad," she said, but Dr. Quail dabbed the milk from the suma root onto the injury.

"This will keep it from scarring." He kissed her forehead. "Now, I can't find my notes on the star-grass specimens. Have you seen them?"

The tree house was a hurricane of crumpled bedsheets, browning apple cores, and manila file folders. "You two are slobs." Fidelia used her toe to slide a Goliath cockroach off Dr. Quail's clipboard. "They're right here."

"What would we do without you?" Ida said. The sloth climbed onto Fidelia's shoulder. When the critter peeked up at Fidelia from under the bonnet, it had one blue eye and one black-and-red eye.

The black-and-red eye started bleeding.

* * *

The sound of gulls clucking woke Fidelia, and the last whispers of her dream fizzled away. It was dark still, the light thin, the stars faint—that strange, uncategorized moment between night and dawn.

She pushed herself up to a sitting position and found her glasses. No sign of any black clouds or tempestuous waters. But there, in the distance, she could see the blurred outline of the horizon climbing, of trees, the corners of buildings.

The mainland.

Glassport—she identified the famous glass dome in the skyline immediately. *This is what Aunt Julia wants for me,* Fidelia thought, rubbing warmth into her arms. A move to a city like this.

A new fire flickered beneath the cook pot. The pirates of the *Rasculat* stood around the sandpit, Niccu stirring a pot filled with Molvanian coffee. Fidelia knew that scent. It was Ida Quail's favorite java—black as tar, strong enough to stand up a spoon in. Blinking hard before the tears could pool, Fidelia swung her legs to exit the hammock—but then she heard Niccu's words.

". . . all the way back to Arborley for her ransom," he was telling the others. "It's not worth the trip."

Fidelia quickly lay back down, pretending to be asleep,

her ears straining to hear the rest of the conversation above the usual din of sailing—chains clanking, the creaking of old wood bending into water, the wind flapping the sails.

"Then what do we do with her?" Hanzi said. "I'm not babysitting."

"We'll sell her to the highest bidder," Niccu said. "There'll be someone in Glassport that'll want her. Matteo, maybe."

"Or Lucian and Crow," Drinka suggested.

Niccu shrugged, sipping his coffee from a tin mug. "Either way. She'll fetch a fine price."

Fidelia's heart sickened. Now what? She didn't want this, didn't want any of this—she didn't want to go with Matteo or Lucian or Crow or any other dangerous-sounding piratical sort; she didn't want to stay with the Molvanian pirates, either.

She hadn't even wanted to leave Arborley in the first place.

A cold fear throbbed in the hollow of her stomach— and a rage. This was Merrick's fault. He was the one who dragged her away from Arborley Island. And now, it seemed, she would have to get herself out of this mess.

If she explained to the Molvanian pirates who she really was, if she promised them some sort of reward money for returning her safely and promptly to Arborley Island . . . Would they believe her? Would Aunt Julia be able to scrape together an amount of cash that would suffice?

She planted her feet on the deck boards, hoping she would be able to bargain her way into a safe trip home. But she stopped.

Merrick, still leaning back against the mainmast, suddenly rolled forward, the ropes that bound him falling silently away from his body and onto the boards. Fidelia gaped, her eyes flickering to the Molvanian pirates. None of them noticed as Merrick stealthily dropped to all fours, crawled to Bloody Elle and Cheapshot Charlie, and sliced through their ropes with the dagger in his boot.

Adrenaline coursed through Fidelia—but she willed her heartbeat to steady itself and considered her choices: She could scream and alert the Molvanians, strangers who were planning to sell her off. What if they wouldn't make a deal with her? What if they refused to take her back to Arborley? She could be bounced all over the world, from ship to ship—she might never get back to Aunt Julia. Or she could stay silent and trust that Merrick would stay true to his word to return her after she helped him to retrieve his treasure.

The monster she already knew or the monster she didn't?

Fidelia chewed her bottom lip as Merrick, Cheapshot Charlie, and Bloody Elle stole across the deck, one light step at a time. Merrick's throat bobbed up and down—a cough tickled, but he stayed silent as the waters.

Could she trust him to return her home when this was all over?

One look into his blue eye, and she knew she had to believe him.

"Scrub the pond scum off this ship," Niccu ordered, giving the chipped, rough railing a severe look. "And find something to patch her up. Oakum, if they have it. We'll fully refurbish her when we have the bread for it."

Bloody Elle crept, ever so quietly, behind a row of barrels, readying a broken board to use as a club.

Meanwhile, Cheapshot Charlie shook the numbness from his arms and climbed up the mainmast like a spider. He began untying the knots holding a tangle of ropes to the mast.

Luca dropped his empty coffee tin and stepped away from the sandpit, and Merrick struck. He seized Luca, pressing his blade into the pirate's neck.

The other Molvanians jumped, yanking out their guns. Before they could fire, Cheapshot Charlie loosed the ropes, trapping the Molvanian pirates in a heap on the deck, where they bobbed like idiot carp.

"Monstrous!" Niccu cried. "This isn't over! I'll have you—"

Bloody Elle charged forward, batting the revolvers from the Molvanian pirates with her board. Cheapshot Charlie climbed down from the rigging and joined Bloody Elle, seizing weapons and restraining the *Jewel*'s invaders.

But in the tussle, Niccu kept a hold of his gun, and, from his position lying on the deck boards, aimed it through the ropes not at Merrick but at Fidelia, who stared back at the revolver. The dark tunnel of the barrel was a tiny black circle across the deck, a shark's eye moments before it rolled back in its socket. Her heart stopped, her feet froze, everything slowing as Niccu's finger inched back on his trigger. . . .

Aunt Julia's face surfaced in her mind, and Fidelia clenched her eyes shut.

Merrick stepped in front of Niccu's gun just as it discharged. As Merrick staggered back, grasping his left shoulder, he dropped his grip on Luca. Bloody Elle seized Niccu's gun from his hand and spun it around to face Luca, who put both his arms in the air. Merrick knelt on the boards and angled his dagger against Niccu's neck.

"Please," Niccu choked, his oily black hair caked in dust. "Kill me quickly."

"I thought anyone from the *Rasculat* would have more sense than to chase after legends," Merrick said, not a shred of pain in his voice. "Especially after losing one of your own to the daisies."

Niccu looked up at Merrick, his eyes wide in fear. "How could I live with myself?" he whispered. "To be so close to Merrick the Monstrous and not try to win his gold?"

Merrick let the tip of his blade drag along Niccu's skin. "How does it feel now? To stare at your death?"

Niccu said nothing.

Fidelia thought she could feel every billow in the sails, every insignificant wave beneath the *Jewel*. Even the morning breeze held itself back, waiting.

"Are you thinking about gold now?" Merrick growled. "Riches? A stockpile of gems?"

Niccu shook his head. "My—my home."

Merrick named it for him. "Molvania."

"Yes." Niccu tilted his head back onto the boards and closed his eyes. "A golden sun over farmlands. Rolling green hills, and mountains, and snow. Frescoes hanging in the village cathedral, older than my grandmother. The house I grew up in . . . only a shack, but my home."

Goose bumps prickled Fidelia's arms. Home.

"Oh, Yanko." Niccu whimpered this, a sad smile on his face. "I failed you, my cousin."

"You'll see him soon enough; you can beg his forgiveness then." Merrick tensed, his mouth a long, bold killing line as he pressed his dagger into Niccu's throat.

Fidelia's insides constricted. "No!" She ran to Merrick's side and held on to his elbow; he tried to shake her off, but she clutched tighter than a barnacle. "You can't kill him! I won't let you!"

"Stay out of this, Quail." Merrick motioned to Cheapshot Charlie, who grabbed Fidelia around her middle and hauled her back.

"I won't help you!" she spat. "I'll throw my Water-Eater right overboard. Then you'll have to figure out some other way to get your precious treasure!" She felt electric, blazing with righteous energy. Bargaining energy.

"Or," she fired on, "you'll have to send me down into the cave alone. Without anything to protect me. Will you really send me down to my death? I'll make you do it." She paused, catching her breath. Would he truly make her suffer the way he was? Was he really that monstrous?

He looked at her, unblinking, his blue eye burning. With a snarl, he stabbed his dagger into the deck and grabbed Niccu by the collar of his tunic. He dragged the Molvanian pirate to the railing, hoisted him up, and held him over the side of the ship. It was terrifying, Merrick's burst of strength—his peacoat flapped open, his shirt beneath unbuttoned, revealing a chest sunken enough to hold water, but still he lifted this bear of a man and dangled him above the water as if he were an empty candy wrapper.

Niccu did not fight back. He didn't kick his legs or throw punches—he simply locked eyes with Merrick and bowed his head. "I will watch for you in the stars," he said—not a threat, but a simple statement. A final blessing, of sorts. A premature eulogy.

"Stop!" Fidelia yanked free of Cheapshot Charlie's hold and rushed over to Merrick—too late.

Merrick threw the captain of the *Rasculat* overboard, and from the deck of the *Jewel*, Fidelia could see a ring of white where Niccu splashed into the water—and then disappeared.

Cheapshot Charlie turned toward the rest of the Molvanian pirates. He removed the tangled ropes, but before he could lay hands on them, the pirates rushed to the rail and, one by one, jumped. Over the side and into the blue.

Fidelia scanned the water, but the *Jewel* moved so quickly—she couldn't see whether the pirates were still bobbing at the surface or if they had already sunk to the bottom like stones.

Merrick nonchalantly checked the time on his pocket watch. "The *Jewel's* aching to stretch her legs, mates. Let's let her run."

Churning, white-hot with fury, Fidelia bubbled over. "You—you *killed* them!"

"I did not kill them," Merrick corrected. "Notice how there's no Molvanian blood on my deck?"

"No," Fidelia seethed, "you didn't slit their throats, but they're as good as dead."

"Glassport is within range." Merrick pointed back at the mainland. "They managed to survive their shipwreck in Molvania. They're obviously strong swimmers."

"But their ship didn't go down during the Undertow. Even the strongest swimmers don't stand a chance!" The sea was too choppy today—the Molvanians were probably already on the ocean floor.

Fidelia slumped at the railing, watching the morning sun hit the waves. "You murdered them."

"Quite the moralizing, coming from a scientist," Merrick said. "Tell me again about your starfish dissections? About how you bleed fish to make shark chum? And tell me again what happened with the silver seal cub?"

Fidelia stood straight up. She knew exactly what Merrick was referencing: *Exploring an Underwater Fairyland.* Her parents' book.

A thousand counterarguments darted through her head at once. The starfish limbs they had dissected to better understand their suction capabilities in tropical waters.

The blood they harvested for chum was from tuna, which they used only because populations were over-saturated near the island.

And the silver seal cub, well . . .

"That cub—" she started.

"Was dying," Merrick said, "and you and your parents did nothing to interfere."

She opened her mouth to protest, but nothing came out. What could she even say?

If she reached into her bag for her observation book, she would find the exact entry that described that day—with far more detail than the chapter from her parents' book:

February 11

Today was a sad day.

Yesterday we found a colony of silver seals migrating east for what Mom calls the "family reunion." Every clan of silver seals from all over the region meet. Mating happens. Babies are taught to hunt for fish under the ice. They stay until spring, and then hightail it back to the glacier fronts to eat the new green shoots and fatten up for the next family reunion.

One seal cub wouldn't leave his mother's side. She barked at him; he cuddled closer. She nipped at him; he tried to nurse. When we finally got a good look at him; we saw why: the cub was blind. Milky-white eyes, a thick film over the pupils. No wonder he acted like the umbilical cord was still attached.

But then the pod started to move. The mother pushed the seal away from the group, off to his own patch of arctic gnome grass. He munched a few blades, and then cried out for her. But she ignored him, flopping along on her belly with the rest of the clan.

"She's abandoning him!" I cried, but Dad shushed me.

When the pod was out of range, the cub stopped his wailing. Maybe he ran out of strength, I don't know—or maybe he sensed what had happened. He sniffed around

*the gnome grass for a few minutes, and then shuffled off
into the wilderness.*

*"We can't just let him go!" I told Mom and Dad.
"He'll die out there!" I grabbed a rope and said, "I'll go
after him and—"*

*"No, Fidelia," Mom said quietly. Like the funeral for
the little cub had already started.*

*This morning, when we were near the penguin bur-
rows, we found the cub's body, frozen solid in the snow, his
white eyes staring up at the sky.*

*I know all about the ethics of observation. I know
about the principle of study—that we can't watch nature
without affecting it somehow. But I see that silver seal cub
every time I close my eyes, and probably will for a long,
long time.*

Sometimes it's hard to be a Quail.

Fidelia gritted her teeth, willing herself to stay where
she was and not charge at Merrick with fists swinging. She
hated him for bringing up that day. That was a terrible day.

"It's not the same thing," she managed to say, shaking.
"It's not the same thing at all."

The Quails' work wasn't about death. It was about
life—and, yes, sometimes that included death.

And was Merrick forgetting how the chapter about the silver seals ended in *Exploring an Underwater Fairyland?* The last words Ida Quail wrote in that chapter were: "The circle of life, the food chain, the give and take of nature—however it is phrased, life always ends in death. Death, yes, that terrifying ending that every living thing is plummeting to, yes—but how wonderful life is, while it endures. . . ."

Merrick's smirk was unbearable. "You're alive for today, aren't you? And I believe you have a set of gills to finish—assuming you are as good as your word."

Fidelia felt his mismatched eyes on her as she left the railing, sat on the bench next to her Water-Eater, and listlessly opened her observation book. How on earth was she supposed to concentrate on work right now?

Bloody Elle picked up the ropes that had bound Merrick. "Charlie," she murmured, "come here."

She showed him a length of the rope; Fidelia leaned forward to eavesdrop.

"He didn't cut it," Bloody Elle whispered.

"Then how . . . ?" Cheapshot Charlie said, his eyebrows furrowed.

Both of them looked across the ship at Merrick, his skinny forearms poking out of the sleeves of his peacoat as he checked the tackle.

"His wrists," Bloody Elle said. She held her hand to her mouth. "Look at them."

Fidelia marveled with them—Merrick's wrists had absolutely wasted away since last night, the bones jutting from the pale skin like knobs on a pine trunk. Was he disintegrating so quickly?

"Charlie." Bloody Elle's voice was small and scared.

Cheapshot Charlie studied her face, then approached Merrick slowly, as if approaching a wild animal.

"Captain," Cheapshot Charlie said. Merrick said nothing.

Cheapshot Charlie nervously scratched the back off his bald head. "That Niccu . . . he said he put his cousin out of his misery. . . ." Cheapshot Charlie hesitated, still watching his captain with something akin to compassion softening his features.

Merrick stared at Cheapshot Charlie, his face as still as chiseled marble. "You have no idea what misery is. Don't speak to me of it ever again." The captain's black-and-red eye throbbed in its socket.

Then Merrick struck.

He stood tall and backhanded his boatswain with his gaunt hand—a wallop that must have stung horribly since Merrick's knucklebones poked out like the tines of a rake.

Cheapshot Charlie staggered back, hand on his cheek.

"Now, set our course south," Merrick said calmly.

Cheapshot Charlie straightened. "Aye, Captain." He headed to the helm, refusing to look up at Bloody Elle as he passed her.

Merrick spotted Fidelia watching, and so she quickly buried her head into the observation book and pretended to work.

Merrick the Monstrous. Not a shred of mercy in his bones.

Not even for himself.

Their good fortune managed to hold out for a few more hours.

Merrick put some space between them and the mainland, and then let the *Jewel* fly. She eased along the breaks at a steady fourteen knots an hour. Fidelia wouldn't have believed it if she hadn't seen the rope herself, dangling over the stern. An impressive speed for a top-notch naval galleon; a scientific anomaly for a schooner in such poor condition.

"She used to go twenty, on a good day," Bloody Elle bragged, spotting Fidelia watching the knots.

Fidelia tried to imagine the *Jewel* as she used to be— her decks scrubbed, the scum scoured from the masts, the beams straightened, the bubbled wood reset and sanded.

She tried to imagine its captain in his heyday, too—and then he bent over the helm and coughed, and the image she'd conjured of him, hale and hearty, vanished into the breeze. He looked like something that had been plucked from a drain and wrung out—had he really once been the terror of the nine seas?

Cheapshot Charlie went up in the cherry picker to mend a few holes in a sail—a job that would have been handled by a rigger if Merrick had a proper crew. But the canvas was patched quickly, a slapdash job, and the sails billowed like strange patchwork blankets.

The sea gusts blew harder and stronger, but the horizon was a bleached blue in all directions. Fidelia breathed easily at the unexpected peace—and then she thought guiltily of the Molvanian pirates. Were they still treading water? Or had the waves already claimed them?

A fighting chance, Merrick had essentially proclaimed it—but Fidelia still couldn't think of it as anything but cold-blooded murder. And she didn't care what Merrick said. Throwing Niccu overboard wasn't the same as the Quails leaving the silver seal cub alone to succumb to nature's grand plan. Not at all.

Why was she surprised? Merrick the Monstrous was a known killer.

But last night, with the fire burning in the sandpit,

and the stars above, the look on Merrick's face when Niccu spoke of the red daisies had seemed so—

Well, whatever she'd seen in Merrick's sapphire eye last night—grace, or fear, or some sort of change of heart—it had clearly been imagined. She'd seen his cruelty in action, and she wouldn't underestimate him again.

She opened her mother's observation book to the diagram of the fish's gills and unscrewed the filtration system from the cylinder. She peered at the tiny holes of the filter, which she had sized out according to this very calculation, here, in her mother's hand.

Well-oxygenated ocean water contains approximately 6 mg of oxygen per cubic foot. Shallow-water fish require 10–14 mg/L per hour; cold-water fish are in the 4–9 mg per hour range.

The idea for the Water-Eater was born of frustration. It was squid-mating season, and Fidelia and her father had just hauled Ida back into the *Platypus* for the third time that morning. The diving suit kept springing leaks. They had to keep patching and reinflating the canvas, and so the hose kept getting tangled, and Ida was exhausted from climbing in and out of the suit. "A pair of gills would sure come in handy," Dr. Quail had said, wiping her sweaty forehead with the back of her ink-stained hand.

A pair of gills . . . The words had burrowed into Fidelia's mind like worms, and while Dr. and Dr. Quail had reeled in the bait lines, Fidelia had scribbled the first spark of the Water-Eater in her observation book.

Dr. and Dr. Quail had listened and smiled encouragingly when she showed them her plans, but had they done so out of parental obligation or because they truly believed it was a good idea?

Now she'd never know.

If your average shallow-water fish needs 14 mg of oxygen per hour, Fidelia figured, her pen scrawling the figures in her observation book, *and ocean water has 6 mg of oxygen per cubic foot, then . . .*

She doodled a few scraggly sea plants while her brain ran the numbers.

Then a fish would need to process two and a third cubic feet of water per hour in order to be fully oxygenated.

Yes, that calculation was right . . . for a fish.

The wind swirled Fidelia's hair into her face, again and again. Finally, she slammed her observation book closed;

maybe Merrick would have an extra handkerchief to tie back her scraggly strands.

She walked across the empty deck and knocked on the door to the captain's quarters.

"What?" Merrick called.

She opened the door, completely unprepared to see a pale, shirtless, strung-out Merrick lying on his rolltop desk, Bloody Elle at his side.

"Ah, perfect timing!" Bloody Elle said. "We could use your scientific eye." She stepped aside—and Fidelia nearly fainted at the sight of a bullet lodged in Merrick's shoulder, the skin around it shattered like a frozen pond.

Bloody Elle pressed a knife into Fidelia's hands. "Try to pop it out in one piece, okay?"

"What?" Fidelia said. "No, I'm not a surgeon!" She dropped the knife on the desk.

Bloody Elle sighed and picked up the blade, then prodded at a flap of Merrick's flesh. "I can't tell if it hit bone," she analyzed.

"So what if it did?" Merrick grunted.

"If we don't set a broken bone, it won't heal properly," Bloody Elle said. "Your whole arm will be useless."

"Considering that very soon I won't be in need of

my arms, broken or otherwise," Merrick cut in, "do get on with it."

Fidelia had never seen a gunshot wound before. She stared at the bullet, how wrong it looked, the way it surfaced out of the flesh like a seal breaching for air. Her eyes couldn't let it go.

Bloody Elle gingerly pressed into the wound—it instantly surged with blood. "You need Lynch for this kind of job," she told Merrick. "This is beyond what I know how to do."

"Yes, well, Lynch is dead, isn't he?" Merrick's blue eye flashed with pain. "Oh, damn it, Elle, I'll do it myself." He seized the knife from her; she threw her hands in the air and stomped out of his quarters.

"Charlie!" Merrick shouted. "Bring me a drink!"

"We're dry, Captain!" Cheapshot Charlie called, and then, after a moment, "Do you want the candy?"

Merrick cursed.

Fidelia told herself to look away, but she didn't. She saw every second of it—Merrick gritting his teeth, digging into his shoulder with the knife, popping out the bullet, his forehead damp as a toad's backside.

Then the blood really flowed. Merrick ripped some lining from his peacoat and dabbed at the wound until it stopped its waterfall. He pulled out a sewing kit and threaded a large needle with thick black floss.

"Aren't you going to sterilize that?" Fidelia asked.

He snorted. "Hardly any point, is there?"

Fidelia nervously picked at a strip of paint on the window-sill, then cleared her throat. "I suppose I should thank you."

"What for?" Merrick bit off the thread and wiped the sharp end of the needle clean on his coat.

She forced herself to meet his mismatched eyes. "I know that bullet would have gone right into my heart if you hadn't stepped in front of me."

"Don't flatter yourself," Merrick said. "I'll sacrifice a lot more than a shoulder, if you can get my treasure."

A set of lungs, a chest, a throat.

A life.

It was becoming quite a list, the things Merrick was forfeiting in the name of this magnificent fortune.

"How are they coming?" Merrick used one hand to close the flopping, oozing flesh so he could make a clean stitch. "Your wonder-gills?"

A tiny flicker of fear sparked in Fidelia's chest, but she merely shrugged. "Fine," she said. *Fine if I was an actual fish,* she finished in her head.

"Good." He grunted. "You've got less than a week to

get them up and running, or else—" He stuck the needle through his flesh and slapped the desk with the pain.

Before she could witness any more carnage, Fidelia charged out of his quarters, taking in gulps of fresh air. Tuna guts and critter blood she could handle, but not the sight of a pirate sewing himself together like a grandmother's quilt.

"Oy, pip-squeak!" Cheapshot Charlie motioned to a puddle of seawater that had sprayed along the lower deck. "Get the mop. Make yourself useful."

Her cheeks burned. "If you wanted a cabin boy, you should have kidnapped one." She marched back to the bench and picked up her Water-Eater's disassembled filtration system, inspecting the holes again with the new numbers in her head. *Two and a third cubic feet of water,* she thought, *and it's been processing way more than that.* But how could she possibly make the holes in the filter smaller? Try to plug them with tar? Find a new filter altogether?

No answers. Not even a whiff of an idea.

She slammed her filtration system back into the box, satisfied when it made a loud noise.

There was no way she could possibly do this. She needed her parents there, needed their guiding comments and their probing questions.

When Merrick found out she couldn't make the

Water-Eater work, what would happen? Niccu's face appeared in her mind, then faded—would that be Fidelia's fate?

She had to try something. Anything.

Slumping over to the tar bucket, she coated the Water-Eater's filter with the gooey, smelly black stuff, spreading it as thick as frosting across all the holes. She'd let it dry until it was tacky. With luck, she'd be able to pierce the tar and make smaller holes. Maybe then the whole system wouldn't flood.

Or maybe she was dead wrong—but she had to try something.

Cheapshot Charlie saw what Fidelia was doing and groaned. "Elle, get her away from the tar." He spoke about her like she was an unleashed puppy. "She's making a mess."

Fidelia dabbed a second layer of gloppy tar over the holes in her filter, making defiant eye contact with Cheapshot Charlie as she did so. "If you don't like my methods, take it up with your captain."

She focused her attention back on the tar—all her attention, except a tiny corner of her brain, which replayed a memory of when she had been working on the Hydro-Scanner.

"It's useless!" she'd growled, shoving the pieces of her

invention across the table as if they were radioactive. "Stupid thing—I'll never figure it out!"

Her mother had set a plate of toast and tomato jam on the table and kissed Fidelia's forehead. "So you're at that stage, are you?"

Fidelia folded her arms. "What does that mean?"

Her father grinned. "You've had this moment with all your inventions. You make that exact face. That frowning, pouting, 'the world's a black hole and everything's ending' face."

Ida demonstrated the pout for her daughter, who immediately wiped her own face clean of expression.

"You always reach this point," Arthur said, kneeling down to Fidelia's level.

"And you always break through," Ida said. "Don't stop now."

"Elle, where's Captain?" Cheapshot Charlie pulled Fidelia out of her recollection before the tears fell.

Bloody Elle was inspecting an old line of oakum between boards. "Fixing up his bullet hole. Why?"

Cheapshot Charlie nodded at the starboard railing. "We're nearly there."

For a terrifying moment, Fidelia thought he meant the cave. How could they have reached it in less than a day—unless Merrick wasn't just monstrous but miraculous as well?

But no—they hadn't even hit tropical water yet. The air still had the crispness of a continental zone. Of course they weren't there yet.

So what had Cheapshot Charlie spotted? Fidelia set aside her tarry Water-Eater and leaned over the railing.

Something poked up through the water. Something that looked like bright-red hands reaching skyward with spiky, curving witch's fingers.

Fidelia recognized it on sight. "Fire coral."

The Coral of the Damned, a rare and dangerous variety of fire coral that sliced and cut and burned through flesh. Its fringes split into sections of six, instead of five—she could've found the exact pages in her own observation book, four-year-old Fidelia's sketch in red pencil, giant flames along the margins to indicate "Ouch! Do not touch!"

"Charlie," Bloody Elle said quietly, "do you think we should call him—?"

"No need." Merrick strode across the deck, a crimson blossom staining the shoulder of his left sleeve like a silk flower. He came next to his crew, resting his limp left arm on the railing.

To Fidelia's shock, Cheapshot Charlie wrapped his arm around Bloody Elle, holding her tight against him.

"Here we are, mates," Merrick said. "Who could have guessed we would sail through here so soon?"

Bloody Elle nodded. "It feels like it was yesterday."

The three pirates stood there like this in silence, Bloody Elle and Cheapshot Charlie entwined, Merrick beside them with his dead arm and stony face. The *Jewel* seesawed up and down on the water; the wind was soft as it trilled through the lines.

Fidelia's stomach gurgled. She nudged a nearby knapsack with her boot, and candy spilled out onto the deck. She wrinkled her nose, about to ask them if they really expected her to survive on BonBon Voyage sweets, when Bloody Elle reached up and removed her headscarf, letting her dirty, white-blond tresses hang loose as she traced her wrist tattoos with wandering fingers.

Merrick had closed his eyes, and he murmured something, words that fell and were lost in the din of the waters.

And then, most surprising of all —

Cheapshot Charlie took a breath and started to sing. Not loudly, not in a language Fidelia recognized, and, if she was being honest, not well — it sounded like a sort of tuneless drone that could cut through fog, meandering through the same three notes.

But even though Fidelia had never heard this song, she knew those notes. She knew that sound.

A mourning song.

"I'm sorry," Fidelia said softly.

Merrick's blue eye was cold and sad as he watched the water break against the fringes of the Coral of the Damned. "You're not the only one who's ever lost someone," he said, and the cruelty in his voice cut right through her.

But it felt that way sometimes. It felt like no one else in the world could possibly be as alone as she was — not even her aunt Julia.

She let Cheapshot Charlie's song wash over her, everything else fading — the *Jewel,* the sea, the pirates. She was back at her parents' funeral, the congregation humming the grief hymn in unison. . . .

She heard all the things everyone had said when they passed by the caskets for the last time. Things that meant nothing, and were meant only to crack open the awful, awkward quiet. Things the world had dictated were the correct, polite scripts for such tragedies. "You'll be missed." "Rest in peace." "Never forgotten."

And to Fidelia: "I'm so sorry for your loss."

I'm sorry . . . that's what everyone said. The constables were sorry, the sailors at the Book and Bottle were sorry, the professors from the university were sorry, Aunt Julia was sorry. . . . But sorry was a blanket that left your feet cold, a thin soup that couldn't fill the aching hunger in your bones. Sorry was the only thing people could offer, and it was a cruel, false replacement for what she had lost.

Everything Fidelia had been waiting to hear—everything she had been waiting to feel—was here, in this boatswain's simple mourning song.

Her chest took in the notes, filling itself with recollection; her tears spilled over. Those three notes, over and over . . .

The breeze picked itself up, drying the tears on her cheeks. The *Jewel* bucked, and Fidelia nearly lost her balance at the railing. Was that the wind howling, or Cheapshot Charlie's song?

Again, the breeze blasted, blowing Fidelia's hair into her mouth faster than she could spit it out, and her insides clenched in fear.

She backed away from the railing, her hands finding the mizzenmast. She clung to it, clawing into the wood. Behind her, Merrick shouted something to Bloody Elle, but Fidelia could hear only the wind, that horrible, deafening howl.

It was back, and with a vengeance.

The Undertow.

The noises alone were worse than her darkest memories of the storm — violent slaps of the canvas sails; the entire ship shaking its boards; wind moaning like a banshee; and above all, the hiss of water, spraying up in fountains above the deck line. It was incredible how quickly the Undertow could accelerate — but to pause and marvel at it was a deadly move.

Merrick was just as swift to respond. "Charlie!" he ordered. "Tie the base down. Elle, take the helm, now!"

The crew members swiftly ran to their positions as the sky dimmed. Everything was cast in shadow now, the sun an empty promise behind the gray clouds.

"Quail!" Merrick barked something to Fidelia, but Fidelia couldn't move. She was petrified, stuck against the mizzenmast, her feet trembling, her lungs unable to inhale or exhale. Louder than anything, louder even than the storm, she heard Cheapshot Charlie's mourning song, playing in her head again and again, a music box . . .

Across the deck, she saw the three observation books blow open on the bench, pages thrashing. She saw it— her eyes took it in, but it meant nothing; her brain was frozen.

"Quail!" Her ears could hear Merrick calling her name, but this didn't register. Nothing did.

Her heart fluttered—such a delicate feeling inside her chest, when all the world around her screamed and swirled.

How close is the storm? Ida Quail's voice, made tinny through the *Egg*'s radio . . .

Fidelia's answer that day: *We have . . . a while.*

The Undertow had found them that day. It didn't give a flying fish that Dr. and Dr. Quail were esteemed marine biologists or that they were beloved parents—it didn't care. And it had found her again.

And now it was her turn.

Fidelia held on to the mast and waited. Waited for the ship to capsize, waited for the inevitable wave to crash over her head and pull her under the steely blue.

You'll be missed. Rest in peace. Never forgotten.

I'm sorry.

"Quail!" A pair of rough, bony hands seized her face, knocking her glasses sideways. Merrick was shouting inches from her face, his good eye wild and electric. "Snap out of it!"

Fidelia blinked. "My p-p-parents—" she stuttered. "My p-p-parents—"

"Listen to me!" Merrick kept his hands on her cheeks, speaking slowly and loudly. "You are not going to die today. Do you hear? Get your things from the bench and go into my quarters."

He pried her off the mizzenmast. She scrambled to the bench, her legs miraculously working despite their shaking. She shoved the observation books into her bag— her mother's, her father's, and hers, all three safe—then grabbed the box with the Water-Eater parts and headed for Merrick's quarters.

Crossing the deck, the wind slanted her sideways—so she dropped to all fours and crawled, reaching the doors of

Merrick's rooms. The wind shoved against her, a corporeal ghost barring her entrance.

Even down on the floorboards, it was chilly and cruel as a winter day in the arctic. The wind stung as it bit at their cheeks, their noses, their hands. A ghostly whistle sounded in the distance — or was it right beside them? Fidelia wanted to huddle up in a ball, just lie there and let the Undertow do its worst.

"Quail, get inside!" Merrick cried. "I won't tell you again!"

With the last of her strength, she yanked on the rusted door handles. The wind kept the doors clenched tighter than a clam's mouth, but at last she flung a door open and tossed her bag into the captain's quarters, before crawling inside and letting the door slam shut behind her.

There she sat, hugging her knees under Merrick's desk, her pulse spiking as she tracked the ship's every rise, every fall. *You are not going to die today,* Merrick had told her, and she tried to let his words ring out above the hair-raising sounds of the Undertow.

The sounds of her nightmares.

"Ship adrift!" Merrick called. "Elle, eyes alert! Steer clear!"

Fidelia lifted her head and found that Merrick's

quarters had brightened. Out the windows, the sky was the dull blue color of a swordfish—the darkest of the Undertow's angry black clouds had fizzled away.

How long had she been sitting here, white-knuckled and frozen? She staggered back on deck and took a slug from the blackjack of water.

"We made it through," she panted, relief flooding her limbs.

"Aye," Merrick said, "but someone wasn't so lucky." He pointed beyond the *Jewel*'s bow, thirty feet away in the water, where the remains of a ship tossed in the waves. It was a cocoa ship—Fidelia would recognize one anywhere. Her stomach hollowed out. The sailors of Arborley dashed through her mind, one by one, as she searched for any significant details in the wreckage—a recognizable ship name painted along the pieces of the stern, a flag floating, anything.

"Ease up," Merrick ordered. "Watch the debris."

Bloody Elle kept a sharp eye as they passed, careful not to let any of the splintered beams barge into the *Jewel*'s delicate, brittle wood.

"Survivors?" Cheapshot Charlie called.

"Do you see any?" Merrick searched the churning waters with his good eye; up at the bow of the ship, Cheapshot Charlie did the same.

Fidelia, too, looked over the railing, preparing herself for whatever tragic sight she might see, whatever familiar face might be bobbing in the water.

But there was nobody, not a soul. Just the broken pieces of a beanie ship. The Undertow had reduced it to its basic parts, lumber and rope and canvas.

"I don't see any lifeboats," Bloody Elle called. "Maybe they got away in time."

Merrick snorted. "Maybe." A rogue burst of wind threw him backward, nearly knocking him over, and a wave reared high on the ocean, touching cloud.

"Brace yourselves!" the captain yelled, and Fidelia clung to the railing, a starfish on a rock. She held her breath, and closed her eyes, and hoped on a whale shark that whatever happened, it would happen quickly.

A merciful death for Merrick the Monstrous, at least. This was her last thought before the wave fell.

But the rush was over in seconds—the Undertow merely sending an aftershock of wind and water. When Fidelia finally opened her eyes, salty speckles dripped down her glasses and the sea was calm again, sunlight sparkling on the ocean swells as they shrank and disappeared.

Fidelia let go of the railing at last, her hands still quivering.

She'd survived the Undertow—not once but twice. How was it possible, when others hadn't fared as well? That broken cocoa ship in the water?

Her parents?

Anything can happen, some unattached voice seemed to whisper to her.

Merrick stood on the lower deck, both feet rooted firmly. His brilliant blue eye shone dangerously. "Hell's bells," he said.

"Cobbers!" Cheapshot Charlie hit the mizzenmast in anger.

The *Jewel*'s mainmast had snapped in two.

"*¡Merrda!*" Bloody Elle ran over to inspect the damage. The top half of the splintered mast rested on a crossbeam at a ninety-degree angle, like a downed tree.

Cheapshot Charlie rubbed his hands along his bald head. "The wind snapped it like a twig—"

"The wood was already weak as cork," Merrick said. "Water-warped and termite-ridden."

"I should have shortened the mainsail." Bloody Elle spat over the railing, cursing again.

"Your captain should have instructed you," Merrick said.

"How could you have known—?"

"I'm the captain," Merrick cut in. "It's my job to know."

He bent over and coughed. When he straightened, he said, "I feel . . . heavy. In my mind. Like I'm underwater. And look." He held out two shaking, splotchy hands: a network of purple and black spindly veins chartered lines across the skin like a spider's web.

"It's happening," Cheapshot Charlie whispered.

"We have to hurry." Bloody Elle's jaw trembled as she stared at her captain's mottled hands.

"We can't make it without the mainmast," Merrick said. "If the Undertow hits again, we'll capsize." He coughed again. "And I don't expect to stay on schedule with the hull as it is. It's already filthy with barnacles."

Fidelia leaned over the railing—yes, the little buggers blanketed the hull in an almost velvety mass. An inevitable occurrence when sailing across the sea.

"We can't careen her, Captain," Cheapshot Charlie pointed out. "Not without a crew."

Merrick closed his eyes, searching for a solution.

"Captain," Bloody Elle said slowly. "Considering our heading—and our current location—we might consider . . ." She cleared her throat.

"No." Merrick's mismatched eyes flew open like window shades. "Not Medusa's."

"Who is Medusa?" Fidelia asked, but the pirates ignored

her. Not even a gruff demand from Merrick that she keep her questions to herself.

"Medusa's is only two hours' sail." Bloody Elle's cautious gaze was still on Merrick, as if he were a bull shark she was trying not to upset. "We'll stay just long enough to repair the mast and clear the hull. Then we'll be on our way and—"

"No."

"What other choice do we have, Captain?" Cheapshot Charlie argued. "Row our way to the tropics? Let the navy catch up to us? Find another ship?"

"I won't sail anything but the *Jewel*."

"Then we either sail to Medusa's Grotto and fix her up," Cheapshot Charlie said, "or we wait for Bridgewater."

Bridgewater. Fidelia had heard that name— Bridgewater was the man who had sunk the *Rasculat*, Niccu said. Some sort of naval officer.

Was Bridgewater chasing Merrick right now?

Merrick pounded his hands on the railing, making Fidelia jump. "If anyone has any other idea of how to get the *Jewel* up and running, I want to hear it." His voice was threaded with rage. "Do you know how to fix this, Quail? Is there some sort of ship-tarring science your parents figured out? If so, I want to hear about it *now*."

The sea rocked the *Jewel*. Fidelia and the two other pirates were silent.

Merrick's glare was lethal. "Make for Medusa's, then."

Cheapshot Charlie and Bloody Elle headed to the lower deck, leaving Fidelia alone with the seething captain.

"What is Medusa's?" she dared to ask again.

Merrick inhaled, his black-and-red eye throbbing in its socket. "A place I thought I'd never go back to." He stalked to his quarters and hurled the doors shut behind him.

Fidelia sank onto the bench, her muscles sore, her belly knotted and sour. Adrenaline drained from her body, the storm inside her waning just as the ocean had, calming itself into a flat blue line.

Merrick's coughs were the only sound on board as Cheapshot Charlie and Bloody Elle set their course east.

Admiral Bridgewater stood at the window in his cabin as the *Mother Dog* cut across some undisclosed stretch of sea. His crimson velvet curtains were drawn back, the lamps in his quarters dimmed. Outside, night was chilly as a Molvanian jail cell—but still, the admiral stood. He watched. He wouldn't miss a ripple.

A huge round moon cast shadows on the decks of the *Mother Dog*, which were empty save for the few men assigned to first watch. The rest of the crew was stacked in their bunks like minnows in a tin, asleep. They didn't have his appetite for justice, the pathetic souls. The pansies needed their beauty rest.

Admiral Bridgewater's own bed was not yet turned down. He wouldn't sleep. Not tonight—not until he had caught that miserable scallywag.

Winter patrols didn't begin until next week. That meant Bridgewater had seven days to find him, seven days to search every wave of the nine seas.

He checked his personal compass against the presentation of the stars from his window. Suppose they headed west. Would that be closer? Or should they continue their slow patrol of the cocoa route — Merrick's favorite playground — and hope that their winds crossed?

Admiral Bridgewater smoothed his mustache, which twitched and bristled in his frustration. It didn't matter what direction they sailed; it didn't matter how carefully they planned and schemed and plotted courses. Over the years, Merrick had proved to be as slippery as a moray, and just as skillful at hiding; whenever Admiral Bridgewater spotted him, Merrick disappeared between the cracks.

"Where did you disappear to, Merrick?" Admiral Bridgewater muttered. "Back to your hidden cave of treasure? Or did you finally sail straight to hell?"

The *Mother Dog* sailed south aimlessly. The admiral barked orders at his men. He tried to do this at least once an hour, to keep them soft and afraid. Every day Admiral Bridgewater endured without Merrick behind bars felt like an eternity, felt miserable. Felt like he could hear someone laughing at him and the Queen's Own Navy.

Other pirates had met their fates. Other pirates, he had crushed like fleas under the boot of the law. But getting rid of the fleas one by one did nothing when the whole mangy dog still roamed free.

"I'll find you," he vowed to the open sea. "If I have to drag the entire ocean, if I have to storm every shore. If I have to swim to the bottom of the sea myself—I will find you."

The sun began its descent, casting a pink glow on the water, and land came back into view.

Fidelia stared as the *Jewel* came closer to the coast. The land stretched forever. Like looking out at the sea, but the opposite—green instead of blue.

The spray was warmer here, the water a more vivid blue—no more undertones of gray, no shingle beaches full of pebbles and rocks. The air even smelled green. Spiced, and fresh.

A brackish whiff hit the ship—the scent of estuaries, those spots where seawater turns into river mouths.

Near a stretch of white shale cliffs, Cheapshot Charlie angled the ship toward the land. The cliffs were straight, a line of perfect tabletop rocks with no visible openings or coves.

"What exactly is this place?" Fidelia asked Bloody Elle, who was tacking the front bottom corner of a sail.

"It's an old . . . hideout of ours," Bloody Elle said.

Merrick pulled his peacoat tighter and hunched under the popped collar. For the first time since he boarded the *Jewel,* Merrick refused to steer, or touch the sails, or do anything except glower over the bow.

"He really hates this place," Fidelia observed quietly.

Bloody Elle's smile was pained. "Actually, just the opposite. Captain loves this place so much, it hurts."

Cheapshot Charlie steered the *Jewel* so it was set to sail right into the wall of shale.

"You're heading for the cliff," Fidelia pointed out.

The *Jewel* held steady.

"The cliff!" Fidelia's voice sharpened. "We're going to smash right into it!" She looked to Bloody Elle and Merrick for their reactions, but they barely blinked.

She marched to the helm. "Charlie," she cried, "I'm not going down in a shipwreck after all you've put me through—"

"Out of the way." Cheapshot Charlie steadied the wheel.

The bowsprit was feet away from kissing the cliffs. "Hang on to something!" Cheapshot Charlie commanded.

Fidelia obeyed, grasping a guard line.

Just before the *Jewel's* needle nose made contact with the cliffs . . . the ship slipped right through, as if the cliff were just a phantom. Clear, cool water trickled down from a river channel in the cliffs—a curtain of water, Fidelia realized. A secret waterfall, which reflected the stony white of the cliffs as it streamed down into the sea. A path camouflaged so well that if you didn't know it was there, you'd never find it.

From behind the waterfall, the opening was clear—a wide arch, leading to a dark grotto, cut out by centuries of waves hurling themselves against the cliffs. The last gasps of sunlight finally disappeared as Cheapshot Charlie steered the ship into the depths of the grotto, deep under the cliffs, into the largest natural chamber Fidelia had ever seen.

The sunlight was gone, yes, but it had been replaced by a radiating blue light, almost as if the water itself were the source. The whole grotto gleamed with it.

Fidelia leaned over the railing and gasped. Soft electric-blue lights pulsed through the water.

Jellyfish.

They were so beautiful, her eyes pooled with tears.

If only Mom and Dad could see this.

"Jellies," she whispered.

"Medusas." It was the first thing Merrick had said in hours.

"Yes, medusas. A whole bloom of them," Fidelia said.

"Bloom?" Merrick repeated.

"Two or more medusas are called a bloom," she explained. Medusa's Grotto—not a person, but an animal.

The medusas flexed their billowing bodies, thin and delicate as chiffon skirts, tentacles streaming ribbons in the water. Not a ripple among them as they floated around the ship. Fidelia's face glowed—she watched the little blue jellies, mesmerized, while Cheapshot Charlie brought the ship deeper into the grotto, until Merrick told the pirates to drop anchor.

She finally peeled her eyes away from the dancing blue ghosts. Merrick climbed down the starboard side of the *Jewel* onto a wooden dock, which was built right into the grotto.

Several tunnels lined the curving wall behind the dock, like a row of hallways. Offshoots, caverns that continued back—how far under the cliffs, Fidelia couldn't tell. Underneath the entire mainland? There could be a whole pirate network underneath the cities of the world, and no one would know.

Merrick spoke to his crew, who were tying off the *Jewel* and assessing the broken mast. "Quail, you help me with the barnacles. Elle, Charlie, the mast." He set his jaw and looked each of his shipmates square in the eye. "There's no reason we should be here past nightfall."

He moved to the hull of the *Jewel,* a steel scraper and

his knife out and ready. "Quail," he barked, "are you going to give me a hand, or do I have to take it from you?"

Fidelia followed him to the bow of the ship, but her eyes stayed on those tunnels. She glanced down one tunnel and saw a room—a round office. An old rolltop desk, drippy walls covered in maps and graph paper, cold-looking candles with blackened wicks, everything buried in dust and cobwebs and time. What else would she find if she slipped away to explore?

"What is this place?" she asked, more to herself than Merrick.

He knelt on the dock, aligning his scraper with one of the barnacle clusters on the *Jewel*'s bow. "It's best forgotten," he growled.

On the dock post behind him, words were carved into the wood: *Merrick + Jewel*.

Fidelia almost snorted. Did Merrick's love affair with his ship truly run this deep?

She peeked down another tunnel and saw a hat stand. "A home is not a home without somewhere to hang your hat," Aunt Julia always said. Fidelia's heart panged to think of her, back in the library, all alone, her niece—her only remaining family—gone.

"Did someone live here?" she wondered aloud.

"Stop with the questions and come pound the scraper for me."

Fidelia tore herself away from the curiosities of the cave and eyed the hull. A colony of barnacles was growing its own city there. Once they cleared the ship of these intruders, Merrick could push the *Jewel* harder, faster. Up to twenty knots, if Bloody Elle was to be believed.

She scrutinized the barnacles. They had hours of work ahead of them, curling upside down to reach the farthest crustaceans, both she and Merrick getting neck aches . . . And without careening the *Jewel,* how would they reach the barnacles below the waterline?

She looked around the grotto, at the eerie blue water, and a pop of orange made her jump. "I have an idea." Unlacing her boots, she scooted to the edge of the dock. "There," she said. "Near that rock."

Merrick frowned. "What am I looking at?"

"Common starfish. *Pisaster ochraceus.*"

He stared at her.

"They eat barnacles," Fidelia explained. "Trust me, this'll be a feast to them." She climbed down into the water. "Ah! Cold, cold!" Her shriek echoed in the grotto. Jellyfish swirled around her, floating blue paper lanterns keeping their distance.

"Mind the medusas," Merrick warned. "They pack quite a punch."

"Don't worry," Fidelia said, wading across the water. "I know how to handle dangerous animals." She stopped, waiting for a jellyfish to drift in front of her. "You'd be surprised how timid most of them are."

"That's exactly what they want you to think," Merrick called. "Then when you're close enough, they sink their teeth into you."

An image flashed to Fidelia: a wide shark's grin, mottled gray skin, a pair of endless black tunnels for eyes. A creature so big, it could swallow her whole—a real monster, some might say, but still, a twenty-foot fish with fresh mackerel blood on its teeth would always be, to her, more fascinating than frightening.

The rock was plastered in pale-orange starfish lying in a heap, a pile of limbs. Fidelia lifted them one by one, gingerly placing them in her outstretched skirt until she had nearly fifty of them.

"Starfish will eat the barnacles," Fidelia recited as she carried her cargo back to the dock, "and then king crabs will eat the starfish. And then people will eat the king crabs. Someone, somewhere, will be dining on these very crustaceans in a fancy seafood restaurant come springtime."

"How wonderful to know I'll be outlived by the crust on my ship." Merrick took the starfish from her, stacking them on the dock. He caught Fidelia's horrified blush and smiled his terrible crooked smirk. "Don't worry, Dr. Quail. Death is a part of life, remember?"

Irritation loosed Fidelia's tongue. "Maybe I'm not as ready to accept it as you are—ouch!"

A sharp sting, right above her knee. She stumbled from the white-hot blinding pain of it, grasping for the dock.

"What is it? Quail? Quail?" Merrick grabbed her hands, holding her steady.

"Jellyfish . . ." she choked out. She tracked the way the venom curled around the wound. First, the sting of the tentacles. Next, the burn of venom pulsing through her skin. In a moment her leg would cut off all feeling—not to shut down nerves permanently but to offer an alternative to fainting from the pain. Yes, here came the numbness—her leg was now dead weight.

Merrick yanked her out of the neon water. "Where is it?" he demanded.

Still horizontal, and stiff as a plank, Fidelia ripped through her stocking and found the sting. The skin was already blistering.

He inspected the sting, using his fingernails to remove

a few stray stingers. "Nothing to do now except wait out the pain."

"Will it scar?" she asked.

"Without a doubt," Merrick said. "But what's life without a few scars?"

Fidelia took in his black-and-red eye, his bandaged shoulder, where a crater from Niccu's bullet still festered. There were a few things she wouldn't mind remembering from this whole journey—these beautiful jellyfish wafting through the water like strange aliens, for one. She'd never seen anything like it. She was certain her mother never had, either.

But she'd rather this journey not leave any permanent marks.

If only her father were here to squeeze a bit of suma root juice into her jellyfish sting to keep it from scarring.

Forget the root—if only her father were here.

The worst of the pain subsided after a few moments, and then Fidelia directed Merrick in decorating the barnacle-encrusted hull with the starfish. To his annoyance, the starfish did not immediately devour the crunchy little pests.

"Give them a minute," Fidelia said.

He coughed. "I don't have very many to spare." He

shifted from his haunches, dangling his legs over the edge of the dock.

Fidelia took a seat next to him, twelve inches of space between them. "How much time?" she asked.

She didn't expect him to answer, but he surprised her: "Who knows." He examined his pocket watch, the water's reflection turning its face blue. "Another few days or so," he said.

"Days!" Fidelia balked. "How fast do the red daisies work, anyway?"

"Fast." He narrowed his sapphire eye at her—enough prying, enough questions.

Only a handful of days . . . "That's why you're in such a hurry," she realized. "You want to get your treasure before you—"

"Maybe I just don't like to dillydally," Merrick said.

Fidelia knew better than to believe him. This was the strange way he communicated, she had learned in the last twenty-four hours with the pirate—saying the opposite of what he meant, in a cruel, mocking way to derail the less clever, to filter weak people from his conversation. A brutal form of sarcasm—how befitting a pirate captain. "But why do you want treasure?" She had to ask. The terrible image surfaced again in her mind—her parents, clinging to life in the *Egg*, their last breaths being taken . . . What whispers came out of that breath? What were they thinking of?

"Your last days of life," she said, her voice sharpening, "and you spend it hunting for gold. Why?" What could someone possibly do with treasure if they were dying?

"Because I'm Merrick the Monstrous," he said. "A vicious, greedy pirate who only cares about gold." He glanced up at the *Jewel*. "What else is there to chase after?"

"Plenty," Fidelia snapped, and when he finally looked at her, a slight surprise in his mismatched eyes, she bubbled over.

"There was this shark," she said, and told him all about the day it happened. The crackling static of the radio. The moment when Grizzle arrived, the reverence in the sea, the electricity in her blood, the excitement. "And he's out there still," she said, "Swimming somewhere, just waiting to be found." *And I thought it would be me who would find him,* she thought, *but then I found the submarine on the beach instead, smashed and twisted, and it tore me in half.*

"So is this what you would chase after, if you only had a day?" he asked, ignoring her tears. "You'd find this shark? Put a tag in its fin and collect your award?"

"It's not about the award," she said. "Don't try to turn this into treasure." Her own words surprised her—it wasn't about the Gilded Iguana or *Adventures in Science Engineering*. Not anymore.

Her eyes went to Merrick's pocket watch, its second hand's slow revolution. "I might not be able to get my parents back, but if I can get *him* back . . ." *Sometimes I think that's the only way I'll ever be stitched back together again,* she finished to herself, sniffling.

Merrick leaned forward. "Listen to me. If you have something important to do," he said, "you do it now. You don't wait until your clock has started ticking. I wish I had—" He sighed, a shaky rattling exhale. "My final days, and this is where I am."

What did Merrick mean? *This is where I am, back in Medusa's Grotto? This is where I am, sitting on a dock, waiting for starfish to eat barnacles off my ramshackle ship that somehow has more lives than a cat? This is where I am, talking about life and death with some kid I took?*

Or maybe he meant something else entirely.

She spared him from any more of her incessant questions. She sat silently beside him, and as the starfish slowly did their work, she and Merrick watched the minute hand of his pocket watch tick around, and around, and around.

Two Years Earlier

Merrick rode the bow of the *Jewel*, watching the break of the waves. He reached for his pocket watch, then remembered it wasn't there. Sweat coated his hands; he wiped them on his linen shirt and metered his breaths, inhaling until his lungs were at full capacity. Why was he so nervous? She met him here every other week, both of them breaking away from their busy schedules to spend time alone.

His hand brushed the box in his pocket. *Because this time is different,* he let himself admit.

The crew guided the *Jewel* into the shallows near the white cliffs of the mainland. Through a secret passageway, under a waterfall in disguise, they sailed the ship into a dark grotto — their hideout, used by the captain and his band of pirates for years.

The *Jewel* moved easily, like a stallion exhausted from a long day of bucking and riding, ready for rest in a stable.

Merrick kept his fingers on the small box in his pocket, its contents a mystery to most of his crew. Only his best people knew about the brooch.

Only his best people knew about *her.*

As they floated through the grotto, the sunlight faded and the strange electric blue light of the medusas pulsed from the water. Merrick smiled—not the wry, crooked half grin he gave to his victims before he pilfered their hold (or worse), but a softer smile. A genuine one.

"Dock her and get her tarred," he ordered his crew. "Shore leave until tomorrow morning. Then we head west. Cocoa season is under way; we want to be there to greet those beanies with flags blazing, don't we?" He gestured to the *Jewel*'s scarlet flag, rippling from the mast.

Hearty huzzahs from his crew—his overworked crew, who were never too tired to give their captain an enthusiastic reply.

Merrick kept smiling as he charged past the tunnels. The largest one led to the captain's quarters; a side tunnel led to an office; a third, to the rum storage.

He turned down another side tunnel, one that meandered deeper under the cliffs to a round, wide, open cavern, a room filled with books—

A library, in the middle of the grotto.

He walked up and down every aisle, past every volume. Except for the characters and ideas and words populating the books on the shelves, the library was empty.

"Hello?" he called. "Anyone here?" His voice bounced off the cavern walls.

In the back corner of the library, there was a stairway carved into the slick gray rocks of the grotto, leading all the way to the top of the shale cliffs. He climbed up until the sun warmed his head and a salty breeze ruffled his hair. He had to squint through the light to see her, sitting near the edge of the cliff beneath a jackfruit tree.

"You're late." She said this without looking up from the gigantic book spread open in her lap. She was sitting sideways with her legs folded beneath her in the shade, her posture straight as a mast. Her feet were bare, pale as shark bait, and bright yellow candy wrappers were scattered by her side—all empty, Merrick noticed with amusement.

"I lost my watch," Merrick said as he knelt beside her, and his voice wasn't a growl or a rumble or a threat, but something . . . tender, a ripple lapping the shore of a periwinkle lagoon. "Forgive me?"

The wind carried her honey-colored hair right into his cheeks. He inhaled, the smell of her like dusty old tomes and polished mahogany and cinnamon tea and chocolate.

"Of course," she said, "but see, now I've started a new chapter, and I need to finish it." Hers was the same smile as his—gently teasing, ready to break into a laugh so happy, it would split the universe into a stained-glass window.

And so Merrick relaxed beside her, one hand in his greatcoat pocket, clutching the box, the other finding hers. She turned pages in her book; he watched the afternoon sun dip lower in the sky, a golden ball ablaze, bathing the world in a saffron light. Dolphins in the distance dove up and out of the water in graceful arcs, their wakes crystallizing like snowflakes in the blue ocean.

When she finished her chapter and closed her book, she looked right at him, and he suddenly forgot everything he'd rehearsed to say to her.

"Choco-glomp?" she offered, holding up a sweet from BonBon Voyage Sweets Shop. "Last one. I saved it for you."

"I—I," he stammered, and she patiently waited, waited for the man who commanded the fear of the nine seas to summon his courage and continue. "I'm so happy," he said, "here with you." It wasn't what he'd planned to say, not at all; apparently his practiced speech had stayed on the deck of the *Jewel.*

But it worked.

She blushed, something in her gray eyes glittering

as she squeezed his hand. "I'm happy," she echoed, "here with you."

Merrick pulled the box from his pocket—were his hands truly shaking? He hadn't been this nervous since the first time the navy backed him into a corner with cannons blasting. "This is for you," he said, "and I want you to know I bought it myself."

"You mean you didn't pluck this from the hands of some . . ." Her banter trailed into silence as she opened the box. Everything happened just as he'd pictured, just as he'd hoped. Her lips fell open in a modest gasp—a sure sign of surprise from a woman who rarely let emotions paint themselves on her face.

"Merrick," she whispered, suddenly at a loss for words despite feasting on them all day in her books. "It's—it's—"

Merrick examined the brooch. "It isn't as fancy as the other things. No pearls, or rubies, or . . . But I thought—"

She stopped his mouth with hers. "You thought right," she whispered.

"Marry me," he whispered back, and her kiss was her answer, and the end of their conversation. He pinned the brooch on the simple white lace dress she wore, and she tucked her head into the crook of his shoulder, where it fit so nicely, and together they looked out at the world.

A world that wouldn't ever understand what force kept them together despite all the odds against them—a world that wouldn't understand his bloodstained hands in her ink-covered ones.

"Now, about that choco-glomp," she said. "How much do you really want it?"

He snorted and unwrapped it for her. "Your stomach must be made of steel."

The sun set. Stripes of vibrant pinks and purples, like watercolors running, streaked across the sky, and seabirds cawed—Merrick felt like he was watching himself watch it. He was . . . happy. Happy enough to think of doing things. Drastic things.

A wife. A home. Dry land.

She sighed, a sound so contented and blissful that Merrick could feel himself unraveling somehow. How did she do it? How did she manage to strip him down to his core and still make him feel boosted up, higher than he'd ever been, in the clouds with the gulls?

There wasn't a speck of the nine seas he hadn't sailed, not an inch of shoreline he hadn't explored—he knew of places not even a maritime cartographer would include on the maps.

And still.

There was nowhere he'd rather be than right here, her chin propped on his arm.

"Read to me," he implored.

She opened her book and read aloud from a story of enchantresses, poisoned arrows, hundred-year sleeps, and first kisses of pure, white love.

When the sun dipped below the horizon, the light shifted. He sat up as if an iron rod had been jammed through his spine. The motion jerked her out of his shoulder nook, where she'd been cozily making daydreams of her own.

"What?" Her whisper was fierce—the only weapon she ever brandished. "What's wrong?"

Merrick didn't answer. He stood and yanked a spyglass from his pocket. When he couldn't get the angle he wanted, he left their spot beneath the jackfruit tree and ran to the edge of the cliff.

Left her behind.

"Bridgewater," he mumbled as the unmistakable sails of the galleon, pride of the Queen's Own Navy, came into view. Its crisp white sails glowed against the twilight water.

"Merrick," she said. "Tell me what's going on."

"It's the admiral." That same mouth he'd used to kiss

her moments ago now curled in rage. "He thought the sunset would camouflage his ship—"

"You said you were done with work for tonight," she protested. "This is supposed to be our time."

"He can't find us, do you understand? He can't find the grotto," Merrick said. "I have to meet him." He collapsed the spyglass. "We'll strike first. He won't know what hit him— pompous old bilge rat—"

"You promised me, Merrick." She stood, and the light hit her new brooch, splintering the last of the sunset into the captain's eyes—reds, fuchsias, deep oranges . . .

"I know." Merrick seized her shoulders and gave her a quick, perfunctory kiss. "But I have to do this. For us."

For us.

It was the falsest gift he'd ever given her.

From the top of the white cliffs he whistled, and from every tunnel beneath, his crew stopped their lounging and frolicking and jumped to attention. Captain's whistle meant all hands on deck.

Captain's whistle meant Bridgewater.

"Get inside the grotto," Merrick directed her, "and no matter what happens, you stay there. Stay until I come for you."

"But what about—?"

"There's food, and water, and books. You'll have everything you need. Please, Jewel," he said. "Do this for me."

Her gray eyes swirled with angry clouds, a storm raging, but he didn't see them. She picked up her book and headed down the stairs into the grotto.

She looked back at him, but he was already somewhere else, his face flushed with the bloom of adrenaline. Hide and seek with the enemy—his greatest game, his greatest passion.

His first love, she realized with a stab.

From inside Medusa's Grotto, she watched his ship disappear under the hidden waterfall, back out to open sea. Then she tucked herself deep in the caverns so she wouldn't hear the stray cannons, the blasts, the ricochets, the ringing of battle. Sounds that made her heart pang and tremble. She ate shrimp, and shellfish, and sweets from BonBon Voyage—he kept them on hand, just for her, and once upon a time this had made her swoon. But now she felt like she could never taste chocolate again without tasting this disappointment, this bitterness of crumbling expectations.

She drank the cool water, and watched the jellies swim, and waited.

We have dedicated our lives to the study of marine biology for more than a decade. We have seen new species emerge from under rocks we've checked a thousand times, as if the creatures were suddenly ready for their debuts. We have seen coral reefs waste away to sad crumbles due to overfishing. We have seen inlets become swamps and beaches eaten away by the ravenous tides. After years of observation, we offer our simple, singular wisdom: everything changes. Change is life. And life is change.

—*Exploring an Underwater Fairyland* by Dr. and Dr. Quail

While the starfish munched the *Jewel* clean of barnacles, Cheapshot Charlie and Bloody Elle restructured the ship to sail on its two remaining masts.

Cheapshot Charlie bound the sails together, his big hands careful and steady with the stitches, and then scaled the unbroken masts, restringing the rigging, creating new knots, new connections. Bloody Elle sanded the masts and the rest of the ship with an old hand-plane recovered from one of the tunnels, her black-ringed forearms bulging with the effort. Merrick paced back and forth along the dock like a caged tiger awaiting his release into the wild. His impatience was all-consuming; clearly he wanted to sail out of Medusa's Grotto right away.

Fidelia stayed sitting on the dock. Her leg still tingled from her jellyfish sting, but she could feel the blood flowing, her nerves awakening. It would be sore, but salvageable.

"There," Cheapshot Charlie said, setting the last sail in place.

Bloody Elle tightened a knot. "It'll slow us down some," she said, "but it's the best we could do." She watched her captain survey his ship. It looked like a failed science project. As if the *Jewel*'s builder had missed half the blueprints.

"Weigh anchor," he said. "Cast us off."

"There's still a few tar lines that need to dry," Cheapshot Charlie said.

Merrick narrowed his blue eye. "How long?"

Fidelia could have sworn Cheapshot Charlie flinched as he said, "The night."

Merrick cussed. "We sail at dawn, then," he said, "and not a second past."

"Captain—" Cheapshot Charlie started.

"We stay on the ship," Merrick ordered. "For the rest of our time here." He slammed into his quarters, and Bloody Elle and Cheapshot Charlie had one of their silent conversations with their eyes.

Cheapshot Charlie noticed Fidelia watching and glowered at her. "Quit wasting time," he said. "All of us. Back to work."

Archipelagos reef, just after sunrise. The fish-finder Fidelia has made for our trawler is working splendidly, just like we knew it would. Our brainy, briny girl.

Fidelia touched the sketch her father had drawn of her wrestling with her Hydro-Scanner, her tongue sticking out of her mouth in concentration. She remembered that day, the first day she'd brought the Hydro-Scanner to an actual field study. How nervous she'd been, fastening it to the wheel of the *Platypus*, praying that all those late nights spent tinkering with the radar screen would pay off.

Her test run in the shallows went swimmingly, but here the water stretches hundreds of feet deep, and still! Her fish-finder located a family of brown marble groupers, hiding in the rocks. I thought Ida was going to jump out of her skin, she was so excited.

If this fish-finder is any indication of the future of Quail Studies, I don't think there'll be a single plant unidentified or a seashell left unturned.

Eyes pooling with tears, Fidelia read the passage over and over until two words stuck in her mind: test run.

A test run.

Of course.

She'd tarred over the holes in her Water-Eater's filter, and if she could find something to pierce new, smaller holes, she could conduct a test run, right here in the grotto. Merrick *had* said to stay on the ship, but she wouldn't stray far. Besides, it was either do the test now or when she was actually in the deep tropical sea, with Merrick's black-and-red eye haunting her from the surface.

A sharp splinter would do the trick. She peeled away a particularly gnarly one from the boards of the ever-flaking *Jewel* and carefully punched through the tar.

There. Holes large enough to allow water flow, but, she hoped, small enough to merely seep the water molecules into the chamber, where they could be stripped of their hydrogen and converted into oxygen.

She screwed the rest of the Water-Eater back into place, then bit down on the rubber mouthpiece and took a few test breaths. The whole thing tasted a bit like mortar, but so far, so good.

While Bloody Elle and Cheapshot Charlie were busy tightening lines on their new mast, she took off her boots and strapped on the mask over her glasses. Bracing herself for the bite of salt on her jellyfish sting, she slipped into the electric blue water.

The water brightened, and soon she could make out the edges of the jellyfish—the closest ones were twelve feet away. Not exactly safe, but safe enough.

Time for the big test.

She inhaled, just a teeny bit, and almost cried when air flowed into her mouth.

It worked! It really worked.

She pursed her lips around the mouthpiece and sucked for more air. But it didn't come.

She inhaled harder—still no air.

For the love of a lionfish! She'd cut the new holes too small.

Her head spun from lack of oxygen. She spat out the Water-Eater and searched for the bottom with her feet, so she could kick off and rocket to the top. Her feet found only blank space, more water—she had spun herself sideways, and now she was lost in the water, disoriented, and out of air, desperately trying to find the surface, blue lights flashing and spinning.

A pair of hands seized her by the collar and yanked her up. She gasped, drawing in the sweet grotto air in heavy swigs. Cheapshot Charlie lay her on the dock and waited for her to choke and sputter herself calm.

"Captain told you to stay on the ship," he said.

Fidelia held up her Water-Eater in one soggy hand. "I had . . . to test it."

Cheapshot Charlie squatted down so his huge head was level with hers. From here, she could see every pore of his umber skin, the facets of his nose jewel, the red vessels in his eyes striking like lighting across the white. "While you are on this ship, you obey our captain, or I will tear your arms off and you can kick your way home. Is that understood?"

He carried her back onto the *Jewel* and set her down roughly on the bench. A failed test run just days before they reached the tropics.

Now what was she going to do?

Dinner was grilled scallops from the cavern pool—only two apiece—and (not surprisingly) candy from BonBon Voyage Sweets Shop. Their supply from Arborley was running low, but Bloody Elle had found a whole crate of the sweets in one of the grotto's tunnels. Apparently candy was an old pirate hideout staple.

Fidelia filled her already sugar-soaked stomach with jelly-jellied jigglers, grumbling with every bite.

"Kids are supposed to like candy," Cheapshot Charlie said.

"We do . . . for dessert after a real meal," Fidelia said. "This feels like a punishment."

"Actually," Cheapshot Charlie said, "this turned out to be excellent sea fare." He examined a glitter cranmeringue. "It tastes exactly the same whether it's fresh or stale."

Bloody Elle was sprawled on the deck, lying on her stomach, her long legs behind her in the air. She unwrapped something from the knapsack and took a bite.

"Is that the last crack-o-mallow?" Cheapshot Charlie asked.

"Don't even think about it," Bloody Elle warned.

Cheapshot Charlie grinned, then tackled Bloody Elle like a crocodile.

"Get off me, you blooming idiot!"

Bloody Elle's face burst up from the tussle, red with fury. Cheapshot Charlie lay across her with his whole weight and dashed into her pocket for the candy, which he gobbled. "Yum!" He licked his fingers. "Good eats!"

"You . . . you *pirate!*" Bloody Elle threw him off with a grunt, then kicked him squarely in the chest, propelling him backward. He quickly recovered and socked her in the jaw, which sent her sprawling.

Bloody Elle jumped sprightly to her feet, rubbing her chin. "Come on, Fidelia, we can take him!"

Fidelia shook her head, backing up against the railing. "You're already more than he can handle."

Cheapshot Charlie furrowed his one eyebrow low. "Captain, are you going to let her insult your best man?"

There was no response.

"Captain?" Cheapshot Charlie called out.

The door to Merrick's quarters was open, his office empty.

"How long has he been gone?" Bloody Elle asked. Cheapshot Charlie shushed her, listening intently to the trickling sounds of the grotto.

"Too long," he determined, and straightened, clenching his jaw. "Let's go."

Bloody Elle secured her pistol, and the two pirates leaped from the *Jewel* and onto the dock, disappearing down separate tunnels.

"Captain?" Bloody Elle was out of sight down a tributary, but Fidelia could still make out a quiver in her words.

"What if he's . . . ?" Cheapshot Charlie's words faded.

Stay on the ship, Merrick had insisted.

Obey the captain, Cheapshot Charlie had barked two inches from her face.

But they had left Fidelia alone.

Could she sail away, leave them stranded in their old hideout? No; she couldn't man the massive *Jewel* alone, especially with its new structure. Maybe she could swim out of the cavern. It would be difficult with the jellyfish, yes, but possible. They might not find her in the dark. She could stay close to the cliffs until she found a way up, then make her way to civilization. To help.

Her breathing was shallow and hot blood coursed through her, making her limbs jumpy.

She'd regret it if she didn't escape now while she could. She knew that.

But a sound pierced her thoughts—a cough, a frenzied one, echoing from the nearest tunnel. Was Merrick sprawled in a cavern, his single blue eye wide and pale as he searched for his next breath?

She hopped onto the dock and ran down the tunnel.

It was dark and damp—her hands quickly became her eyes.

"Merrick?" she called weakly. This wasn't her search—she knew this. Not her people, not her captain. Not her concern. But before she could shake away her sympathy completely, she spotted the faint gleam of a candle's light, flickering off the rock walls in front of her. She followed it like a beacon, stepping through the tunnel and into a massive cavern, large enough to be a room.

Not just any room.

A library. Unmistakably, a library.

There were bookshelves, tall, lined in a row to create aisles, and endcaps, proper space for an entire catalog system to be in operation. A stalactite dripped water onto one such shelf—the source of the rancid, earthy smell of rotting wood that filled the room.

A pillaged, abandoned library in a pirate's grotto.

Fidelia had seen many incredible things in the last two days, but nothing so unexpected as this.

The books remaining on the shelves were crumbling, a consequence of their age and state—forgotten. Some books, the fibers exposing the spines like human vertebrae, lay in sad piles, collecting dust. A few books had gooseneck barnacles coating their covers; a family of sea spiders made their nest beneath the loose pages of a broken atlas.

"I told you to stay on the ship." Merrick's voice crackled from the corner of the library.

Fidelia found him in a dirty, worn-out plush armchair, a mostly empty rum bottle balanced at his side. "Bloody Elle and Cheapshot Charlie are looking for you."

Merrick's head lolled back. "Those two . . . best mates I ever ran with, really." He took a drink.

"You look . . . awful." It was an understatement—his mismatched eyes were sunken, creating dark hollows beneath them; his face was pallid, the skin stretching thin over his cheekbones.

He snorted. "I'm dying. Isn't that to be expected?" He lifted the bottle to his mouth, straining with the effort required to hold it there so he could drink.

Fidelia stepped over a puddle of seawater. A stale sea bird's nest, long ago forsaken, rested on the shelf next to her like a bookend.

"Go ahead," Merrick said. "I can see your head swimming with questions. Let's have it."

"Just one," Fidelia said. "What is this place?"

"Isn't it obvious?" Merrick waved his arms. "Look. Books."

"I've just never heard of a vicious pirate having his own private library." She pulled a volume from the shelf. "What are these, treasure maps? Encyclopedias of foreign weapons?" She opened the book, only to find a soggy, blotted mess of unreadable pages.

She tried a different book, a fat red one, and found a familiar title looking back at her: *Exploring an Underwater Fairyland* by Dr. and Dr. Quail.

Her heart stopped. She ran her fingers along the spine's gilded lettering and opened the front cover.

"Hey!" she said. *Property of Arborley Library*—there was the telltale stamp, right on the inside flap. "This is a library book."

"And I'm a pirate." Merrick coughed, staring at the cavern walls.

Fidelia swallowed, pulling the book tight to her chest. "I've been thinking. My father, he is—or, was—a botanist. The greatest marine botanist to ever live, actually, and he won awards to back it up—"

"The point, Quail. Get to it."

"Maybe—maybe he knew the cure." Fidelia pushed the words out in nervous, excited exclamations. "Maybe there's an antidote written down in his observation book somewhere, and I've just never noticed it—"

"Oh, you sweet, stupid girl." Merrick's bottle slipped from his fingers, leaking the last drops of sticky rum onto the library's floor. "There is no cure for the red daisies." He looked up at her, his blue eye catching the candlelight, burning past her spectacles and into her brain. "There is no cure for a black heart."

"I want to help," she whispered.

He took hold of her chin, his rough, skeletal hand as

gentle as he could manage. "You want to help?" he said. "Get that treasure. Don't let me lose it before I go." He dropped his gaze. "Now get out."

Fidelia backed away from the pirate, *Exploring an Underwater Fairyland* still tucked under her arm. A lone tear tickled as it traced down her cheek. "Charlie!" she managed to call. "Elle! I found him!"

A pirate dying—why did it matter? Not just any pirate, but Merrick the Monstrous. Wanted for robbery, burglary, arson, murder—and now kidnapping.

So why did it matter?

She leaned against a tunnel wall, sliding down until she was sitting. Why did it matter to her?

Because every rattling breath Merrick took reminded her of her parents. Because she looked at his sapphire eye, wide and searching, and saw a fear, so out of place with the rest of him, and she thought of her parents—

No, that wasn't it.

She thought of *herself*. The before and the after. Fidelia, before her parents died, unafraid and busy and bold, and the Fidelia after—just a shell, hiding in a library.

Because losing Merrick reminded her of what it was like to lose her parents. The awful before and after, all over again.

Watching Merrick die was like looking into a mirror—watching her lose herself.

"Where is he?" Bloody Elle slid to a halt in front of Fidelia, scanning the tunnel. Cheapshot Charlie was three seconds behind her.

"Down there." Fidelia pointed toward the candlelight, which glowed even brighter, battling the grotto's darkness. "In the library, drinking." She laughed, once, and it came out tasting like bitter sea melon. "If the red daisies weren't already killing him," she said, "coming back to Medusa's might have—"

"Do you smell smoke?" Bloody Elle interrupted.

As if on cue, black smoke curled down the tunnel, searching for a release. The light intensified, orange as the morning horizon.

The three of them hurried back to Merrick, the tunnel walls suddenly warm to the touch. When they reached the cavern, Fidelia threw the hem of her dress up over her mouth to block the smoke.

The library was on fire.

The flames devoured the books as heavy smoke billowed up into the stalactites. Fidelia blinked, her eyes peppery hot.

"Where is he?" Bloody Elle yelled.

"He was in an armchair!" Fidelia squinted, trying to see through the smoke to the corner where Merrick had slumped in his chair moments ago.

Cheapshot Charlie and Bloody Elle dashed through the flames, into the smoky black belly of the fire.

This could be it, Fidelia thought. *Merrick, taken by fire and smoke before he could cough himself to death.*

The fire raged higher, kissing the cavern ceiling. Every book, every shelf, gone. Rendered to ash by the flames. Fidelia sputtered and paced, counting the seconds—any moment she'd hear the screams as Cheapshot Charlie and Bloody Elle succumbed to the fire.

Just before Fidelia gave up hope and ran out of the library to save herself, all three pirates staggered out of the fire. Cheapshot Charlie and Bloody Elle carried Merrick between them, whose head lolled against his chest, his legs dragging along the floor behind him. They raced him out of the tunnels, and Fidelia followed behind, her eyes stinging.

"What happened?" she cried when they finally collapsed on the dock.

Merrick lay on his side, limbs splayed like a broken marionette doll. "Alcohol," he rasped, "is very flammable."

A typically vague Merrick answer—she stared at him, her eyes leaking. Did he trip over the candelabra? Had it fallen?

Or was this one of Merrick the Monstrous's violent acts of arson?

An accidental fire or a deliberate one?

Why did it matter?

He coughed, Fidelia coughed—all four of them coughed now, a regular symphony of burnt throats and lost breaths.

"Come on," Bloody Elle croaked, pulling herself to standing. "The fire's spreading." She and Cheapshot Charlie took their captain into his quarters on the *Jewel*.

Fidelia checked the hull as she boarded the sloop—the starfish had eaten away most of the barnacles, leaving the water-warped beams of the *Jewel* clean—as clean as a lake-scuttled, dilapidated old lucky ship could be.

The pirates worked to cast off the *Jewel*.

This time, Fidelia pitched in. The grotto was quickly filling up with clouds of the black smoke, and the tunnels all glowed the same white-orange—the fire was moving down the tributaries and would soon make ash of the grotto's dock. Amber light shone above the water, neon blue light in the water.

By the time the fire finally burned out, Fidelia realized, nothing would be left in Medusa's Grotto but black marks on the walls and a pile of fat, happy orange starfish.

And the medusas, pulsing eternally through the water.

The medusas, who had seen all the grotto's secrets.

Through the secret waterfall the *Jewel* sailed, back into the open sea. Fidelia let Cheapshot Charlie and Bloody Elle give her orders, and they sent her scrambling to the yards to fix the rigging or had her hold the wheel while they tightened lines. The work of a cabin boy, yes — but she was grateful to keep her hands busy.

Hands busy, mind busy.

Merrick stumbled out of his quarters to watch the cliffs vanish in the distance. Medusa's Grotto faded out of reality and into memory.

"Good riddance," he grumbled. But Fidelia could see his sad blue eye. *How it aches to say good-bye* is what he really meant.

Fidelia stood behind him, clutching *Exploring an Underwater Fairyland* to her chest, listening to his coughs until all they could see of the grotto was the pillar of smoke on the horizon, white against the star-speckled sky.

19

"Sir!" A naval officer burst into the admiral's quarters without knocking, his face flushed and sweating.

"What is it?" Admiral Bridgewater had just poured himself a third glass of spirits, which meant his jaw had loosened and his skin was as pink as a boiled ham.

"The horizon, sir. You'll want to see!"

Admiral Bridgewater pushed himself in front of the officer and dashed up to the deckhouse. The night air was cold, the wind putting up a fair fight.

"There." Another officer pointed. "Ten o'clock. It's smoke, sir."

The admiral took the officer's spyglass and squinted his tiny eye. Just southwest of their bearings, wisps of smoke, billowing into the night sky—faint, but undeniably there.

"Fire. On the jack-tree cliffs." Admiral Bridgewater stretched his face into a grin, a rare and somewhat unsettling sight to the rest of the silver-buttons.

"Merrick." He chortled. "At last, I'll have you."

"Sir?" an officer timidly asked. "Are we certain it's him?"

"Without a doubt," Admiral Bridgewater said. "Merrick's the only one crazy enough to brave the Undertow."

The officers glanced at each other, the obvious follow-up to this statement dancing between them. Neither would say it.

"Shall we steer toward the smoke, sir?" an officer asked.

"No," Admiral Bridgewater said. "Merrick never stays in one place for long." Especially the last few months—something had Merrick scared, darting from hiding place to hiding place like a mouse running from a hawk.

"Make for the cocoa route," Admiral Bridgewater ordered, "but luff the sails when you come within range of the tropics. We have the element of surprise—don't lose it." He collapsed the spyglass and shoved it into an officer's chest. He suddenly surged with new energy.

He could take on a hundred Merricks tonight, if he had to. "We've got him now."

When Fidelia woke, the *Jewel* was back on open water. The mainland was nowhere in sight—every direction was just flat and blue. Medusa's Grotto was behind them, a blackened stain in a corner of nature no one would ever find.

She stood and stretched her arms, and waved good morning to the pirates. Bloody Elle nodded back, but Cheapshot Charlie blinked at her and went back to the rigging.

She watched the boatswain work for another moment. She saw the extra force he used to tie his knots—the punches and swings of a man angry because his captain was dying and there was nothing he could do to stop it.

Death affected everyone—the ones who left, and the ones who were left behind. No one knew this better than Fidelia.

She walked down the deck to where the candy pile was stashed, then chose an astrobloomer and a kaleidorainbow fig and munched on them for breakfast. The *Jewel*'s sails caught the wind and billowed, mirroring the fat, puffy white clouds in the sky above. She ran her hands along a railing; the wood was rough, dinged from when the mast split and fell in the Undertow.

"You know," Fidelia said, "if I squint, it *is* a pretty ship."

Cheapshot Charlie looked at her, then puffed up with pride. "Back in its heyday, any sailor would have given his right arm to sail the *Jewel*," he said. "Even Admiral Bridgewater's probably tempted to clean it up and add it to his fleet. That is, if he docsn't bury Captain in it."

That name again. This time, Fidelia gave in to the curiosity. "Who is this admiral?"

Cheapshot Charlie tightened a sheet. "Admiral Percival J. Bridgewater," he finally said, surprising them both. "Top wig in the Queen's Own Navy. Royally bestowcd with the task of catching pirates along the cocoa route and bringing them to trial. But he's made a special mission out of the captain."

"What kind of mission?"

Cheapshot Charlie pulled a slack line. "His only mission. Bridgewater won't rest until the captain's hanged."

Fidelia thought about this as the *Jewel* hit a gentle bump. "But Bridgewater's already brought the *Jewel* in once, hasn't he? And he's caught Merrick how many times?"

"At least a dozen. What's your point?"

Fidelia tried to say this delicately. "So why isn't Merrick . . . you know?" *How hard is it to kill a pirate?* she wondered.

Cheapshot Charlie narrowed his eyes. "You're a smart enough girl—you can figure it out."

Astern, at the wheel, Merrick coughed, and Fidelia could hear his insides rattle.

"The treasure," she realized.

"Bridgewater wants the captain dead," Cheapshot Charlie said, "but not until he's got his hands on that treasure."

Fidelia's jaw dropped. "An admiral in the Queen's Own Navy shouldn't be drooling over treasure."

Cheapshot Charlie raised his eyebrow. "People aren't like your infernal sea creatures. You can chart their behaviors, observe their habitats, make predictions, but . . ." His gaze suddenly left Fidelia; she followed it behind her to the stern, where Merrick stood at the helm.

"But people don't always act the way you expect them to," Fidelia finished for him.

Cheapshot Charlie snapped his attention back to her, glaring at her as if she were a seagull who had stolen his meal. "Stop pestering me and get back to your ridiculous contraption. We'll be there by morning."

Fidelia's stomach plummeted. That meant she had less than twenty-four hours to figure out how to make her Water-Eater work.

Or else she'd be diving down to the bottom of the sea with nothing but her lung capacity and her courage.

The *Jewel* moved for hours, flying through the water so smoothly, someone could have composed a watercolor masterpiece while standing on its decks. The nervous, bustling energy that had defined the voyage so far was gone—now everyone stayed mostly quiet, concentrating on their tasks.

Fidelia could feel the air shift warmer, the sun beating down on her skin. The Undertow had left the forefront of her mind; instead she pored over her parents' observation books, searching for answers. Any answers.

"Mind the sails," Merrick announced at noon. "Keep her steady. We're nearly there." A charred bit of paper untangled itself from his hair and blew past Fidelia— a remnant of the fire. She studied him, searching his good eye for that flicker of sadness she'd seen the night before.

Medusa's Grotto was probably the closest thing Merrick had to a home, besides the *Jewel*. Fidelia had already said good-bye to her own house, but she still had Arborley Island, still had the sailors, still had the Book and Bottle, and the beach—at least for now. And when she moved away to the mainland, she would still have Aunt Julia. Home wasn't a place, she realized; it was a feeling. Right here in her observation books, right here in her memories.

What did Merrick have, though—besides this dilapidated ship? He had his mates. His own name. And he had his treasure. All that was left to say good-bye to.

And it was up to her to help him find it.

That was how they remained as the day shifted into night—solemn and steadfast and mostly silent. Fidelia unwrapped candies from BonBon Voyage without complaint and nibbled her sugary meals—astrobloomers for lunch, kaleidorainbow figs for dinner, choco-glomps for dessert.

Her test run in the grotto had failed, terribly—the Water-Eater didn't give her enough oxygen to dive twenty feet, let alone dig through the sands of an entire tropical stretch to find a lost treasure.

She twisted the filter out of its chamber and ran her

fingers along the rough tar. It had been a good idea, creating new, tinier holes—a good idea in theory.

Now she had to try something else.

A shadow loomed over her. "Finished yet?" Merrick asked.

Fidelia curled herself over her dismantled invention, protective. "You still haven't told me anything about where we're going," she said in defense of her poor progress.

"So?"

"So if my Water-Eater is going to work, I need more information about the type of environment I'll be diving in. The water temperature, the region, the climate, the plant life—"

"Hot." Merrick looked up at the west star.

"Hot." Fidelia scoffed. "Really? That's your idea of a climate description?"

"I already told you, we're sailing to the tropics," Merrick said. "Tropics are hot."

"Not all of them," Fidelia argued. "Three of the major islands are mediterranean, technically, and only one of them has mangroves—"

Merrick glanced down at her again, one of his gold

teeth blazing in the bleak illumination of the lamplight. "We are traveling to the most beautiful stretch of ocean you or your brilliant Doctors Quail have ever seen. The water is clear and turquoise. The ocean floor is the color of cherry blossoms in spring. Black trees grow from the islands and snake their roots down into the water like sea serpents. I have no idea the type of flora or fauna that thrives in such waters; suffice it to say it's a paradise on earth." He stopped. "Descriptive enough for you?"

Fidelia blinked, then pushed her glasses up on her nose. Sea serpents . . . a pink seabed . . . turquoise water. He could certainly be poetic when he wanted to. Her earlier conversation with Cheapshot Charlie flashed through her mind—*people don't always act the way you expect them to.* "Yes." She flipped through her father's observation book, a memory niggling. "Reef territory, do you think?"

But Merrick was done talking climate. He vanished from her side, and moments later Fidelia heard his dry, grisly cough as he concentrated on navigating.

Fidelia turned the pages more rapidly, searching for March 16, a day the Quails worked in a tropical sea-grass meadow and found a whole colony of silky reef sharks.

Aha!

March 16

Silky sharks are mangrove dwellers normally, but the ones in this region have developed an affinity for juvenile cuttle-fish, which make their nurseries in the sea grass. Ida's already tagged one of the large maternal females, whom she's dubbed Myrtle, and Fidelia's using the university camera to snap a few photographs.

Below the passage, off in the margin of the page, her father had sketched a long, thin, fernlike leaf, with such thick, fibrous fronds that it almost looked like a feather.

Fidelia turned the book sideways. *Parrot-feather leaf,* her father had labeled it.

Low salinity and high temperature waters, tropical and subtropical. Anchored in rock beds, low drag. Fibrous leaf structure allows for air filtration and maximum surf flotation.

Filtration.

That word jumped out at Fidelia like a mako caught on a line.

She scoured the rest of the page for any information

about the leaf, but the only other notes Arthur took on March 16 were to describe algae that grew on the bellies of sea lions.

Parrot-feather leaf!

Fidelia's brain churned and whirred like a well-tuned engine. She found a blank sheet of paper in her observation book and, again, sketched out a prototype of the Water-Eater—the mouthpiece, the cylinder, the oxygen chambers . . .

This time, in lieu of the filtration system she had created—the tarred filter with the holes—she drew a parrot-feather leaf, placed gently sideways between the faux scales and the chamber. She reran her calculations.

It could work, she realized. It could really work!

The tropics were full of sea-grass meadows. In the morning, when daylight was on her side, when the *Jewel* was closer to their destination, she'd scope one out.

It would work. It *had* to work.

Bursting with the sort of confidence that always accompanied these frizzled, harebrained breakthroughs of hers, she dropped her pen on her observation book, sat back, folded her arms, and actually grinned.

It was then that she noticed the shadow, again, hovering above her. Merrick stood beside her, blue eye glinting.

"So you did it," he said.

She nodded. "I think so."

"We'll find out tomorrow, won't we?"

An ominous thing to say.

But nothing Merrick said could crush her now. This feeling, this rush of solving the puzzle, the flutter of possibilities flapping through her mind . . . This feeling was a memory, and she nestled into it, snug and content.

She would not let herself think about the fact that her parents weren't around to join her celebration.

She would not.

A week later, she finally crawled out to meet the day and had to remove her peach spectacles to peek at the sun; she'd grown accustomed to the darkness of the cave, to the dim candlelight above her as she read book after book. She'd read all the novels in the grotto and had even paged through a fair number of sea charts and encyclopedias, until there was nothing left to do but sit, and worry, and wonder, and finger the brooch on her chest.

The brooch. *Marry me,* he'd asked as he pinned it to her dress, and she would have done it that very night.

Her eyes adjusted as she walked down the cliffs to the stretch of beach, and that's when she saw him.

Just a body, lying in the shallows, crumpled like a wad of paper.

It was Merrick.

She ran to him, tearing across the sand with weak legs, and lifted his head onto her lap. He was alive, barely, and he croaked with closed eyes, "Bridgewater . . . almost had the *Jewel* . . . Swam back here alone . . . the others, the others were . . ."

He looked at her.

"Your eye!" She soon realized it didn't matter how many times she used the hem of her white dress to wipe away the blood that pooled on his face. The eye was permanently red, almost turned inside out. She gagged at the sight of it, at the sight of him.

"Cannon hit the mast . . ." he said. "A splinter ricocheted . . . hit my eye . . ." He shuddered. "We outran him, but barely . . . Charlie's hiding the ship on some island . . . He and Elle are okay, but the rest of them—the rest of them—he's got them on the prison barge—"

He suddenly tried to stand.

"Hold still." She pressed down on his chest. "You have to lie down. I'll bring you some water."

"No, no." He clutched her arm. "Stay. Stay just a little longer."

A plea to stay. *How the tides have changed,* she wanted to shout, wanted to slap him and swim away with the dolphins. But she stayed.

"Jewel," he murmured. "Jewel . . ."

It was his pet name for her.

But her heart sank, down past the waves and the reefs, to the bottom of the sea, because she knew he wasn't calling for her.

His ship. The *Jewel*. His greatest love.

Merrick's eye was gone. That much was certain. Inside the grotto, she cleaned it as best she could, but what remained of the pupil had already begun scabbing, a film of red tissue building over the injury, the socket darkening and deepening. But the damage to his eye was the least of her concerns.

There was something else missing from Merrick, something delicate that had dried and hardened. A steel exterior that had always existed to everyone else, never to her—and now, it was all she could see when she looked at him. Cold and reflective. A mirror, her own confusion blinking back at herself.

"But if he is there . . . and we attack him from the north . . ." Merrick made conversations only with himself as he poured over his sea charts, his maps of the known and unknown world. He schemed day and night, pausing only to sip from one of his reserve bottles, draining the rum like it was medication. She tried to slip him bowls of fresh water, plates full of jackfruit cut into hearts, candies from BonBon Voyage Sweets Shop, but he acted like they were as invisible as she was.

Bloody Elle and Cheapshot Charlie made their way back into the grotto, one at a time, and Merrick barely greeted them beyond hammering out instructions for his strike on the prison. Then it was the three of them plotting on maps, sketching out possible courses — circumnavigating whole continents if they had to, all to surprise the Queen's Own Navy and break out their crew. The three of them ignored her as she withered away in the grotto, as if she were a prisoner of Merrick's instead of his supposed future bride.

And so nobody noticed when she slipped out of the grotto in a dory. Not even Merrick did, until he called for a book on tidal shifts in the tropics, and instead of receiving yet another lesson on the library's card catalog system, there was only quiet.

"Where'd she go?" Merrick held up a handkerchief to catch the blood seeping from his black-and-red eye and listened — for the sound of pages rustling, for the sound of her breathing. But all he could hear was the dripping of a stalactite, the faint softness of the faraway waterfall.

"Captain." Cheapshot Charlie pointed to the docks. "A dory is missing."

Merrick's arm muscles burned as he steered the *Jewel* out of the grotto and into daylight. Cheapshot Charlie and Bloody Elle did their best to rush the ship across the sea.

They searched her hometown. No sign of her. They backtracked and searched the mainland's every coast, every library, every bookstore, every sweets shop—no sign of her.

"Where else would she be?" they asked, perplexed.

And suddenly Merrick knew.

But even as they accomplished the impossible, manning a fifteen-person ship with a crew of three, Merrick rarely thought of her, basking in the shade of a jackfruit tree, the new brooch pinned to her white dress. He was fantasizing about a beet-faced man in uniform dropping to his knees, begging Merrick for mercy. Every hour spent dealing with her dramatic escape meant Bridgewater slipped farther and farther away.

And so, a week later, when he rowed one of the *Jewel*'s dories along the stretch of turquoise water, near the beach with the white sand and palm trees that he and his men had frequented over the years, his hands were tense, his face hard, impatience shining from his remaining blue eye.

"So you finally looked up," she said, her oars jutting out at odd angles into the water.

He snorted. "Do I truly have to defend my voracious reading to you?"

"You don't have to do anything," she said. "Not anymore." Rowing the dory had blistered her palms; she flinched as she took a drink of water from a blackjack.

"You didn't row all the way here," he said.

"No," she answered, her mouth a long black line. "Hopped a ride with a beanie ship, then sneaked away with their longboat and a whole crate of cocoa beans when the ship was asleep." She raised her eyebrows. "I'd make quite a pirate, wouldn't I?"

"Come back to the grotto," he said. "As soon as I free my crew, I'll take a break from—"

"We both know that's not true," she said. "You can't resist the admiral." She smiled, but behind her peach glasses, her eyes were sad. "As long as he's still alive, there's only one way it will end. Either you die or Admiral Bridgewater dies."

"Bridgewater is the one who dies," Merrick growled, "and then you and I—"

"Do you have any idea what it's like? To be set aside, like a task to be gotten to later? When I saw you on that beach—" Her voice broke; she cleared her throat and tried again. "There's a reason pirates don't live long enough to retire," she said. "Your life is gunfights, and enemies, and danger. There's no room for anything else." *Or anyone,* she clarified to herself.

She held the brooch in her palm; Merrick hadn't even noticed that it wasn't pinned to her chest. The pewter didn't catch the sunlight or reflect it; it absorbed it, somehow. Like a little gray storm cloud in her hand.

Images flashed through her mind: a week spent pacing and fretting in the grotto . . . the way her heart had stopped when she found him strung across the sand like dried-out kelp . . .

"Jewel, please," he said, and he made his words soft again—quite the trick, she thought. "As soon as Bridgewater is gone, we can go anywhere. I'll take some time off work— a whole year. We'll see the world—"

"A year is not enough." She gritted her teeth to keep from yelling. "I want more. I want a lifetime—a proper lifetime, not just a pirate's."

"I can—"

"I want you to stop." There. She'd said it. "Stop pirating. Stop and be with me."

Before he could hold it in, he laughed—threw his head

back and laughed, and she experienced, for a moment, what it was like to be ambushed by Merrick the Monstrous.

"I can give you anything in the world," he said. "Anything at all—just not that."

She shook her head, her face incredulous. "You really won't stop. Not even for me."

Merrick stared at her with his remaining eye—sapphire blue and cold as the polar seas. "Why not ask the moon to become a daylight creature?" he said. "Or ask a shark to give up his teeth? This is who I am. This is the man you love."

"And what a fool I am for it," she said softly.

Marry me, he'd said.

No, he'd ordered it. Ordered, as if the whole world were his ship and he the captain of it all—as if she were his to command.

Her sister had been right. She'd been a fool to trust a pirate with her heart.

She tilted her palm. "Here's another piece of treasure for your cave," she said, and she dropped the brooch into the water, where it sank down, down, to the mouth of the cave. His beloved cave, with his beloved gold and jewels.

She didn't bother to watch the pewter disappear in the shimmering depths; she picked up her oars and rowed away.

"You're being ridiculous," he snapped. "Come with me. I'll take you home."

But she kept rowing.

"Jewel! Where are you going?" Merrick didn't shout this until she was already a dot on the horizon. Such a display, from a woman he thought was all tenderness and books. Her behavior would have been worthy of a flogging if she were a member of his crew.

And this is how he had to think of her, to keep himself from shattering—as if she were just a lowly deckhand who had mouthed off and mutinied and now carried herself to her own exile. Marooned herself.

He glanced into the water. Something inside him twisted to think of the pewter brooch in his cave, touching his gold. Tainting it. He wished she'd hurled it into the waves like a broken seashell—lost in the ocean where it belonged.

Now he'd have to see it again someday.

Back in the grotto, Cheapshot Charlie and Bloody Elle had barely tied off the *Jewel* when Merrick leaped onto the dock and began packing ropes, food, and booze.

"Get your things," he said. "We leave now."

"Leave for where, Captain?" Cheapshot Charlie dared to ask.

"A thousand blue notes says Bridgewater's camping out up near the prison barge. He'll be expecting us." Merrick refilled his pistol with fresh ammunition and practiced aiming it, his damaged eye already squinted for accuracy. "Let's not disappoint him."

"Captain," Bloody Elle said, "where is she?"

Merrick rolled up his sea charts and placed them in a knapsack. "Gone," he said. "Now, where's the tar?"

His comrades exchanged a look. "Aren't you going to go after her?" Bloody Elle pressed.

"I did," Merrick said. "I did chase her. And she made her choice." The gleam in his remaining eye said it all: end of discussion. "If we leave now, we'll reach Bridgewater by morning. So pack the coffee and cast off."

A drop of rain falls from a cloud and lands on a mountain peak. Another joins, and another, and another; a trickle, and a creek is born. The creek runs down the mountainside, gaining speed and momentum, and becomes a river, loud and crushing, a living thing. The river cuts through the land and empties into the ocean. Our ocean is made of these droplets, smaller than pebbles.

A tiny drop of water on its own may barely wet a parched throat, but an entire ocean of droplets becomes the most powerful force on the planet.

—*Exploring an Underwater Fairyland* by Dr. and Dr. Quail

21

Fidelia fell into memories of what it was like to spend days at a time on the water: long spans of tedium followed by mild insanity. The *Jewel* had covered an incredible distance in a small amount of time—had sailed through three oceanic climates, down most of the mainland coast, and had even survived a run-in with the Undertow. "We're close," Merrick said between coughs, and as soon as the sunlight was strong enough, Fidelia parked herself near the port side railing with her binoculars and began scanning for sea-grass meadows.

The ocean levels had shrunk. The *Jewel* was cruising through water depths of less than a hundred feet now, and Fidelia spotted the many animals of the sunlit zone: a lone bluefin tuna, who darted away from the ship at double speed; three or four hammerheads, their strange craniums oscillating as they swam; a few men-of-war undulating like tissues in the water; and a common white surf clam.

A clam! She watched it closely as they moved past it; it yawned open, basking in the sunlight on its massive pink tongue, then sank back down below the surface.

Fidelia smiled. It felt like a message from her parents—
Hold on. You're so close.
Just get his treasure, and then you'll go home.

"There!" She pointed to a patch about fifty yards away—dark and amorphous, swaying under the water like a fluid sea monster, its strands floating to the surface like green mermaid's hair.

The captain, at the helm, was huddled in his pea-coat despite the warm temperature of the tropics. But he motioned for Bloody Elle to climb down the rope dangling from the stern and pick a few leaves.

"You're putting your life in the hands of a leaf?" Cheapshot Charlie stared at the parrot-feather leaf with utter distrust.

"Absolutely," Fidelia said. She took the leaf to the bench, unscrewed the Water-Eater, and placed her new filter in its position. It fit perfectly, just as she'd known it would.

Bloody Elle appraised the contraption from over

Fidelia's shoulder. "That thing is really going to let you breathe underwater?"

Fidelia turned the Water-Eater around and around, a final check for any kinks or wrinkles. "If I'm truly the inventor Merrick believes I am, then yes."

"Captain wouldn't get this wrong," Bloody Elle said. "It's too important." She reached out a hand and touched the dried tar, her swallow tattoo fluttering its wings as her fingers moved. She watched Fidelia looking at the bird. "You said you've been to Canquillas?"

"I've been to the coast," Fidelia said.

"Then you know Canquillas is the most beautiful country in the world," Bloody Elle said. "Those crystal-clear lagoons. The white-capped mountains. Yucca on every hill. But it is very poor. So poor that I was picking pockets by age four, and by age ten, I was the breadwinner in my family."

Fidelia set down her Water-Eater, listening.

"With a dead mother, two younger sisters, and a crippled father, what else could I do? I stole food, coins, shoes, anything that wasn't strapped down," Bloody Elle said. "Every time *les bofies* caught me, they locked me in the *bostiel* for the night and slapped one of their brands on me." She held up a wrist; the bold, black lines circumnavigated her flesh. "Canquillas puts permanent cuffs on their criminals.

That way every villager knows, when you reach out to shake their hands, that you're a thief."

Fidelia ran her eyes along the tattoos, losing count after twenty lines. "How many times were you caught?"

Bloody Elle lifted the billowing sleeve of her blouse — the black lines continued all the way up her bicep. "They ran out of room by the end. But my family always had rice and beans, and so did the widow next door, and the homeless dog that scratched at our back door for bones."

Fidelia pointed at the swallow tattoo on Bloody Elle's hand. "What does the bird mean?"

Bloody Elle smiled. "I got this the night I stole a uniform."

"A uniform?"

"Took it right off a member of the royal guard," Bloody Elle said, her eyes twinkling. "I found him staggering drunk by the river and persuaded him to go for a dip." She grinned. "I ran off with his velvet tunic and bearskins and strolled right in to the *bostiel*. Unlocked a few of my friends, and anyone else who asked to be released." Her expression turned serious. "There was only one prisoner who didn't cry out for me to break him free."

"Merrick," Fidelia guessed.

"Yes," Bloody Elle said. "'You're wasting your talents

here,' he told me. 'This village is too small for you. Come work for me, and your only bounds will be where the seas end and the sky begins.' But I told him I wouldn't leave my family behind to rot. And he promised to see them taken care of, if only I would come to his ship right that minute and become a thief on the sea." She laughed. "He also threatened to slit my throat if I said no. 'That threat's emptier than the mayor's wine jug,' I told him, 'considering you're still behind bars.' But then he held up the keys, and jingled them—I still don't know how he lifted them off me. He opened his cell and put his knife to my neck, and that's when I knew I'd found my captain."

Bloody Elle's iron eyes went soft and misty as she immersed herself in the memory. "See, the lines around my wrist were from the *bostiel.* Chains. Black reminders of a black life. But the bird is because I flew away." She traced a finger along the swallow's outspread wings. "Captain helped me fly away. As soon as we hit open water, he inked this himself."

Fidelia frowned. "And what about your family?"

"Captain was true to his word," Bloody Elle said. "He saw that they were taken care of. Whenever we sail past the Canquillian coast, I can see my family's manor on the cliffs. They have gardens now, and servants." Finally she looked right at Fidelia, her face once again hardening into sun-scorched cheeks and wind-weathered lines. "When Captain says he'll do something, he means it—so when he tells you he'll kill you if you don't find his treasure, you'd better believe him."

She patted Fidelia's knee as she stood, then left Fidelia alone to study her Water-Eater yet again—her only tool against Merrick the Monstrous's cruelty, and suddenly she could see it the way the pirates saw it: a bunch of garbage glued together, tarred and punctured, now with a piece of seaweed stuck in the middle of the mess.

Her last hope.

Just when Fidelia recognized the looks on everyone's faces—about to topple from mere boredom into stir-crazy—Merrick suddenly pointed. "I see our stretch."

Cheapshot Charlie and Bloody Elle hurried to slack the sails. Fidelia shot from her seat like a firecracker.

The *Jewel* approached a sandbar, a spot in the sea where the water became shallow—turquoise, glassy clear, still as a mirror. Fidelia guessed it was about thirty feet deep. Nearby, maybe another mile's sail, a tropical island's mangrove trees lined the white shores, the roots dipping down into the sea like legs, testing the water for warmth. Mangroves. They were hubs for all sorts of hot-water species: mud lobsters, sponges, brown pelicans, hawksbill turtles. Oh, how her parents would have loved to see this. A feast for the fish lover's eyes.

She watched the multicolored fish darting through a coral reef, bodies glittering like jewels through the water, until a cough brought her back to the grim reality of her situation.

"Quail," Merrick said, "time to prove your salt."

Fidelia took a deep breath and joined the pirate captain at the stern of the ship. Cheapshot Charlie and Bloody Elle had dropped anchor and flanked Merrick with faces like stone gargoyles, no gratitude for Fidelia helping them escape from the Molvanian pirates, or helping them tie down loose lines, or helping them remove the barnacles from their ship. They were there to intervene, should she cause any trouble for this, the big moment. This was it—the reason they had taken her.

"I'll be blunt." Merrick's blue eye burned bright against the clear sea. "The cave is filled to the brim with treasure. Everything I've collected for nearly a decade." He coughed. "It is the result of sweaty, bloody work, both my own and my crew's—"

"You said—you said . . ." Fidelia's voice threatened to crumble, her entire body seizing up in fear. "You said you weren't sending me into the cave." Her Water-Eater was supposed to separate oxygen from water; she had no idea if it would work as a death-pollen filter.

"I'm not." Merrick's nostrils flared as he coughed—his patience was as thin as the lining of his lungs. "You are not to go inside the cave." He paused, wiping the speckles of blood from around his mouth.

"You will bring up one thing, and one thing only: a brooch."

"A brooch?"

"A small pewter brooch."

Fidelia frowned. "But pewter is junk metal," she said. "It's probably been eaten away by the salt water. It isn't worth anything—"

"It's worth everything," Merrick growled.

Fidelia blinked at him, waiting for the bottom line. But Merrick was silent. "That's it? You want me to dive down and find a pewter brooch?"

"Easier said than done," Merrick said. "It's lost somewhere in the seabed."

"Lost?" Fidelia asked. "Lost how?"

"I pulled it out of the cave, but I dropped it in the algae when—" He ended his sentence with a cough. "It's down there," he growled, "but it's up to you to find it."

"All of this for a pewter brooch." Fidelia was incredulous.

"All of this, and much more." Merrick coughed his horrible cough, and his meaning couldn't have been clearer. "Now, put on your wonder-gills and go get my treasure."

She untied her boots. "Follow the reef down, about twenty feet," Merrick said as she held up the Water-Eater for one more inspection, her hands shaking.

The Water-Eater . . . This time, if it didn't work—

No. Best not dwell on the negative. Arthur and Ida would never have allowed such pessimistic what-ifs. *Just pretend it's another test run,* she coached herself. *Pretend Mom and Dad are here, and you're just doing one more analysis before you send the blueprints off to the patent office.*

She tried to rub the fog off the mask, then spat into the visor.

"That's vile," Merrick wheezed.

"But effective." She secured the mask over her glasses and sat on the edge of the *Jewel,* glancing at the pirate captain. "Did you or did you not kidnap me because of my diving expertise?"

"I did not," Merrick said, and broke into coughs. "I kidnapped you because of your shark expertise."

Before Fidelia could fully process what he had said, Merrick pushed her backward off the ship and into the water.

Underwater, the world was quiet.

Fidelia gently eased her eyes open. A trace amount of seawater leaked into her mask—typical of even the best diving equipment. It made her head feel like a pitcher, sloshing with every movement.

After a moment, her eyes adjusted to the dimness of life beneath the surface. She glanced up, where the *Jewel* floated like a giant lily pad. The water blurred and distorted the dry world above. Bloody Elle and Cheapshot Charlie peeked over the *Jewel*'s railing, their faces stretched long and bulbous as though they were looking through funhouse mirrors.

Merrick stared at her, too, blue eye narrowed in concentration. His black-and-red eye hung dead, magnified through the sea.

Her lungs felt wrenched. All the oxygen she'd taken in at the surface was gone. It was time to take a breath.

She steadied herself in the water, made sure her lips were fully sealed around the mouthpiece, and inhaled.

Oxygen seeped into her mouth, just as it had in the grotto. So she didn't celebrate yet.

Another inhale—and more oxygen!

A third inhale, filling her lungs to capacity, and she knew it was working.

The parrot-feather leaf! It filtered the oxygen at just the right rate. Leave it to the ocean to grow the perfect substitute for gills.

If only her father were here to see this.

She kicked her feet, propelling forward. Downward.

The light shifted. The oranges of the sun flowed down to the sandy pink ocean floor, swirling with the turquoise water in a river of color. Fidelia had seen many shoals before, and sandbars, and continental shelves—but none as rich or vivid as this.

The scientist in her kicked in. She analyzed the area and took mental notes. Water depth, from surface to seabed? Approximately twenty feet, at the shoal's highest peak. Climate? Subtropical. To her right, the coral reef; to her left, the sea-grass meadow, swaying in the current.

Here and there, piles of blackened wood splinters were half-buried in the sand—remnants of ships that had run aground or wrecked along this very stretch. Schools of fish darted around the ships as if they were gauntlets to be bested. Where were the rocks responsible for these shipwrecks? She noticed tatters on the seabed: the navy's flags, there and there, and an old shredded skull and crossbones leering up at her from the sand. These vessels had been sunk by man, not by nature—by one man. By Merrick.

The reef reached to the surface, deep purple, and braided, and beautiful. Reefs always attracted the most bizarre of creatures, as if nature used this habitat to experiment with every possible design. A red frilled dancer bent and gyrated past Fidelia's nose. Dainty garden eels popped their heads out from the coral's many pockets, sensing a visitor. Down on the carpet of algae along the reef's base, a row of giant purple clams pursed their lips.

Fidelia arced her body down in the water, swimming around the reef. The water brightened, and the row of clams twitched their lips, kissing the sunlight streaming from above. Everything on the seabed glittered and shone as Fidelia swam down.

The cave. She spotted the opening at the base of the

reef. That gaping black mouth—the cave where the red daisies grew. The source of the legends.

The cave that killed Merrick.

Just inside its dark entry, she could see treasure piled everywhere. A wooden chest overflowed with strands of pearls in all sizes. Expensive-looking silvery rope coiled on a golden bed frame. A ritzy crystal chandelier was now home to a family of sea horses. She spotted bowls of emeralds, and ruby rings, and gilded goblets with engravings around the sides, and blue-and-white china dishes in stacks. Starfish rested atop mountains of doubloons; piles and piles of gold coins cascaded into the algae lining the floor of the cave.

Fidelia scanned this litter of treasure. Merrick could be living like a king, she realized, instead of hiding as an outlaw. This was the kind of wealth that allowed a person to relocate. Live as someone else. Disappear forever. Why hadn't Merrick done that?

Why had he risked everything for some junky brooch?

She shook the mystery from her head. The brooch—the thing she was here to find. She would find it, and then she would go home.

She searched with both hands, her fingers melting through the slippery algae that coated the base of the coral.

Finding this brooch was like hunting for a pewter needle in a haystack. She'd never be able to find it this way, one square foot at a time — it would take her days.

No, she had to do this logically. Like a scientist.

No. Not like a scientist.

Like a librarian.

She darted up to the surface and removed the Water-Eater, breathing deeply. "Merrick!" she called. "Get the book out of my bag!"

"Which book?"

"Exploring an Underwater Fairyland," she called, treading water. "I saved it from your bonfire."

"You mean you stole it." Merrick found the book and flipped through its pages. "Should I toss it down to you? See if knowledge floats or sinks?"

"No!" Fidelia said. "Find the section on spring gales, and tell me which wind blows the Undertow clear."

If she knew exactly which direction the tides pushed come springtime, then she would know whether the sand and algae had come from the west, bringing residue from the nearby island's mangrove roots, or from the east, bringing the bulkier, brinier sands of the mainland.

Merrick tore through the pages. "West," he finally said. "'Mid-oceanic islands near the continental margin experience a shift in currents semiannually, both with the arrival of the Undertow and the dispersal of the Undertow, when western winds and showers bring in the springtime and chase the Undertow offshore.'"

Softer, siltier residue, then.

She took another breath, replaced the Water-Eater, and dove back under.

As she plunged back to the bottom of the sea, she plotted out the brooch's drop into the water, refiguring where it could be with the westerly shift in the currents.

The water's pull wouldn't have brought it toward the cave; it would have brought it . . .

The clouds shifted again, darkening Fidelia's view momentarily. She tried to find the light, but the shadow moved with her.

A torpedo-shaped shadow, circling above her. She looked up — and froze.

Shark!

She swam to the other side of the reef, legs tingling with nerves, and peeked through the coral at the beast.

Her Water-Eater nearly fell out of her mouth.

Grizzle!

She could never forget that bone-white scar wrapping around his dorsal fin. Or that mouth, as big around as

Arborley Library's double doors, teeth hanging down like icicles.

She felt like she might explode in her own skin. Of all the reefs in all the seas, Grizzle was here!

But this isn't a field study, she reminded herself. She couldn't hide behind the reef and observe this glorious creature until daylight faded—no, her very life depended on finding Merrick's brooch—a task that had just become even trickier.

A shark's tail was a metric for reading its emotions, just like a dog's. Grizzle's tail was relaxed, straight as an arrow; he was still only curious about the underwater visitor hiding behind the reef.

If his tail flicked in small, annoyed movements, that meant aggression—which meant trouble.

Keep calm . . . The voices of the Drs. Quail echoed in Fidelia's mind. *Find the brooch. Get back in the ship. Grizzle doesn't have to be a dangerous factor. Just focus.*

Westerly winds. A spring gale, pushing tides west. *Look for the mangrove root residue.*

That patch of algae, there, dusted with a fine layer of silt. Nestled right where the coral sprung from the ocean floor. That's where the brooch would be.

Keeping an eye on Grizzle, she moved as gracefully as

she could—water resistance was draining, and she needed to conserve her energy. Breathing slowly through the Water-Eater, she kicked farther down, stretching to the seafloor.

Grizzle passed her again, giving her a bit of a nudge with his blunt nose. Her brain fizzed and smoked with warnings—the shark's attitude had changed. He dropped his pectoral fins and swam from side to side in an exaggerated pattern.

This was predatory behavior.

Fidelia reached the sea bottom and dipped her hands into the soft, slippery algae. It had to be here. Where was it? *Where was it?*

The shark nudged her again, harder, throwing her off-balance. Desperate, she searched faster, her fingers sliding in and out of the algae. The brooch, the brooch, the brooch . . .

Grizzle bumped her again, and this time it knocked her mask clean off. She squeezed her eyes shut and fumbled for it, panicking as she felt it float out of her grasp. Prying her eyes open, she swallowed a gasp when the salt stung. It was uncomfortable, yes, and everything was blurry, even with her glasses—but she had to find that brooch and get out of the water. Grizzle's patience wouldn't last much longer, and then she'd be at the receiving end of one of his bolder moves. A bite, perhaps.

She sucked in air, trying to calm her heart, and strained for air.

Her Water-Eater! The oxygen was thin, barely enough for a mouthful.

What had happened to the parrot-feather leaf? Why wasn't it working?

Searching the algae in a frenzy, she glanced over her shoulder for the shark—as if it would help when she could barely see two feet in front of her. Her brain was practically shouting instructions at her: *You can't see! You need air! Go tell Merrick the brooch is lost forever! Do it before Grizzle loses his temper!*

But then her fingers touched something small and hard.

The brooch!

A pewter brooch with scalloped, lacelike edges, any other detail rotted away by the seawater. She pulled it from the algae just as the massive dark shape jetted right toward her.

She kicked off the seafloor, brooch in hand, and Grizzle cruised underneath her feet. A deliberate miss—a shark Grizzle's size never missed his prey. She knew it would be her last warning.

Fidelia scrambled for the surface, her lungs burning and her legs tingling, expecting at any moment to receive a chomp—but the shark didn't follow her. He swam in circles around the base of the coral, his tail flicking.

She had to get air. Now. Every fiber of her body was screaming for her to break the surface and breathe.

But why didn't the shark follow her? He'd exhibited all the signs of predatory behavior, and had clearly viewed her as a threat. Why was he still hovering by the reef?

She paused and peeked back into the depths.

Her view was fuzzy, but she saw why Grizzle wasn't coming after her—he was guarding his own precious treasure.

Three shark pups darted out of the algae on the seafloor, each about a foot in length. They snapped their jaws at each other, sibling rivalry ingrained even at this early age.

Baby Grizzles—Grizzlings!

Fidelia's heart twittered, her entire body itching with joy. She wished she could stay and watch. So little was known about larger sharks and their parenting behaviors—particularly the males. But her primal instincts took over, and her legs kicked until her head broke through the water as if she had shattered a window.

When she spat out the Water-Eater and her lips finally found air, she drank it greedily, her body convulsing with relief. She was too tired to swim, to tread water, to kick to the boat . . .

Her head bobbed back under the water.

For the third time in as many days, Cheapshot Charlie grabbed under her arms and lifted her into the *Jewel*. Seawater drained from her nose.

"So your super-gills worked," Merrick said.

Fidelia hacked until her throat was clear. "So . . . it seems," she retorted, and Merrick grinned at her cheek.

Bloody Elle draped a dry tunic around her shoulders, and Fidelia pulled apart her Water-Eater to examine the filtration system—the parrot-feather leaf was shredded, only fibers. Of course! After a certain number of breaths, the harsh salt water had dissolved the leaf past the usage point. Even though it had nearly killed her, she smiled, because she had figured it out. Her next prototype would allow for easy removal of the leaves so a diver could replace the filter when the oxygen slowed.

She'd actually done it. And she'd done it without her parents.

But of course, she knew they had still helped her solve it. Their observation books. Their blood flowing through her veins. Their lifetimes of research.

Even in the midst of her glee, her heart panged.

If only they were here to see her, to see what they had helped her create.

To see the daughter they had raised.

Merrick coughed as he searched her over for wounds with the scrutiny of a surgeon. "That shark started patrolling these waters the last few times we visited," he said. "I knew I needed the very best shark expert to deal with him and get my brooch."

"Well," Fidelia said, opening her palm, "here it is. I hope it was worth it."

She finally got her first good look at it with clear eyes.

It was . . . ugly. A dingy piece of jewelry, and not salvageable at all—not worthy of any money, not becoming for a fashionable woman to wear. Not worthy of Fidelia's life. The salt water had decayed most of the shine, and the fastening pin on the back was broken, irreparable.

"All this trouble for a piece of garbage," Fidelia said, then winced.

But Merrick didn't snap at her. He stared at the rotted piece of metal in her hand, then pierced her with that haunting blue eye of his. "Thank you," he whispered.

He took the brooch from her. His skin was more purpled than flesh-colored; the veins bulged between his hand bones like rivers between skeletal peaks.

A dying pirate, drowning in his own phlegm and blood, all for a pewter brooch . . . She had to know why. "Why this brooch?" she asked, so only he could hear. "What's it for?"

Before he could answer, a shout rang out: "At last I have you, Monstrous!"

A huge frigate approached, its red and blue flags waving boldly in the breeze. Even from the distance, Fidelia could make out the guns—at least twenty of them on this side alone—jutting from the ship like spines on a sea urchin, and all of them aimed at the *Jewel*.

A hoglike man stood at the helm, his golden blunderbuss drawn. A haylike mustache twitched above his lip, and a dainty pair of spectacles perched at the end of his lumpy nose.

"How many times must I kill you, Merrick?" the man hollered.

"At least one more time, it would seem, Bilgewater!" Merrick called back. Fidelia saw new life surge in his face. He clenched the brooch until his bony knuckles whitened.

"Bridgewater." Bloody Elle's lips crimped in a hateful sneer. "Look at him—his eyes are so close together, he should be wearing a monocle."

Fidelia studied the man on the frigate. So this was the dreaded Admiral Bridgewater.

But he didn't look like much of a nemesis for Merrick. Sort of like a grandfather with a pooch around his middle who made everyone listen to his war stories and refused to take off his decorated uniform.

"I see you've managed to resurrect the *Jewel*," Admiral Bridgewater said. "What's holding that pile of driftwood together? Pure luck?" He lifted his nose in disgust. "The ship matches the captain, I always say."

"Would you like a ride?" Merrick asked. "There's a spot down on the hull for you. You'll get a nice view of the seabed."

Naval officers in cobalt-blue jackets burst from the *Mother Dog*'s hatches like bees leaving a hive. They rowed to the *Jewel* in longboats, enough to be a scourge.

This wasn't like the Molvanian pirates' takeover of the *Jewel*. This was an admiral of the Queen's Own Navy. This was the rescue Fidelia had been waiting for.

But even if she reached for it, she couldn't feel a shred of relief.

She didn't want to leave Merrick's side, she realized. Not like this. Not when he was so fragile. Merrick must have seen her tense, because he placed a hand on her shoulder. "Steady," he murmured. "This will all be over soon."

Fidelia exhaled a shaky breath. *Steady,* she repeated to herself.

The navy's longboats rowed closer.

Cheapshot Charlie pulled his pistol from his belt. "Our orders, Captain?"

Bloody Elle snaked her white-blond hair back into a braid as she glared—if her eyes were weapons, Admiral Bridgewater would be tattered in the water. She, too, readied her gun, and kissed the barrel for luck.

"Surrender now, Merrick," Admiral Bridgewater called, "and I'll make sure the sharks can't get the biggest pieces of you!"

The *Mother Dog's* longboats knocked into the side of the *Jewel*—a horrible sound, like the drumbeats of war.

"Captain!" Cheapshot Charlie said. "They're here. What are your orders?"

Merrick took his gun and spat out a gob of blood. "Your orders are to jump," the captain said, and aimed his gun right between Cheapshot Charlie's eyes.

23

"Captain, no!" Bloody Elle cried. "Bridgewater will shoot you as soon as he gets the treasure—"

"I am a dead man already," Merrick said. "Bridgewater will take the treasure, and he will take the *Jewel*. And then he'll hang the two of you, if he doesn't kill you right here."

Cheapshot Charlie didn't move, Merrick's gun still pointed at his forehead. "We stay and fight," he said.

"This is an order from your captain." A bead of sweat rolled down Merrick's forehead as he cocked his pistol. Cheapshot Charlie and Bloody Elle didn't even flinch.

The naval sailors were scrambling up their grappling ropes.

"I'm warning you, Charlie!" Merrick's hand shook, his pistol rattling. "Jump now or I'll shoot!"

"Then shoot me," Cheapshot Charlie said. "I'm not leaving."

Merrick cursed—then lowered his aim and pulled the trigger.

The shot hit Cheapshot Charlie's leg—the pirate doubled over with the pain, clenching his muscle as blood soaked his pants.

Fidelia screamed, the burn of gunpowder piercing her nostrils.

"Captain, stop!" Bloody Elle whipped off her headscarf and pressed it into Cheapshot Charlie's wound.

Merrick readied another ball in his pistol, aiming it at Bloody Elle this time. "I said go." His black-and-red eye twitched in its socket.

"What are you doing?" Fidelia yelped.

The *Mother Dog* was now parallel, close enough that Fidelia could see the sails of the *Jewel* reflected in the frigate's shiny guns.

"I'm giving them a fighting chance," Merrick said. "Which is more than Bridgewater will give them."

"No! I won't abandon my captain!" Bloody Elle's lips trembled.

"Nor will I," Cheapshot Charlie gritted out. "Not until it's finished."

"Please, go." The sound of Merrick begging, even as he held his pistol steady—it broke Fidelia's heart. "This is your last order."

But it was too late—naval seamen leaped over the railing, swarming the *Jewel's* warped deck.

Bloody Elle and Cheapshot Charlie were tackled and cuffed. Merrick's wrists and ankles were bound, his pistol thrown overboard, sinking to the seabed—perhaps finding its way into his cave of treasures. He lay trussed on the floor of his own ship like a worm, coughing miserably at the strain.

A pair of sailors seized Fidelia's arms and held her, unsure of what to make of her. Fidelia let them; she had no fight left in her.

Merrick had shot his own man. His own boatswain.

But not out of monstrousness, no. Out of mercy. It was as unexpected and jarring as seeing Grizzle—massive, toothy Grizzle, the most powerful and primeval of all sea creatures, a terrifying living dinosaur—protecting his three pups.

Merrick the Monstrous, yes—but not a monster. And that was, perhaps, the most unsettling discovery of all.

The inevitable transfer happened—Bloody Elle, Cheapshot Charlie, Merrick, and Fidelia were lowered into a longboat and rowed over to the frigate. Officially in naval custody.

"Search that sorry excuse for a ship!" Admiral Bridgewater commanded his officers. "Every board, every cranny! Find it. Find it all!"

"Go on and search, you old—" Before Merrick could finish his insult, he erupted in a fit of coughs, flopping against the *Mother Dog*'s railing.

Admiral Bridgewater's grin only brightened, his eyes replaced by two gold coins. "Run that mouth of yours all you want, Monstrous," he said. "Because today, at last, I have it."

The naval crew spread across the *Jewel* like cockroaches swarming a larder; they touched every inch of the ship, lifted every loose board, jammed the butts of their guns into knotholes to widen them. Bits of wood flew from the ship, a storm of splinters.

Merrick watched in silence as the navy violated his ship, his face chiseled in stone—so calm.

Fidelia spotted his left hand, tied behind his back, squeeze in his ropes. The brooch. He still had it. Bridgewater's men hadn't found it—not yet.

The most valuable of all of his treasures, he'd called it.

Merrick had pulled a lot of tricks—scuttling the *Jewel* in a forest lake to keep it hidden, escaping from the navy's inescapable prison—and those were just the ones Fidelia knew about.

But as the sailors swept the *Jewel* for treasure, she hoped, with every bit of Quail blood she had, that he had one final card to play, one last trick in him: a way to keep that brooch. After everything he'd done for it—he had died to get it.

The navy crew found nothing aboard the *Jewel*—of course they didn't, not on this rickety old ship held together only by slivers and nostalgia. Fidelia waited for an outburst from the admiral, for gunfire and threats. But Admiral Bridgewater wasn't fazed. He raised a hamlike fist in the air and called to his men, "Bring me the suit."

His officers carried a sea chest from the admiral's quarters out to the main deck, and Fidelia started when they opened it.

"The diving suit!" she cried. So that's why it wasn't in the garden shed back on Arborley Island—the admiral had stolen it for himself.

The admiral turned his beady eyes on her. "You're their daughter, aren't you? Those fishy scientists, the Pheasants."

"It's Quail," Fidelia said. Admiral Bridgewater sniffed; he couldn't care less about names. Her name, their name.

"That suit and helmet are university property," she informed him.

"My men commandeered it, in the name of the queen." Admiral Bridgewater yanked the canvas suit up and over his body, somehow managing to zip his bulk inside the rubber. "Shall I have Her Majesty personally sign it out?"

Fidelia watched him secure the diving helmet, one of his officers twisting the corselets into place. *Break off,* she ordered fiercely. *You old rusty screws—fall off!* She willed any of the usual problems the Quails had with the diving suit to manifest: a crack in the glass visor, a split in the canvas, a leak in the rubber . . . But the admiral looked every speck the part of a real diver.

He opened the helmet's visor, holding his arms aloft while the officers inflated the suit. "I knew I'd catch you, Monstrous. I knew I was the bigger, stronger, faster animal. How does it feel now, to have my teeth around your throat?" He grinned, his cheeks flushing triumphant pink. "And here comes the bite."

To his officers, he said, "If any of them attempts even a whiff of escape, blow their heads off. That includes the girl."

He snapped the visor shut and tipped himself backward over the railing of the *Mother Dog,* splashing into the turquoise water. A weighted net was lowered over the side of the *Mother Dog,* and it sank into the water after him.

Silence washed over the two ships, broken only by a ghastly wet cough.

Then they waited.

June 4

Today's the day.

> *I'm so anxious, I can hardly write straight.*
>
> *Today's the day I try my new submarine!*
>
> *We picked the perfect spot for a test run—a continental reef ledge on the east side of Arborley that attracts all manner of pelagic creatures during the summer: crustaceans, octopuses, sea turtles, and of course—sharks.*
>
> *On a hot day like today, it's going to be shark city.*
>
> *I've made smaller-scale submersibles before—the Ocean-Soaker, the Aqua-Flood, the Wave-Walker—but nothing as ambitious as this.*
>
> *The* Egg *is a full-size mechanical submersible with propellers. It's capable of hundred-foot depths—at least, I think it is. I've made sure the chambers are properly pressurized for deep-sea diving. I'm calling it the* Egg *because it's shaped like one. The chandler was running a sale on some old cans of aquamarine paint.*

Fidelia watched Merrick's face. Hog-tied and breathless,

there was no crooked smirk, no hardened jaw, no inferno in that blue eye of his.

Merrick got what he wanted, she reminded herself. That pathetic brooch in his hand.

Still, her heart ached for him. He was about to watch his worst enemy pull up his life's work. Bridgewater would spend every bit of this great wealth that had taken Merrick years to compile . . . and Merrick would be fertilizing daisies.

We've just sailed out. It's a perfect sunny day — nothing but blue sky and blue water. It's teeming out here, busier than the canal on a Monday morning. I tried tracking fins — I lost count at thirty sharks. We've got a bunch of duskies, tons of blacktips, some nurses munching on crabs, and a tiger shark (who took off as soon as we anchored the boat). They're all hovering around the drop-off, right where the reef ledge ends and deep water begins. Right where we're going to lower the Egg *and see if it works.*

Dad's going to man the Platypus *while Mom and I go below.*

Crossing my fingers, my toes, and all my insides that this works.

The net emerged from the sea, and despite herself, tears fell from Fidelia's eyes, steaming up her glasses. There it was, a net nearly the size of the frigate itself, full of the world's largest accumulation of wealth. Sparkling gems. Gold doubloons. Silver chandeliers.

Admiral Bridgewater sputtered as he wrenched open the visor of the diving helmet. "Reel me in!"

Fidelia looked at Bloody Elle and Cheapshot Charlie; they were shockingly still. Bloody Elle stared down at her own toes, and Cheapshot Charlie's gaze was already beyond the horizon—finding anything else to focus on while their cave was plundered.

Stop him! Fidelia wanted to cry. *You're the greatest pirates who ever lived—break free from your ropes and get your treasure!*

Merrick met her eyes, and she brushed her tears onto her shoulder. Wait until all the sailors back home heard that the legend of the red daisies ends with a cheap pewter brooch.

IT WORKS!

I'm writing this from the inside of my very own submarine!

A very curious nurse shark keeps bumping her nose against the porthole.

"Tell her to come on in; it's nice and cozy!" Mom said, and held up her tea in cheers. That's right, tea—the Egg is working so well and it's so smooth that we've been down here for nearly three hours! Mom went topside for a bit so Dad could have some time in the sub.

"This is going to change everything," he kept saying, using the Periscope-Anchor to spin the Egg three hundred and sixty degrees around. "You wait and see, Fidelia. You've just revolutionized our line of work."

I don't know which I'm more excited about—the things that happened today or the things that could happen tomorrow.

Admiral Bridgewater's officers pried the suit off his uniform, still pristinely ironed and starched beneath the canvas. The treasure was carted off to the admiral's quarters; it took two dozen men several trips each to carry all of it.

"What happens now?" Fidelia asked Merrick softly.

He clicked his tongue. "Don't let him scare you, Quail," he said. "He'll get you home in one piece."

Her throat strained. "I meant what happens to you?" Another one of her incessant questions.

There. There was that crooked half smile. "Don't you worry about me," he said. "You just tell that old aunt of yours—"

He toppled over in a fit of uncontrollable coughing. Blood flecked the spotless deck.

"Stand him up!" Admiral Bridgewater said.

Officers snatched Merrick and pulled him upright; he wavered, still coughing, until at last he found his balance.

Admiral Bridgewater came inches away from the pirate. "In another lifetime, Merrick, you and I could have made a team for the ages. If only the navy had beaten all that sauce out of you." His piggy eyes disappeared into the flesh of his face. "You could have been the next me."

Merrick lifted his chin. "I would've tied my own noose, if I ever became a bilge rat like you."

The corners of Fidelia's mouth sprang up. This was why Merrick would always win, she realized. Admiral Bridgewater didn't really want to kill Merrick—he wanted to kill Merrick's arrogance. Tame him. And since the admiral never would, he'd have to settle for killing Merrick the Monstrous instead.

Admiral Bridgewater's elation was blown clean off his face. "We shall all see the great Merrick the Monstrous hang. Just like every other black-hearted pirate. That's right,

Monstrous," he whispered as he leaned over Merrick, seawater dripping off his soggy mustache. "You may have fancied yourself the king of the nine seas, but you're going to die in the same way as every other sea dog who decides to sail under a red flag—dancing the hempen jig where anyone who wishes can watch you take your last breath. But first." He rubbed one of his silver buttons, polishing it spotless with the tip of his thumb. "Gunners, at your ready!"

The *Mother Dog*'s cannons were already powdered, loaded, and aimed; the gunners awaited their signal. Fidelia followed their sight lines, and her heart leaped into her throat.

"Do something!" she said to Merrick and Charlie and Elle. *Save your ship, your lucky ship,* her heart screeched as it flapped into her mouth, circling and desperate.

Merrick's face was still marbleized.

With some relish, Admiral Bridgewater shouted, "Fire!"

The cannons were deafening. They exploded with black clouds of smoke, blasting giant, splintering holes into the side of the *Jewel.*

Tears fogged Fidelia's glasses as the *Jewel*'s toppled foresail caught fire. She could still see the ghost of Bloody Elle, her long cornsilk hair whipping in the breeze as she inspected a line. And there—her eyes found the spot on the boards that Cheapshot Charlie had scoured with the holystone, scrubbing away pond scum—gone now, only ash.

"Again! Fire at will! Take it out." Admiral Bridgewater had fallen under a spell—his eyes glazed over, the hairs in his mustache standing at attention, emanating steam and fire and red.

His men reloaded and shot, and shot, and shot.

Fidelia's ears rang. Somewhere she thought she heard singing—was that Cheapshot Charlie again, droning his three-note mourning song?

No, the boatswain's mouth was closed. He looked like he would never sing again.

The shots finally ended—whether by Bridgewater's command or because they had run out of ship to shoot at, Fidelia didn't know. When the smoke cleared, the *Jewel* was a pile of kindling, and Fidelia watched each little blackened stick fall through the water. The red flag, thundered through with grapeshot, floated for a second on the sea's surface before it, too, sank and was lost forever.

Fidelia buried her face with her hands and sobbed.

"Take them below," Admiral Bridgewater ordered, "but keep them separated. And put a gag on Merrick. He's spoken his last words."

"What about the girl?" an officer asked, clutching Fidelia's elbow roughly.

Admiral Bridgewater considered her. "Put her in the barracks," he finally prescribed, "but if she gives you any trouble, take her below with the others."

Cheapshot Charlie and Bloody Elle were removed first, dragged to a hatch and pushed inside. Fidelia stared at the trail of blood left by Charlie's injured leg.

Two sailors carried Merrick down to the hold, not even giving him a chance to use his legs—just towing him off like a rabid dog on a leash.

The *Mother Dog* set sail, heading north. Back to civilization, back to the real world, where pirates were criminals to be hanged, not comrades, not men to be pitied, not clever or brave or hopelessly tragic. A world where a cave of red daisies could exist only in sailors' yarns.

A world where a girl who was kidnapped would be best off just forgetting all about it.

Fidelia was escorted to a dingy, dark bunk on a lower deck, and she couldn't tell if the sound of howling was the wind, thrusting them back to Arborley much faster than she wanted, or Merrick, moaning and coughing beneath the deck boards.

Two Years Earlier

Water held ships. It held creatures of all shape and form and disposition.

Water also held memories.

It was the perfect vessel for them—Merrick would be sailing across the white arctic sea, weaving through a labyrinth of ice caps, and the water would suddenly gift him a remembrance of the day he defected from the navy—his first battle with Admiral Bridgewater, a success. A happy day, happy memory.

He would be sailing across the golden waves of the Molvanian coast, and again, the water would present him with a memory, as if it had been storing it for him—the memory of his first raid, that first pillage of a beanie ship and the giddy night he spent counting gold in his quarters. That night he didn't think of all the things he would buy, but of how this would be considered a dismal amount of gold, pathetic compared to how much he'd take before the reign of Merrick the Monstrous came to its glorious end.

He could sail across the blues and grays of Arborley Bay and remember the first time he saw her. A green dress flapping on the boardwalk, hair blowing free, her eyes on him and his ship as though she'd never seen something so wild. A bittersweet memory, to be sure—these days more bitter than sweet.

But for all its good memories, the water also offered up the wretched ones. The time he'd lost her, the one honest thing he'd ever given her falling between the waves as if it were just a brooch made of cheap metal and not a piece of his very heart.

Even that—even that—paled in contrast to this latest memory.

The worst battle he'd ever lost. Losses too horrible to face. He wished he could remove the memory of this night completely from his mind. Drop it into the sea like an old bone, hear it plop and watch it sink into the silver churn, the sharks snatching it up.

But the water couldn't keep it forever. It would stir the memory up if he ever came this way again, if he ever sailed across the Coral of the Damned again. Then he'd remember.

The slick of his deck boards, blood rolling along their surface and dripping off into the sea.

The sight of a head lolling against his feet—one of his crew members, but drenched, and disfigured, like a bruised fruit.

The sounds—oh, god, the sounds of the slaughter.

The *Mother Dog*'s braying cannons, hurling great balls of terror, and the *Jewel*'s pitiful retaliating gunshots, tiny nips from a puppy in comparison.

The cries of his crew—grown men and women who had lost limbs for him over the years, and tattooed their skin with the tips of their blades on a wavering sea, and survived the near starvation and mental torture of long journeys. Never, never had Merrick heard them cry like this—the wails of beasts, trapped and awaiting their certain death.

And above it all the sound of Bridgewater laughing— *laughing*—as he carried out his butchery.

Merrick's crew was picked off one at a time with the guns, or in whole groups by the cannons, until once again there was only Merrick and Bloody Elle and Cheapshot Charlie, who helped him move the pulverized *Jewel* away from the scene at last, skimming through the shallow waters of the Coral of the Damned, where the *Mother Dog* couldn't follow.

Merrick the Monstrous, retreating like a wounded animal.

In the waters below, his men and women sank until their bodies bumped the sand — that's what they were now, just bodies. Bags for their bones, meat for the bottom-feeders.

And soon they, too, would just be sea and salt and memory.

Merrick had plotted out the trip perfectly: He would sail to the prison barge, and Cheapshot Charlie would distract the guards. Bloody Elle would take care of the dogs. Merrick would let everyone on the prison barge loose, crew or no, because the more people wandering free in the world who were like him, who were pebbles in the admiral's shoe, the better.

And this is what happened.

They broke them out of the prison, everything unfolding according to plan. The crew had set the *Jewel* at a fair clip, and were already cheering their captain's victory, when Admiral Bridgewater ambushed them.

And then the bloodbath.

A dreadful memory. One of the worst simmering in Merrick's mind.

But then why, only a week after losing his crew, was it a different memory that kept pushing to the surface? A different loss?

Her face plagued him day and night, awake or dreaming—the coldness in it as she dropped the brooch overboard; the feathery sound of her voice; the feel of her twirling around him as they danced, the softness of her lips against his skin.

The memory of her was relentless.

They sailed aimlessly for a week, trying to gather their bearings. Merrick watched the sea's spray cleanse the *Jewel* completely of blood. He watched, silent. After a week of hollow sleep and nightmares in waking daylight, Merrick spun the helm east.

"Captain?" Bloody Elle said—a question and a concern, all in one word.

"We're going to the market," Merrick said, his jaw tense.

"Good idea," Cheapshot Charlie said. "We need to tar this hull before she springs a leak—"

"You do that," Merrick said, "but keep her ready to make a quick exit. Molvania is not going to like the storm I'm bringing."

Bloody Elle and Cheapshot Charlie exchanged a look—they'd been doing this lately, Merrick noticed. Of course he noticed; that was his job, as the captain. To oversee.

He didn't care. Let them worry.

* * *

Merrick stalked through the wet market with single-eyed purpose.

The posters advertising for his dead-or-alive capture had tripled on the walls of the hash house. He barely noticed.

Without a word, he walked up to the jeweler who had sold him the brooch and held his pistol against the jeweler's throat.

"My watch," Merrick said. "Where is it?"

The jeweler lifted a shaking finger. "The table."

Merrick's old watch, given to him by his father. The only thing Merrick had that was his. And he was taking it back.

"That brooch you sold me was garbage," Merrick said.

"I told you, you should have brought her diamonds," the jeweler replied, his breath stinking of tooth rot and fear. And then as he regretted his cheek, his eyes widened, just white holes with black circles floating, and he braced himself for the kill shot.

But instead of blowing his head off, Merrick just laughed.

He laughed the entire walk back through the market. He laughed when he got to the patched-up *Jewel,* and as their lousy, shaken three-man crew brought her to her full twenty knots, he laughed, and laughed, and laughed.

The stench of death was thick in the air as we approached the carcass. There, a mere mile off the mainland coast, a sperm whale floated, belly up, its ventral grooves black with decay. We circled the whale—and then we saw the sharks. At least six of them, four great whites and two tigers, moving in to tear chunks of meat from the whale, as casually as if they were dining at a local buffet. Their teeth grappled the whale expertly, their jaws working with a thousand pounds per square inch of pressure, their bodies violently shaking the flesh loose—a display to birth a thousand nightmares.

But also a testament to nature's great cycle of life. A whale dies; the sharks feast. An apple is eaten, its core discarded; a bird plucks out the seeds. A tree's leaves fall and rot; the nutrients released provide sustenance for an entire forest of trees. In nature, death not only makes way for life; it *fosters* life.

The death of things that come before us is the only reason any of us receives a turn on this planet in the first place.

—*Exploring an Underwater Fairyland* by Dr. and Dr. Quail

Fidelia stared up at the ceiling. The beams of the *Mother Dog* were impeccable—no slivers, no wood rot, no termites. As if the oak trees had grown branches already sanded and shaped.

Her mind felt too tangled to sleep, her heart too wounded. Merrick was finally caught.

Logically, she knew he was dying anyway. He'd signed his death sentence when he went into the cave of the red daisies. What difference did it make whether he was hanged by Admiral Bridgewater or blown up with the *Jewel* or left to wheeze and cough and sputter while his lungs slowly collapsed?

But it *did* make a difference, Fidelia knew.

It made a difference whether a great shark was reeled in or left to fight and lose its battles out in open waters.

And what about Cheapshot Charlie and Bloody Elle? Admiral Bridgewater would hang them, too, without a doubt.

So much unnecessary death.

Her adventure was over. She, too, was being hauled back like a fish on a barbed line. And after everything that had happened over the last week, nothing had really changed. Her parents were still gone. Grizzle was still untagged. Aunt Julia was waiting in Arborley with her books and her turtle soup, and they would still be moving to the mainland.

She still buzzed with questions unanswered: Why did Merrick send Fidelia into shark-infested waters just to see an old brooch one more time?

And for that matter, why did he search through the deadly cave in the first place?

What was the brooch for, really?

And what would happen to it when the admiral inevitably found it?

Long after the lamps had been extinguished, Fidelia resisted closing her eyes, certain it would be a sleepless night for her. But her eyelids grew droopy in the darkness, so she rolled over onto her side and slept. Dreamlessly and silently.

* * *

Sometime in the night, she was suddenly awake.

The bell must have rung, signaling the changing of the watch. Or perhaps the ship had rocked, or—

It didn't matter. She was up now, and she knew what she had to do.

She threw her covers off and shivered. The air was crisper, chillier than the muggy tropical counterpart. They were back on the cocoa route, on their way to Arborley. To the gallows.

She tiptoed, the boards cold beneath her stocking feet, up to the quarterdeck. A line of marines stood along the railing, keeping guard, and Fidelia approached them, clutching her stomach.

"The admiral told you to stay in your cabin!" one of the men barked at her.

"I know. It's just . . . I think I'm going to be sick." She put a wasted look on her face and gagged, then rushed between two of the men and leaned over the railing, heaving dramatically.

"Don't you get any of that on the boards," one of the men said. "You make sure you pitch it way out."

At last she stood up, wiping the back of her mouth delicately. "That's better." She sucked air through her nose with a little quaver. "I'm sure I cleared the ship."

As expected, the guards dashed forward to inspect the side of the ship; Admiral Bridgewater would no doubt blame them if even a drip of vomit hit the *Mother Dog*. When their backs were turned, Fidelia carefully plucked a set of keys from one officer's waist and sneaked to the hatch, lifting it slowly.

It was a dark, damp space. Creaks from the deck above echoed through the hollows of the ship; the ocean pounded against the sides in muffled rhythm. Fidelia had to duck to avoid hitting her head on the ceiling.

At first, nothing. Just the scratching of rats.

Then something moved in the shadows.

Cheapshot Charlie and Bloody Elle sat on the benches in their cells. Water sloshed around their ankles.

Bloody Elle snoozed; Cheapshot Charlie nudged her gently and said, "We've got a visitor."

"And the visitor has a gift." Fidelia glanced behind her, just to be sure she hadn't been followed, and pulled the set of keys from her dress.

"How did you . . . ?" Bloody Elle said.

Fidelia smiled. "You three have been a bad influence on me."

She unlocked their cell doors and uncuffed them. "Where is he?"

Bloody Elle rubbed her sore wrists, then pointed to the farthest corner of the hold.

"Merrick?" Fidelia inched forward until she found him, and her breath abandoned her.

He was cuffed to the wall. His wrists, feet, and neck were all enclosed by tight metal hoops and linked by a heavy chain to the ship's boards. A sort of steel cage was fixed over his head and around his mouth—a muzzle. Admiral Bridgewater was either afraid Merrick would talk his way to freedom with his clever words or he was tired of Merrick's insults—or both.

Merrick was slumped against the wall, his labored breathing audible even over the hold's noisy groans and shudders. He coughed every few seconds, an awful, grating sound.

Fidelia's stomach clenched at the sight of him— shackled. Exhausted. Defeated.

"Merrick," she said.

He didn't even look up—his chin stayed tucked to his chest, coughing, sniffling, breathing that rattly breath. . . .

She unlocked his cell and stood beside him, waiting for him to expose his cuffs so she could free him.

"Lean forward, Captain," Bloody Elle said.

But Merrick didn't move, or make any indication that he'd even heard them.

Fidelia looked at Cheapshot Charlie and Bloody Elle. "What's wrong with him?" she whispered, her voice weak. "Why won't he let me unlock him?"

Merrick slowly angled his head up and coughed, and Fidelia winced at his black-and-red eye—swollen, and black as ever, leaking some darkish fluid down his cheek.

Cheapshot Charlie studied his captain. "He's not coming," he finally surmised. Merrick coughed, his whole body straining, chains jangling, blood spraying through the bars of his muzzle. For a moment, Fidelia thought, *This is it. His last breath.* But Merrick somehow found his air, then dropped his head again.

"No!" Hot tears stung Fidelia's eyes. "No, you can't just surrender like this. You're Merrick the Monstrous—you always escape! Do your disappearing act before Bridgewater hangs you."

But with every shaky inhale Merrick took, it was confirmed the pirate captain was all but finished. He'd never survive an escape. He'd never be able to swim away, and Cheapshot Charlie and Bloody Elle were in no shape to tow him to land. They were both weak from their all-sweets diet, drained from the tussle with the navy, and Charlie's leg wound was festering with pus and crusted blood. It would be a miracle if the two of them made it to safety.

Was Merrick trying to speak? Fidelia couldn't tell—his jaw muscles were blocked by the iron gate of the muzzle.

"Go," he croaked.

Bloody Elle dropped to her knees and gripped Merrick's skeletal hands. "Captain . . ."

But there was nothing more to say. If Cheapshot Charlie and Bloody Elle had any chance of escaping, they'd have to leave Merrick behind.

Merrick raised his head again and met the faces of his crew, his two best mates. The ones who had survived by his side. Slowly—so painfully slowly—he nodded.

It was all the answer Bloody Elle and Cheapshot Charlie needed.

"You have to hurry. They'll know I'm out of my bunk any minute." Fidelia could barely stand it, the heaviness of this moment, the agony.

Cheapshot Charlie and Bloody Elle slipped up the ladder in silence, off to hide themselves somewhere on the massive flagship until the opportune time to jump. No good-byes, no hugs, no final message to their captain or their captive.

Fidelia needed to get back to her bunk before the

admiral was alerted, but she couldn't make herself care. What did it matter if they caught her? She couldn't save Merrick. Just like when her parents died—she was helpless against the ebbs and flows of life, the triumphs and the losses. Creatures were born, and played their part in the great ecosystem, and then they died.

And there was nothing she could do to stop it.

She swiveled around and marched to the ladder—she had to get back to her bed so she could pretend to be waking at dawn. So she could feign innocence when the officers realized Bloody Elle and Cheapshot Charlie weren't in their cells. So she could act like everything was fine.

"Quail . . ." The moan was barely detectable among Merrick's strained breaths.

"Thank . . . you."

Thank you? For what? For retrieving his brooch? Well, he had forced her. Taken her away from Arborley, sailed her across the world, threatened her with all manner of violence if she refused to complete the task . . .

But he hadn't made her care. No pirate on earth could have forced such a thing, not with a thousand pistols.

Her tears spilled over as she climbed the ladder. No sign of Cheapshot Charlie or Bloody Elle on the deck. Perhaps they'd already dived overboard, or perhaps they were hidden safely out of sight, waiting until the opportune moment to make their getaway. Either way, she wished on every swell of the sea that they would make it.

Soundlessly she replaced the hatch to the hold, then threw the set of keys overboard, and when she climbed back into her bed, she stared at the ceiling until morning.

Twenty knots. That's what the *Jewel* could do, back in her heyday. So said Cheapshot Charlie.

The *Mother Dog* could barely reach twelve knots—she was much too big to be as nimble as the *Jewel*—but she made up for her lethargy with sheer gusto. Goose pimples broke out on Fidelia's arms with every swell, but the ship powered through any threat of storms with the strength of ten blue whales.

Still, slow as she was, the *Mother Dog* was flying, making record time. The crosswinds, Fidelia realized, were almost nonexistent. The Undertow was not only sparing them its chaos; it was actually pushing them back to Arborley.

Too fast! Fidelia wanted to cry to the wind and the waves. *Slow this down; make it last. These are Merrick's final moments. Stretch them out.*

But on they sailed, and by the afternoon of the second day, the *Mother Dog* cruised past the Coral of the Damned without fanfare or ritual. Fidelia, seeing the red fringes poking up out of the water from the porthole in her bunk, closed her eyes and hummed a tuneless three-note song, and she didn't open her eyes again for a long time.

The officers had discovered that two of their four prisoners were missing. (Fidelia counted herself in this group because although she wasn't cuffed in the leaky hold, she was no longer allowed to leave her quarters.) Admiral Bridgewater sent some of his men out in longboats to scan the ship's surroundings for any clues to their whereabouts, but to no avail. The pirates were gone.

On the evening of the third day, an officer came to Fidelia's bunk.

"The admiral wants to see you." An order, not a request.

Admiral Bridgewater's cabin was spacious, larger than Aunt Julia's loft at Arborley Library. Fidelia took a seat at an elaborately carved table that seated twelve—a war table, for plotting out battles, she figured. How many plans to catch Merrick were made at this very table, only to be thwarted on the seas?

Silhouetted in the bay window, the admiral stood across from her. His uniform jacket was currently being ironed and starched by a sailor in the corner; instead he had donned a burgundy velvet smoking jacket and lounging cap.

"I am trying," Admiral Bridgewater said, "to get an exact accounting of what happened to you." He walked to his drinking cart and poured himself a glass of spirits, then sipped it with a grimace as if it were a tonic.

"Let me guess what happened here," he said as he circled the long table. "Merrick took you against your will. He brought you to his cave, and he would have made you fetch his treasure for him if we hadn't shown up and saved you." His piggy eyes were squinted, focusing on Fidelia as if she were a very small, indecipherable treasure map. "Is that accurate?"

How could she possibly explain to Admiral Bridgewater that it was all a bit blurrier than that? Yes, there were pistols in her face when the pirates came to the Quail family home, pistols that motivated her to board the *Jewel* and do as Merrick said — she'd believed him when he said he'd hurt her. He was Merrick the Monstrous, after all.

Yes, it was easy to measure a beast by the size of his teeth and the power of his jaws . . . But there was more to a beast than just his bite. And somewhere along the way, things with Merrick had shifted. She'd *wanted* to help Merrick, to grant this dying man his last request. Even though it meant risking her own life.

"Yes," Fidelia answered honestly, "but—"

"What doesn't make sense," Admiral Bridgewater went on, "is why a victim of Merrick the Monstrous would be so distraught when we finally caught and bound her captor. Am I mistaken, or did I see tears when the *Jewel* sank?" He sneered and smoothed his velvet lapel. "And then there is the matter of the missing prisoners. Two of my men reported seeing you on deck—in direct violation of your orders to remain in your cabin—on the very night the pirates escaped. The coincidence is rather remarkable, isn't it?"

His smile was terrible, pompous as one of the medals on his uniform. "A victim of Merrick's will be returned safely home and given Her Majesty's guarantee that the vermin will hang until dead." He swished his glass of spirits so the ice clinked against the sides. "But his accomplices," he continued, "will swing next to him."

His stench of alcohol and body odor soured Fidelia's nostrils as he stepped even closer.

"So what are you?" Admiral Bridgewater enclosed her in his shadow. "Are you one of Merrick the Monstrous's unfortunate pawns? Or were you a willing participant?"

The right answer was obvious: All she had to do was condemn Merrick, disintegrate into cries of relief at being rescued, and recap the nightmare she'd had, spending those days on the *Jewel* in terror with the outlaws. All she had to do was name Merrick for the devil he was, and the admiral would be satisfied.

She looked into Admiral Bridgewater's face. There, between the jowls and the scorn, she saw it—fear.

A fear she recognized. That fear you get when something massive is dangling on your line, and you'll do anything to reel it in—and you're scared you'll lose the biggest catch of your life.

Admiral Bridgewater had Merrick. He had Merrick's great treasure. And he'd do anything to reel this all the way in.

So why couldn't she do it? Why couldn't she give the admiral the answer he was looking for?

Admiral Bridgewater watched her flail, scrunching his face. "Did you know that Merrick was in the navy?"

She nodded slowly, wary of a trap.

"Do you know how he left?" Admiral Bridgewater stroked his mustache and took a seat right next to Fidelia— she could smell the sharpness of his cologne, the sweat between his chins. "Merrick was top of his class. The best gunfighter we'd ever seen, a pro with schematics and navigation, a master sailor. But even more than that—he was a thinker. He'd devise ways out of battles that didn't require a single cannon fired. A mind like that, I thought, will spoil faster than Molvanian goats' milk if we don't channel it. And so Merrick was on track to being the youngest vice admiral in the history of the Queen's Own Navy."

Yes, that sounded like Merrick. A man who hid his beloved ship in a lake knew how to think sideways, how to come up with plan Z when plans A, B, and C were ruined.

"I knew, of course, how bright he was—but I had no idea the things he was truly capable of. The horrible things. I should have seen it—I should have put out that twinkle in his eyes, wiped away that laugh in the corner of his mouth. I should have stopped him." Admiral Bridgewater sipped the melted ice in his glass.

"I have caught and hung the most notorious pirates to ever sail the nine seas," the admiral said. "But I've never seen a monster like Merrick. He didn't just abandon rank and leave the base as any decent officer would have done. No, he had to make a grand exit. He and that—that fiend Charlie, they took one of the frigates one night and threw its crew overboard. They set off explosions all along the fort. Those who weren't blown completely into pieces had to search for their own legs among the debris."

Fidelia shuddered. She shouldn't be surprised. She knew Merrick's legacy. She knew how monstrous he was.

And yet she'd seen it, in his one remaining eye—a shred of humanity. There was sadness there—deep, abiding sadness. And immeasurable gratitude when she brought him that brooch. It didn't excuse what he'd done; of course it didn't. But it made it impossible for her to write him off as simply a monster.

"So please believe me," the admiral finished, "when I say you are lucky to be alive. You are lucky to be in one piece. And whatever sympathy you may have for this . . . this animal, well—toss it overboard, where it belongs."

Arborley Island.

Smog hung thicker than she remembered, and the plants seemed yellowed and dried compared to the lush green fronds in the tropics. Everything about the island looked stale. Bleached. Sad.

The *Mother Dog* made berth at the main wharf, and the officers exited the ship in rank—the seamen first, the warrant officers, then the lieutenants. A lieutenant strong-armed Fidelia off the ship and took her to a bench on the boardwalk. They wrapped a scratchy, colorless, navy-issue blanket around her.

As if she, and not Merrick, were the one infirmed.

Admiral Bridgewater came down the *Mother Dog*'s gangplank, his beery red eyes scanning Stony Beach as if he expected a royally commissioned parade to greet him and celebrate his victory. But the beach was empty. "Bring him out," he ordered.

They dragged Merrick out of the hold completely uncuffed; the thirty marines' bayonets aimed at his head were more than enough to keep him tethered. Fidelia winced at the sight of him—he shivered and coughed, soaking wet and stinking so strongly of mildew that she could smell him from where she sat. The officers marched him down the gangplank, then dropped him onto the shingle beach like a half-drowned rodent.

His arms were yanked out of his peacoat. His shirt was peeled from his body. The faded tattoo of a red daisy stained Merrick's sunken chest, just above his heart, his rib cage visible enough to play like an instrument. The hardened purple veins on his hands had spread, weblike, up his arms, onto his knotty back, and onto his neck.

He crumbled, a shower of bloody phlegm coating the pebbles under him, and he balled his fists from the pain.

In one of those hands, Fidelia realized, *Merrick still has the brooch.*

"Merrick von Mourne," announced Bridgewater, "you are convicted—again—of piracy, evasion of the navy, and the kidnapping of a minor. All are capital crimes under Her

Majesty's rule. You are hereby sentenced to hang by the neck until dead."

"Or . . . until . . . you blink," Merrick wheezed.

Admiral Bridgewater strode closer to Merrick, until the pirate captain's face was mere inches from the admiral's well-polished boots. The admiral lowered his voice. "Legally, I have to hang you. The queen prefers that enemies of her kingdom have public deaths. But when you attempt whatever hackneyed escape you're planning"—here, the admiral leaned down, close to Merrick's ear, which, Fidelia noticed, her gut twisting, was also bleeding—"I will be the one to shoot you."

Merrick raised his head. "Looking . . . forward to it." The pirate stared, his two-toned eyes firing holes into the admiral—but just when Fidelia was bracing for the admiral to throw punches, Merrick coughed. He coughed right in Admiral Bridgewater's face, and red spittle clung to the admiral's mustache like raindrops.

Admiral Bridgewater pulled one of his white gloves off and wiped his mustache clean. "You hang at dawn," he said, "and then I'm finally free of your black soul."

A nod from the admiral, and the brutes in silver buttons swept Merrick down the boardwalk, into the cobbled street, and out of sight. They were taking him to a holding cell, an iron box where he'd wait for death.

And this time, Fidelia knew, death would find him. Whether Merrick truly could make a grand escape from the noose or whether he gasped his last breath in that cell, it didn't really matter. Merrick the Monstrous was done.

Admiral Bridgewater went back to his ship, leaving a small group of marines to patrol the beach. Fidelia barely noticed them. She stayed huddled on the boardwalk. A soft rain fell.

She rubbed her glasses dry on the hem of her dirty, threadbare dress and sniffed the ends of her hair. She positively reeked. Enough dirt coated her arms that she could have planted carrots. Aunt Julia would dunk her in a bath right away and pour that awful violet tonic all over her—if she even let Fidelia inside. Maybe she'd just make Fidelia wash off in the rain.

Here she sat, again, staring out at Stony Beach, again. Just as she had done weeks ago. She'd sailed almost around the world, and she'd come back to see the same view. The Undertow swirled just beyond the harbor, crackling, a stormy commander gathering troops for weathery destruction.

Beneath the bridge, a canal boat approached, splashing grimy water onto a murder of crows congregating on the cobblestones. Fidelia barely noticed; she was too busy watching the waves in the bay go from ripples to mountains.

"Fidelia!"

At first Fidelia thought it was the crows crying, the sound was so inhuman. But when she turned, she saw a woman hobbling across the boardwalk. It took a moment to realize it was Aunt Julia. Her aunt was wearing the same beige dress she'd worn the day Fidelia was kidnapped, only it was covered in ink blots and tearstains and smudges from who knew what. And her hair—Aunt Julia's usual tight, perfect chignon was a gull's nest of greasy tendrils. She was a person undone.

Fidelia got to her feet. Aunt Julia ran along the slats, the gap between them closing smaller and smaller, until—

Her aunt collided into her and clutched her so hard, it felt like the wispy librarian might snap in two.

"Oh, god, you're all right." Aunt Julia buried her face in that crook between Fidelia's neck and shoulder, muffling her words. "Thank goodness. They told me—they told me you'd been taken by *pirates*! But you're all right!"

You're all right. . . . Was Fidelia all right? "I'm home now," Fidelia said, her words mechanical, stroking her aunt's back.

Aunt Julia landed a kiss on Fidelia's forehead and searched her face. "Fidelia, what happened?"

"Aunt Julia," Fidelia croaked. "The book."

"The book?" Fidelia dropped the military blanket and pulled *Exploring an Underwater Fairyland* out of her bag.

Aunt Julia went pale as a turtle's egg. She opened the front cover, shuddering when she saw the stamp—*Property of Arborley Library*. Aunt Julia took hold of her shoulders, her magnified doe's eyes blinking fiercely behind her peach spectacles. "Tell me what happened, Fidelia. Tell me everything. Right now."

So there, on the boardwalk, rain pitter-pattering down into their hair, Fidelia told Aunt Julia everything—a skeletal version. She told her aunt that she'd been taken by Merrick and Charlie and Elle. When she said his name, Merrick the Monstrous, Aunt Julia closed her eyes, and kept them closed for a full five seconds before she seemed ready to see the world again.

"What did he want?" Aunt Julia's voice was strangled. "Did he tell you why he took you?"

"He needed me to get his treasure," Fidelia answered. "Lost treasure. From an underwater cave—"

"From the cave of the red daisies," Aunt Julia whispered. Her cheeks were gray.

"How do you know—?" Fidelia said.

"I'm a librarian." Aunt Julia shook all over. "Did you

go into the cave? Tell me now, Fidelia—did you breathe in the pollen?" She clamped Fidelia's wrists with cold, bloodless fingers.

"No," Fidelia managed, and pulled her wrists free. "No. The navy came, and they took it all, and . . ."

"Where is he now—Merrick the Monstrous?"

"He's locked up somewhere." She didn't mention that Merrick was dying. She didn't mention that all he wanted from the bottom of the sea was some old pewter brooch. She didn't mention that watching him die was horrifying, and would haunt her for the rest of her days—like seeing a fish drown on dry land. "The admiral is hanging him tomorrow morning."

Her aunt bloomed red with anger. "Good." Aunt Julia's teeth were clenched. "Let him hang." She wiped her palms on her skirt.

"But . . ." Fidelia didn't know how to tell her aunt that there was a spark of humanity in Merrick—or there had been, before the admiral captured him, before he was muzzled and beaten and locked in the hold of the flagship. "I don't think he should die like this."

"He kidnapped you," Aunt Julia said. "He would have let you die—"

"But he didn't," Fidelia said. "He could have been so cruel. He could have kept me in ropes the whole journey—he could have held his gun to my head and made me dive into the cave. He could have just let me breathe in the pollen. But he didn't." She glanced down at her boots. "I know he's Merrick the Monstrous . . . But I don't think he's all bad."

"He's a pirate, Fidelia." There—there was a whiff of the stern Aunt Julia Fidelia had left behind. "How could he possibly be anything but bad?"

Fidelia looked out over Stony Beach, at the slate-blue water folding over itself, the foam climbing the shore. There was so much still to tell, but she was out of strength. Out of words.

Aunt Julia reached out and tucked a strand of Fidelia's ragged hair behind her ear. "Are you hungry?" she finally said.

Her aunt's hand lingered in her hair; Fidelia could feel the warmth of the familiar touch radiating through her entire being.

"That depends," she said with a weak grin. "Are you cooking?"

"Huzzah for Fidelia!"

The howling of the Undertow was nothing compared to the storm inside the Book and Bottle. Fiddles whinnied and sailors sang and danced around the tables as Fidelia and Aunt Julia slurped their bowls of Shipwreck Stew.

Shipwreck Stew, hot and robust, a hundred flavors to decipher: lobster and littleneck clams and tarragon and cod. And above all, the taste of familiar.

The taste of home.

"This island isn't the same without a Quail!" Old Ratface drained his fourth mug of ale and hiccupped.

"Long live the reigning Quail!" the pub chorused.

Fidelia smiled at each of them, most already drunk and red-nosed. Some of the sailors gawked at her, as though they were looking at a ghost. Some regarded her with mugs raised, clearly impressed that she had endured Merrick the Monstrous and lived to tell the tale. And a few grinned stupidly, glad she was back safely, no doubt, but also pleased to have an excuse for merriment.

Then she thought of a few other faces missing from this circle.

Ida's and Arthur's, yes. *Of course,* yes.

But also Bloody Elle, her rough, tanned skin, her black ringed tattoos, her loyalty to her captain, her earnestness. And Cheapshot Charlie, his long face and bald head and grouchy eyebrows and his brambly disposition—his way of protecting his captain, Fidelia now understood.

And Merrick, of course. His contrasting eyes—the piercing blue, for all of his cleverness and grit, and the black-and-red eye. A dead eye.

She missed them all.

Her chest suddenly gave a little tremble. The celebration around her dimmed and muted itself. Everything was coming up fast, a rush of sky, as though she was surfacing too quickly from a deep-sea dive. She'd survived a kidnapping. Survived pirates—and not just any pirates, but *the* pirate, the most dangerous outlaw who had ever sailed. She'd survived the Undertow again, survived a breakneck trip to the tropics, survived an encounter with a territorial shark, survived finishing the Water-Eater.

And she'd survived losing her parents.

She folded herself in half over the table, buried her face in her hands, and cried hard.

"Shhh." Aunt Julia patted her back with soft hands. "Let's get you home." Her voice echoed, faraway to Fidelia.

Aunt Julia led her out of the pub and into a canal boat, the sailors lining up to watch her leave, like a processional. She managed to stay awake long enough to see Arborley Library—still massive, still beautiful. She managed to get out of the canal boat and up the marble steps.

Then Fidelia collapsed, the weight of the last few weeks—the last few months—making her too weak to stand. She felt Aunt Julia lift her—small, wispy Aunt Julia carried her up all three flights of stairs, tucked her into bed, and didn't let go of her hand until she fell asleep.

Two Years Earlier

When they reached Medusa's Grotto, Merrick shut himself in his personal tunnel — the captain's quarters — and locked the door behind him.

Bloody Elle and Cheapshot Charlie kept busy. They cleaned their wounds from the great naval massacre, bandaged cuts, repaired themselves as best they could with the primitive first-aid supplies they kept on the *Jewel*. They scrubbed the ship of barnacles, refitted new wood along the boards, tarred the dry rot. They caught fish, grilled shrimp, and guzzled rum while staring, silent, at the fire in the sandpit. They slept, rose, and slept again.

Merrick's door didn't budge. If he came out to find sustenance or drink, it was in the night, while his comrades were snoozing.

"He's been in there too long," Bloody Elle said after a week, her fingers following the lines of her wrist tattoos, around and around. "I'm breaking down the door."

Cheapshot Charlie held his arm in front of her. "He needs more time."

"He needs water!" Bloody Elle cried. "And food! And air!"

Cheapshot Charlie gripped her shoulder. "He'll come out when he's ready," he said. "I know Merrick. He loves to fight . . ." The boatswain stared at the door. "But he also loves to brood."

"If we open this door next week and find a skeleton with one blue eye, I'm telling Merrick's ghost it's your fault," Bloody Elle grumbled. But she let the captain alone.

Cheapshot Charlie, who had known Merrick for more than a decade—who had first met the ambitious, glib pirate captain back when he was a fresh-faced, silver-button-wearing, goose-stepping member of the Queen's Own Navy—Cheapshot Charlie was right.

One morning when Bloody Elle and Cheapshot Charlie walked past the captain's quarters, the door was ajar.

Their captain sat on the edge of the dock, his bare feet dangling in the water. Jellyfish swirled dangerously close but didn't sting him.

As if they sensed he'd been through enough.

His greatcoat, once the pride of his wardrobe—black velvet lined with silk, white embroidered ivy along the collar—was flung over a post, ruined. He bought that coat after his first raid, a ceremonial purchase from a fur stall in Molvania. And now the coat was trashed: tails tattered, embroidery unstitched and frayed, the lining stained with giant scorch marks from the admiral's cannons.

Bloody Elle and Cheapshot Charlie approached their captain slowly; wounded animals were often desperate enough to lash out for a last taste of blood in their final hours.

"Greenlegs," Merrick said, after a moment. "The great pirate." He skimmed his toes along the electric-blue surface of the water. "He died young. Only thirty years old."

"I remember," Cheapshot Charlie said.

Merrick continued. "Iron Chest Shelley also died at thirty. And Captain Walden. Crowfoot Callum died two weeks' shy of his thirtieth birthday. And how did they all die?" He didn't wait for them to answer. "Swinging in the gibbets, wearing noose neckties. Or shot down at sea by the navy." He kicked at a jellyfish who pulsed too close. "All of them, caught."

"What are you getting at, Captain?" Cheapshot Charlie asked.

Merrick finally glanced up, his cheeks gaunt, his good eye distant and cold. "I'm thirty this year,'" he said.

"You're twice the pirate any of those others were," Bloody Elle said. "Even Greenlegs."

"Yes," Merrick agreed, "but I'm thirty. I'm due." He jerked a loose button from his overcoat and skipped it along the glowing pool, watching the ripples until they stopped.

"Some would say those pirates went out in a blaze of glory," Cheapshot Charlie offered.

"More like a dying star," Merrick said. "A puff of smoke, and they're gone. Forgotten. Replaced by whatever new sailor decides to turn sour."

"Is this about your—your legacy, Captain?" Bloody Elle said.

"No," Merrick growled. "Legacies are for the living. Why should I care what they say about me when the worms have eaten my ears? No, I'm concerned about more . . . current events." He slid his feet out of the water and used his old greatcoat to dry them. "She threw her brooch in the cave." He put his feet back into his boots and stood. "I'm going to get it back."

Cheapshot Charlie balked. "The cave, Captain?"

"Aye." Merrick climbed aboard the *Jewel,* beginning preparations for the voyage.

"But, Captain—" Bloody Elle began.

"I'm maggot food anyway, aren't I, mates?" Merrick burst out. "It's only a matter of time before one of Bridgewater's cannons finally hits my melon. I'm already slower than I used to be. I can feel it, feel death creeping up on me." He put his hands on the railing. "Now, I am going down into that cave, and I am going to turn over every piece of eight until I find that brooch. You can help me sail to the tropics, or you can stay here. I don't rightly care. It won't be easy to man the *Jewel* alone, but it's possible."

"You really think this'll work, Captain?" Cheapshot Charlie asked. "You think she'll take you back if you bring her the brooch?"

"This isn't about getting her back." The cold shock of this realization sank in—it was true, then. She really was gone forever. He shook his head. "I'm a wanted man. I can't run forever. And I won't put her through that. She deserves better. She deserves—" He stopped, clearing his throat of something that had collected there, some sorrow. "I'm the pirate who threw away the greatest treasure he ever got his hands on. The biggest fool to sail the nine seas. And I have to make sure she knows I know that. Make sure she knows I'm sorry—before I'm gone."

Bloody Elle climbed aboard the ship. Cheapshot Charlie, however, took a few more seconds of contemplation.

"You know I would follow you to the ends of the earth, Captain. Off the maps entirely." His eyebrows pressed down so hard, they seemed to knit together. "Are you sure this is what you want to do?"

"I never should have let her go," Merrick said.

"Are you sure this is how *you* want to go?"

He knew why Cheapshot Charlie asked. The same dilemma had cycled through his mind in the last few days, over and over, like a bad sea shanty—to do this went against nature itself, didn't it? Willfully dying, instead of waiting for the universe—or whoever made such decisions—to turn him into fish food?

Merrick didn't even pause. "Without a doubt." A death on his own terms. A death with a purpose.

Still, Cheapshot Charlie hesitated.

"You've been with me for a long time, Charlie," Merrick said.

"Since the beginning," Cheapshot Charlie replied quietly.

"If this is too far for you, then go. Go now."

363 ᔐ

"Captain—" Cheapshot Charlie started.

"You will never be my enemy," Merrick finished, walking to the helm, giving his boatswain space to decide.

Within an hour, the *Jewel* cruised across open sea at a fair clip. Cheapshot Charlie trimmed the mainsail, worry lines wrinkling his bald head as he watched his captain.

But his worry was unfounded. Merrick was like a greenie, taking in everything with a fresh eye—

The sight of the seabirds, dipping their wings into the water.

The sun hitting the water, the waves glittering.

The marble in the salted meat.

The way Bloody Elle's lips disappeared when she concentrated on a knot; the way Cheapshot Charlie watched Bloody Elle, secret yearning in his eyes that he thought was well hidden.

He would miss it. All of it.

But not as much as he would miss seeing her smile one last time.

Merrick slipped into the turquoise water and swam straight into the cave. He crawled out of the water and took his first breath without fanfare. The air in the cave didn't smell different, didn't taste poisonous, but he knew the pollen was all around him — invisible and deadly.

A single breath inside the cave, and it was already too late.

For hours he searched for the brooch under the watchful gaze of the happy, yellow-eyed daises coating the cavern walls.

If the water could hold a pirate's memories in its fluid, otherworldly matter, then each piece of his treasure was a tangible, touchable memory. Each piece jetted him back to where he stole it, whom he stole it from, and how it came into his possession: Through coercion? Through blood? Through trickery? Through all three?

A chain of rare emeralds, taken from a Canquillian cocoa ship.

A giant golden cross necklace, lifted off a priest's barge passing through the channel.

Rubies, diamonds, pearls — and it could be tossed straight onto a bonfire in hell, for all he cared.

The brooch. That was the only memory he wanted.

And at last he found it.

Just as evening crept out of the palm trees on the islands and the turquoise water became a place of stripes and shadows, he found it.

With one last deep breath of toxic air from the cave, he swam into the open water, brooch in hand—

Only to be met by the largest, most terrifying mouthful of teeth he had ever seen.

A shark—a tank of a fish almost twenty feet long— whipped its tail as it patrolled the mouth of the cave.

Merrick reared back in the water, and the brooch fell out of his fingers. Frantically he grasped for it as it sank through the water, but at the very moment his fingers brushed it, the shark charged.

Merrick dodged out of the way, then arced his body downward and immediately began pouring his hands through the slimy algae.

But the brooch was gone. Frantically he searched, until his lungs were on fire and his brain sent explosive warnings.

The animal, to its credit, did not strike; it herded him to the surface, then left him alone and paced the seafloor near the cave, as if hired to act as guard.

When Merrick broke the surface, his mates threw down a rope. Their hearts sank into their stomachs like peach pits: after their captain gasped for air, choking on the sweet purity of oxygen after breathing in the pollen, they expected him to flash a conquering smile. But Merrick's expression was stoic as he climbed into the *Jewel*.

"I dropped it," he said, spitting up seawater. "I dropped the brooch."

"Where is it?" Bloody Elle asked.

"I don't know!" Merrick blasted. "A shark, a huge one—it surprised me—I dropped it beneath the reef somewhere—" He stopped talking and coughed.

A small cough, dry and innocent. It could have been his lungs trying to wring more water out of his system. It could have been the chills, or the bends, or the beginnings of a nasty cold.

But Bloody Elle and Cheapshot Charlie knew what that cough meant. They looked at him with wide, unbelieving eyes.

"Now I have to find that brooch," Merrick said. "Or I'll be dead for nothing." He coughed again.

He didn't stop coughing as he worked on a new plan, didn't stop coughing when they reached their mark. They anchored the *Jewel* in the gray, stormy bay off Arborley Island. Coughing, and coughing, and coughing.

He was thirty, after all.

He was due.

To explore the offerings of the great ocean, you needn't put yourself through a perilous sea journey, or stare into the mouth of a dangerous animal, or master the art of deep-sea diving. Simply visit a tide pool. Count the legs on a starfish, run your fingers along the shell of a mollusk, watch the way a sea urchin's spines move. Look for the seabirds, the way they dip their wings into the swell. Follow a crab home. Keep your eyes open, always, and the marvels of the ocean will be there, waiting.

The sea is always welcoming to those who don't mind getting a bit of brine or adventure on their sleeves.

—*Exploring an Underwater Fairyland* by Dr. and Dr. Quail

A thunderclap.

Fidelia awoke in the darkened, dampened dawn. She waited for the pelting of rain on the loft window but heard nothing.

She let her eyelids flutter shut, disregarding the noise as a dream. The room was silent, the couch warm, and she snoozed.

Another thunderclap.

Fidelia rolled off the couch and stumbled to the loft window. The streets were mist-shrouded, the sky hazy and purple in that perplexing time that was both moonless and sunless.

It wasn't a thunderclap, she realized. It was the navy's cannon. The naval base.

"Tomorrow at dawn." That's what Admiral Bridgewater had said.

And now tomorrow was today.

The navy sounded its cannons for all public hangings. The first cannon fired when the noose was strung. The second cannon, when the convicted dangled.

A third cannon blast meant he had ceased his kicking and was gone.

Two cannons had fired. Merrick, right now, hung from the gallows, noose tight, face red, purple veins bulging.

Fidelia held her breath.

The third cannon came.

Fidelia bit down on her fist, trying to rid her mind of the image of Merrick's lifeless body twisting in the morning breeze. What about the brooch? The brooch he'd given his life for?

Had the admiral found it in Merrick's final moments and tossed it in the garbage? Or had Merrick managed to stash it somewhere? Did he pitch it back into the sea before they hanged him, where the salt water might eventually finish it off, eating the pewter until it became brine?

She heard a noise in the other room.

Padding around the corner, she found Aunt Julia sitting up in bed, staring out her own window with tears streaming.

"Aunt Julia?" Fidelia asked, her voice creaky with sleep.

Why was her aunt crying? Happy tears, because Fidelia had returned safe? Sad tears, because Ida and Arthur had not?

"Are you all right, darling? What is it?" Aunt Julia discreetly wiped her cheeks.

"Bad dream," Fidelia lied. "But I'll try to forget it."

She went back to the couch, but sleep eluded her.

Stony Beach was a wasteland of wood splinters, broken shells, jute bags lost from cocoa ships and torn apart in the storm, and the sun-bleached bones of a sea creature. A kitchen sink, of all things, had washed ashore, its porcelain already decorated with acorn barnacles. Kelp was everywhere, dried, clinging to rocks. Low tide brought a fishy sulfur stench to the beach, but Fidelia breathed it in as if it were her first taste of air.

Her heart pitter-pattered. Ocean as far as she could see. The shift of pebbles, to course sand, to foam beneath her boots . . . Some things, at least, never changed.

She flipped open her observation book before the tears came and traced a finger along the outline of Grizzle's sketched tail.

Sickle-shaped. A tail built for power. For speed. A sweeping tail that made the whole ocean shudder.

Fidelia shut her observation book and looked around.

It was midday. The bay wrinkled in the beginning wisps of a storm. Waves kissed the harbor and retreated, swelling higher every second. Old thunderstorms blew away; fresh rain moved in. The windows of all the buildings turned into mirrors, making the whole city feel like the inside of a cumulonimbus cloud.

She hadn't been able to save her parents. She hadn't been able to save Merrick.

But maybe, if she hurried, she could save herself.

If you have something important to do, Merrick had growled to her in Medusa's Grotto, while the starfish ate the barnacles decorating the *Jewel*'s hull, *you do it now.*

Now.

Inside the library, Fidelia found Aunt Julia stamping catalog cards for a few new atlases. "Aunt Julia? Can we talk?"

Aunt Julia considered her niece, then nodded. "Let's go upstairs. I'll put the kettle on."

In the loft, she brought two cups of tea and sat across from Fidelia, quietly waiting at the little green table.

Taking a deep breath, Fidelia opened her observation book to the sketch of Grizzle, then pushed it toward her aunt. "On the night that Mom and Dad . . . died," she said, noting that she had managed to say the word without flinching or hollowing out, "this shark swam into the bay. I was so close to tagging him, but then the Undertow hit, and . . ."

Aunt Julia reached out a hand, gripping Fidelia's chilly fingers.

"He's out there still," Fidelia said. "Puttering around the tropics, untagged. And if I don't track him down and tag him, someone else might."

Aunt Julia sipped her tea.

"I know you feel like this is my parents' work," Fidelia said, "and that I am just a girl, but—"

Aunt Julia shook her head. "No, Fidelia. I was wrong." She took a deep breath. "You are not just a girl. You are a Quail. And I can't think of anyone better to continue with the Quail family research." She traced a finger along the floral print of her teacup. "I've never been the bravest person in a room—the quiet of books, that's what I've always preferred." Aunt Julia pushed her round glasses higher on her nose. "And it's cost me dearly, in the past. It cost me—" She cleared her throat. "I think I could learn a lot from you, Fidelia. If you would be willing to show me."

Fidelia came around the table and gave her aunt a hug.

"They would be so proud of you," Aunt Julia whispered

into Fidelia's hair, and Fidelia felt a tingle of warmth trail down her spine.

"Now, then," Aunt Julia said, turning her attention back to the observation book. "Tell me more about this fish."

Fidelia spent the rest of her day in the library, drawing maps and making plans for a spring trip to the tropics. Aunt Julia promised they could leave as soon as the Undertow ran its course, and so Fidelia wrote a to-do checklist (fix the *Platypus,* replicate the Water-Eater, reorder a few essential supplies) while Aunt Julia hunted through the archives for any mention of shark-migration patterns.

It almost felt like a normal day—a day from before, before her journey with the pirates, and before losing her parents. Fidelia ran her fingers along the outline of Grizzle's powerful tail and the old fizzle and whisper of adventure charged down her back like a current.

This was really going to happen—she was finally going to put a tag in Grizzle's fin and give him his scientific name.

"So it's settled." Aunt Julia closed her ledger at five o'clock, an ink smudge on her forehead. "The day after the Undertow blows out of town, so do we."

"And we don't stop until we find that shark," Fidelia said, her insides full of shooting stars.

Aunt Julia blew a gust of air out of her mouth and grinned at her niece. "I'm famished! What do you think about going out for dinner? Maybe at La Fruits de Mer?"

"La Fruits de Mer?" Fidelia repeated. It was the fanciest restaurant in Arborley. Fidelia had been there only a handful of times with her parents, usually to celebrate a university grant or a major research breakthrough.

Aunt Julia took their empty teacups to the sink and rinsed them out. "I think we deserve a gourmet meal. Salmon cakes to start, I think. And lobster bisque, and the lemongrass mussels . . ."

Fidelia's stomach growled. "Sounds perfect." She glanced down at her plain blue frock, brown tea dribbled on the collar. "I'll go change."

"Oh!" Aunt Julia dashed into her bedroom; Fidelia followed. Her aunt dug around in the very back of her closet. "Ah. Here it is."

She turned, holding out a lovely pale-lilac high-necked sheath dress, with a sheer lace bib, ivory lace trim, and ribbon on the cap sleeves. A pair of lilac, lace fingerless gloves were draped over the hanger, as well as an ivory sash.

"Was it Mom's?" Fidelia breathed, gliding her fingers along the fabric.

"No," Aunt Julia said. "I wore this. To your parents'

wedding." Fidelia was shocked—her aunt Julia had once worn this? This dress that barely had sleeves? She couldn't picture her aunt in anything so stylish.

She let Aunt Julia fasten her into the dress, and together they looked in the full-length mirror.

It was like looking at Ida Quail herself. Was it the evening light, softening Fidelia's usually angular nose and jawline? Was it the way the dress lengthened her neck, making it elegant instead of scrawny and pencil-like? Even her hair seemed less scraggly once Aunt Julia pinned it back over her right ear.

"You look so much like her," Aunt Julia whispered.

"So do you," Fidelia said, and meant it—Julia was ten years younger than her big sister but shared the same gray eyes, the same closemouthed smile, the slight gap in her front teeth. "Now, what about you? Are you going to get ready?"

Aunt Julia looked down at her clothing. "I am ready."

Fidelia stared. Aunt Julia was in her typical librarian uniform: a modest, ankle-length gray skirt, sensible flats, and a starched-and-pressed button-up cream shirt. A gray chiffon scarf was tied around her neck, to cover the last remaining inch of skin.

"Oh, all right," Aunt Julia said. "I suppose I could

change things up." She removed her scarf and reached for a slightly different scarf, chartreuse green, hanging from a hook in her closet.

"Wait!" Fidelia caught a glimpse of something on her aunt's neck and leaned over to inspect it. It was a violet scar, prominently dark against the rest of Julia's porcelain-smooth skin.

"A jellyfish scar," Fidelia whispered. If she hadn't already recognized the scar from her childhood with marine biologist parents, she could have matched her aunt's scar with the one on her shin. Fidelia's was fresh and still raw, yes, but they were otherwise identical.

"From—from when I was younger." The green scarf went around Aunt Julia's neck, tied with an extra knot. "Shall we?"

Fidelia nodded, and was still nodding when Aunt Julia slipped down the stairs, the impression of the scar's outline etched in her mind like a lightning strike.

Dinner at La Fruits de Mer was delectable. Flaking, buttery cheese biscuits, fizzing white grape juice, and the seafood smorgasbord—Fidelia had never seen her aunt put away so much food.

"Shall we order another serving of clams?" Aunt Julia asked after Fidelia had taken what she swore was her final, final bite of baked octopus.

"Are there any left on the island?" Fidelia groaned.

Aunt Julia laughed but put in another order. They ate every morsel.

When the two of them were stuffed to the gills, they left the restaurant and found an abalone sunset battling the Undertow's gray clouds for supremacy of the sky—the pink was winning at the moment.

Aunt Julia put her hand over her heart. "Sometimes I think the darkness almost makes it . . . more beautiful."

Fidelia tilted her head. Yes, the Undertow did make the brights brighter, the gasps of sunlight louder. A dramatic display, this skirmish between light and dark, life and death.

For a split second, Merrick's mismatched eyes flashed through her mind—a dazzling, deep-blue eye, spilling over with vitality, and the gruesome blackness of the dead one.

"Darling?" Aunt Julia touched Fidelia's shoulder. "Are you all right?"

Fidelia nodded.

"You have that look on your face," Aunt Julia pressed. "I've seen it a few times today."

Fidelia sighed. "It's nothing." Then she met Aunt Julia's bespectacled eyes. "Actually," she retracted, "there is something, but I'd rather not talk about it. Not here. Not tonight." Not after today, the closest thing to a perfect day she'd had in months.

Aunt Julia, gratefully, accepted this, squeezing Fidelia's shoulder briefly. "There's something I would like to talk to *you* about. Regarding our move to the mainland."

Fidelia waited, looking at her aunt.

"Well, would you be terribly disappointed . . . if we *didn't*?" Her mouth twitched in the hint of a smile.

Fidelia's heart leaped, like a whale breaching the surface. "Really?"

"Darling, I can't take you away from here. This is your home. It's in your blood—your memories live here, and—" She took a deep breath. "It's my home, too. It's where my own memories are. The good ones, and the less-than-good."

"We'll make plenty of new ones," Fidelia said. "Wherever we decide to be." She meant it. Home wasn't a place—she'd learned that these last few weeks. It was a feeling, a state of being.

It was a person.

"Wherever we decide," Aunt Julia echoed, and offered the crook of her arm.

Fidelia linked elbows with her aunt, and they walked down the boardwalk.

She was having such a good time, she wasn't prepared when they turned the corner and she spotted the mint green door of BonBon Voyage Sweets Shop.

Fidelia stopped cold. A tidal wave of memories hit her: the taste of choco-glomps as the moon rose over a water-warped main deck; a kaleidorainbow fig munched down between high-rising waves; astrobloomers washed down with a gulp of cold water from a blackjack.

"What's wrong?" Aunt Julia searched her niece's face. "What is it?"

Fidelia gestured to the door. "Do you think we could pop in for a minute?" she asked.

Aunt Julia was unreadable, her expression murky. "You know I don't care much for sweets."

"Please, Aunt Julia," Fidelia implored.

Aunt Julia pursed her lips. "Oh, all right."

Fidelia thought of Merrick's reaction when Cheapshot Charlie pulled out that knapsack of stolen sweets. Back in the Quail house, when Fidelia was first taken captive by them—back when she was still terrified of Merrick the Monstrous. Back before she knew he had a soft center, deep under the layers of stone, a softness that was reached only with a junky metal brooch.

When Aunt Julia opened the front door, a string of bells sounded, jarring Fidelia out of her nostalgia and back into reality.

One step into BonBon Voyage Sweets Shop, and they were transported into an alternate world, one made of cotton-candy clouds and chocolate thunderstorms. The walls were soft pastel pink, textured like spun sugar. Yellow sconces gave the store a lemony glow. Black and white tiles checkered the floor, and as Fidelia walked through the store, a different scent seemed to inhabit each tile: coconut, marzipan, hazelnut . . .

Crystal jars of rainbow-colored candies were in rows along the counters. Fidelia read the labels, remembering every flavor: apple crantruffles, peach creme fizzers, apricot popcorn.

"Choco-glomps, and crack-o-mallow bars, and butter turtles, and jelly-jellied jigglers," Aunt Julia read. "I haven't had these in ages."

"Get one of each," Fidelia suggested.

"Bold," Aunt Julia said. "But I think I'll just take a sliver of this dark chocolate—"

Glass shattered behind them. Someone tumbled through the storefront window, knocking over a table of canary cobblers and rolling onto the tiles.

Amid the shrieks from the customers and staff, a familiar cough burst from the man as he clambered to his feet.

Fidelia's heart stopped.

It was Merrick.

For a crazy moment, she thought he was a ghost. He looked like he'd dragged himself from the grave. A river of red spittle trailed onto his bare chest—he wore his peacoat over his naked torso. His network of veins was now black, crisscrossing his body like spilled ink.

Fidelia waited to feel Aunt Julia's hands digging into her arm, holding her back. But her aunt was frozen to the rack of chocolate bricks, staring at the pirate as if he had crawled out of her nightmares.

"H-how?" Aunt Julia whispered, her voice trembling. "How is it possible?"

"You know . . . the saying," Merrick wheezed. "Anything . . . can happen . . . in the Undertow." He stumbled forward, strain in every step.

A pit opened in Fidelia's stomach. "Why?" she whispered, her teeth chattering. *Why did you come here, of all places, to die? Why are you going to make me watch, after all the death I've already seen? After I already mourned you?*

Merrick came toward her. Between coughs, he murmured something, a single word, repeating it louder and louder until finally Fidelia could hear it: "Jewel . . . Jewel . . . Jewel . . ."

Walking around Fidelia, he stood close enough to Aunt Julia that the flaps of his greasy peacoat skimmed her crisp white blouse. "Jewel," he whispered, lifting one bony hand to her cheek, and Aunt Julia flinched.

Before Fidelia could register what she was seeing, the front door blasted open, kicked clean off its hinges.

"Merrick, you demon! Why won't you die?"

Admiral Bridgewater stumbled into the sweets shop, aimed his blunderbuss at Merrick, and fired.

The bullet missed, ricocheting off the back wall.

"No!" Fidelia shouted. Aunt Julia screamed. The shopkeeper ducked behind the counter, and the remaining customers escaped through the shattered window, disappearing down the street.

Someone else ran through the broken door, pistols blazing — Bloody Elle.

Without skipping a beat, she shot at the admiral, who dove behind a stand of astrobloomers. Blueberry sprinkles flew everywhere.

Cheapshot Charlie hobbled into the sweets shop behind her, dragging his right leg as if it were a tagalong — the leg Merrick had put a bullet into, back when they were ambushed by the admiral in the tropics.

Charlie and Elle! They had made it! They were alive! Joy shot through Fidelia — only an instant of relief before the admiral fired a shot that nearly hit Cheapshot Charlie's neck.

Cheapshot Charlie shot back, missing the admiral. "Captain! The streets are swarming with silver-buttons. You have to get out —"

"Not until . . . it's done!" Merrick gasped.

The next shot from Admiral Bridgewater nearly grazed Cheapshot Charlie's shoulder — he rolled out of the way, knocking into Bloody Elle. Both their guns skittered across the checkered floor.

Fidelia felt as if she were watching everything in slow motion, underwater. Bridgewater's mustache, curling up in a smile as he leveled his blunderbuss at Merrick. Cheapshot Charlie and Bloody Elle struggling to their feet, grappling for their weapons.

Then suddenly, Fidelia was moving. Free from the range of Aunt Julia's desperate grasp, past the candy aisles, and directly in front of Admiral Bridgewater's gun.

"Out of my way, girl!" Admiral Bridgewater tried to shove her aside with the flare of his gun, but her boots gripped the tile, and she didn't budge.

"Fidelia, no!" Aunt Julia cried.

"Quail—!" Merrick immediately doubled over, coughing horribly.

"I won't!" Fidelia's nerves hummed, her chest full of fire. "I won't let you die like this. Not when—not when—" *Not when you're so close,* she finished in her mind. *Not when it's already over for you.*

"Accomplice!" Admiral Bridgewater jutted a sausage finger at Fidelia, his blunderbuss shaking with his rage. "I warned you, didn't I? I told you anyone who aided Merrick the Monstrous would dangle beside him at the gallows."

"You already got his treasure," Fidelia said. "Now leave him be!"

The admiral let out one short laugh, almost a bark. "He is the treasure," he said. And with jubilation glowing in his eyes, the admiral raised his gun and pointed it at the center of her chest.

A shot fired, and Fidelia panted, her heart slamming into her ribs. She waited for the pain, the sear of a bullet in her chest, the acrid smell of gunpowder. The blood.

But Admiral Bridgewater hadn't shot her. His blunderbuss was still pointed at her, his cheeks still red as snappers. The smoke wafting in the candy store wasn't coming from his weapon. It was coming from —

The doorway, where Niccu and the other Molvanian pirates stood clumped together. Niccu's antique silver flintlock pistol was pointed at the ceiling, smoke curling from the end; he lowered it and aimed right at Admiral Bridgewater's head.

"Drop your weapon, Admiral."

29

Fidelia's blood was ice, her muscles stone. She had been so concerned with the Molvanians' survival when Merrick left them bobbing in the ocean, but she felt no satisfaction seeing them here. Niccu's guns may have been pointed at the admiral, but she couldn't imagine the Molvanians would leave unpunished the pirate captain who tossed them overboard like rotten fish heads.

Admiral Bridgewater sneered at Niccu's gun, dropping his own blunderbuss with a clatter. "My men will be here any minute," he said. His tricorne hat had fallen off his head; Fidelia thought his head looked very small and sweaty without the three corners of black felt to fill it out.

"How perfect; this will only take a minute," Niccu said. He turned one of his pistols onto Merrick, who clung to the closest candy rack for support, like a bivalve on a rocky shore. "I'll ask you only once," the *Rasculat* captain said. "Where is the treasure?"

Merrick coughed. "Ask . . ." He gestured to the admiral; the effort to speak was too much.

Niccu turned his full attention back to Admiral Bridgewater, whose face drained of all color like a pierced vegetable.

"Confiscated," the admiral said, untucking his chin and trying very hard to look the part of the dignified royal soldier. "It's all in Her Majesty's possession, being accounted for—"

"*Razat,*" Niccu said, stepping closer to the admiral. "Mule's *razat.* Where is it?"

Outside, the rain began to fall in heavy sheets.

"It's hidden," Admiral Bridgewater said. "Hidden from the likes of you or any of your black-hearted cohorts. And there's nothing you can do—"

"I will give you Merrick." Thunder rolled above BonBon Voyage Sweets Shop; the sound of crashing waves echoed along the boardwalk.

"'Give me Merrick?'" Admiral Bridgewater said.

"I will let you finish him," Niccu answered. "You will tell us where the treasure is, and we will leave him to die at your hands. If he is, indeed, such a great prize to you, then this is an easy bargain."

Merrick coughed.

Fidelia's forehead was damp with sweat; she watched the pirate captain bend in half, searching for his next breath, searching, searching . . .

Niccu tensed. "Quickly, Admiral, quickly. You don't have much time." He bowed his head slightly toward Merrick. "It could happen any second."

Admiral Bridgewater twitched his mustache, confused. "What the blazes does that mean?"

Niccu studied the admiral's blank, flobby face. "You mean you don't know?" He tipped his head back and laughed. "Listen to Merrick's cough. Listen to his inhales. Look at his hands. He's finished, do you understand? He's rub on a wooden leg."

Admiral Bridgewater cocked his head, staring at Merrick as the pirate captain wheezed and hacked. Like a slow submersion in cold water, Fidelia watched the realization hit the admiral.

"The pollen of the red daisies." Admiral Bridgewater's jowls shimmied as his jaw dropped. "Then . . ."

"Yes," Niccu said. "He's dying."

The Molvanian pirate twirled his gun. "So now you will make your choice. Tell me where the treasure is, and Merrick is yours to end. Or I blow his head off now and we still take your treasure."

Admiral Bridgewater's top lip quivered in pure madness. He studied Merrick, his face darkening. Through clenched teeth, he finally said, "In the hold beneath the lower deck of the flagship. A special chamber, just below the bilges."

Niccu bowed and tucked his revolvers into his belt. "Thank you, *pralipe*. And to you," he addressed Merrick, "the stars are calling. We will watch for you in the skies." He stepped backward until he was out of BonBon Voyage Sweets Shop, then he and the other Molvanian pirates headed down the cobbled street, straight for the *Mother Dog*.

In an instant, Admiral Bridgewater was back on his feet, blunderbuss in hand—aimed once again at Fidelia, who still blocked Merrick from the admiral's fire, though her knees were shaking.

"Last chance to move," Admiral Bridgewater growled at her. "Merrick is mine."

"After . . . all this time," Merrick rasped between coughs, "you'll let . . . the great treasure go . . . just so you can . . . be the one . . . to pull my trigger?"

Trickles of yellow spit flowed down the admiral's chin as he spoke. "I have been waiting ten years to kill you," he said. "Ten years of chasing you so I could have this moment." His whole body quivered. "And to think, you almost stole it from me." The admiral shoved around Fidelia, pushing her to the floor, and placed the flared barrel of his weapon directly on Merrick's bare chest.

Merrick pointed at himself with a hardened, purpled thumb. "Pirate," he breathed with a grin.

An infuriating grin to the admiral, Fidelia knew—and she tried to match Merrick's complacency, even as tears gathered in the corners of her eyes. Death for Merrick, at last.

Admiral Bridgewater reached into his pouch for powder and shot, and found nothing.

The admiral was out of shot.

Merrick chuckled—an awful drowning sound.

"All that gold," the great pirate sputtered, "all those gems . . . All the wealth from the stories . . . and you're about to let it go . . . back into the hands of pirates."

Somewhere above the din of the growing storm, a whistle blew. Admiral Bridgewater tilted his head like an old bulldog—the sound of men, now, shouting from the harbor.

The *Mother Dog* was under siege.

The Molvanian pirates were fighting for the treasure, everything that had been down in that cave.

Fidelia, Aunt Julia, the pirates—they all watched Admiral Bridgewater survey Merrick with fury, then disgust, then mere annoyance.

"Rot in hell," he said, and spat on Merrick. He ran out of the sweets shop, chasing after his treasure.

Along the boardwalk, a bell rang—the constables had been alerted. Any second they would cruise down the canal in their patrol boats and investigate.

"Captain." Cheapshot Charlie's deep voice trembled. He and Bloody Elle took a step—a step toward the door.

Fidelia swallowed. If the constables found them here, they'd be jailed and hanged. They had to get out now.

"Go," Merrick commanded. Just as he had on the *Jewel*, back in the tropics.

"But—" Bloody Elle started, and Merrick coughed in her direction, cutting her off.

"No good-byes," he said. "You've saved . . . me enough times. . . . Let me . . . save you." He reached for breath and managed to choke out, "Best . . . mates," and Fidelia felt her chest bulge, threatening to split.

Bloody Elle opened her mouth, but whatever she was going to say stayed a secret. Instead the two pirates placed their hands on their hearts, turned, and slipped out of BonBon Voyage Sweets Shop and into the night.

Fidelia looked around her. The candy store was a devastation of sugar and sprinkles and fallen shelves. Aunt Julia huddled in a corner, arms wrapped around her middle as if to keep from falling apart.

Merrick pulled himself to standing, his breath rattling, and walked right to Aunt Julia. He seized the librarian's face with both his vein-riddled hands.

Just as Fidelia cried out, ready to rush to her aunt's side, Merrick kissed her.

Then he collapsed.

30

BonBon Voyage Sweets Shop was silent but for the crash of the waves in the bay, and the splatter of rain, and the wind's mourning through the broken glass of the front window—and Merrick's pocket watch, spilling from his trouser pocket, its ticks the loudest sound to Fidelia as she stared, unblinking.

Merrick's body lay in a crumpled heap beneath Aunt Julia. He coughed; blood sprayed from his mouth and onto the black and white tiles. A morbid red rain.

Then he was still.

"Merrick," Aunt Julia said softly, falling to her knees. Fidelia held her breath.

For an uncomfortably long time, there was quiet.

But Merrick stirred, and twisted his body around so he lay flat on his back. He coughed. "Jewel," he said.

Jewel. Fidelia's heart thumped so hard, she thought it might jet out of her chest and onto the floor next to the captain. "You . . . you know him?" she said to her aunt.

"I know him," Aunt Julia said. "I know him very well." She pulled Merrick's head onto her lap, running a hand along his grimy black hair. "Is it true? Is it the red daisies?"

"It's . . . death," Merrick growled. "Not so pretty . . . is it?"

Aunt Julia took off her chiffon scarf and used it to wipe the blood around his mouth. Her jellyfish scar, the one on her neck, was an iridescent lilac in the storm's light.

Suddenly, Fidelia felt things click into place—a radar's scan, complete: "The library book back at Medusa's." She looked at Aunt Julia. "That was yours."

"You took her to the grotto?" Aunt Julia balked.

Merrick opened his mouth to speak, then burst into coughs, and they rolled out of him without mercy, one right after another. Wave after wave, unrelenting peaks.

Over Aunt Julia's shoulder, Fidelia stared. Merrick's face was white, his mismatched eyes both retreating into his skull. The black-and-red eye was raw, bloated, a full blood moon, its shiny film the only thing holding it together. He sucked in air with his colorless lips, which were shriveled like dried bait worms.

397 ↄ

"It's done, Jewel," he grunted. "I'm . . . open market . . . on the maggot buffet."

With each breath Merrick took, his lungs squeezed, the air rattling. It took him forever between inhales, but he somehow summoned the strength to keep breathing . . . and to open his hand.

There, resting on his palm, like it had always been there, was the tarnished pewter brooch.

Aunt Julia's pale-gray eyes grew. For a woman whose livelihood was words, she seemed to struggle to find any. "But I threw this into the cave," she finally said. "This was supposed to be gone forever."

Merrick smoothed the brooch with the tip of his thumb, skimming the scalloped edge. "Now it's back."

"How did you—? How on earth did you—?" Again, Aunt Julia fished for words, turning the brooch over and over until the realization washed over her. "Oh, Merrick. No." She removed her peach glasses, which were beginning to fog. "You went into the cave to get this back for me."

The wind blew sideways, sending a drizzle of chilly rain through the broken store window. Merrick coughed, then took Aunt Julia's hand. "I would do . . . anything for you . . . Jewel."

Jewel. The word pulsed in Fidelia's ears.

The names carved into Medusa's grotto, the ones on the wall. *Merrick + Jewel.*

Merrick loved Julia so much, he named his ship after her.

"That's not true." Aunt Julia narrowed her eyes. "You wouldn't stop your pirating." She considered their interlaced fingers, her nostrils flaring with some old rage. "Nothing could have convinced you to give it up. Not the law. Not death. Not even me."

"We are . . . who we are. . . . Haven't your books . . . taught you . . . as much?"

Aunt Julia sniffled. "If we are who we are," she said, "then you're a damn fool."

The pirate coughed. "I gave up . . . my life . . . when I gave up you. . . . I wanted . . . you to know that . . . before it was . . . too late." He shook his head. "You're right . . . I am a fool . . . who never stopped . . . loving you."

A sound came out of Aunt Julia's throat, visceral, a howl. "And I never stopped loving you."

Merrick lifted his pocket watch from his pocket, and the three of them listened to its ticks, the clicks of time passing.

Aunt Julia kissed his cheek, kissed his forehead, kissed the sharpness of his jaw. She combed her fingers through his hair, her tears falling onto his head like anointments. He nestled into her lap and closed his blue eye, content to spend his last ticking seconds here, just touching her, breathing the same air as her.

Fidelia knew she should look away, give Merrick and her aunt privacy during this intimate moment, but she couldn't. She watched this outlawed pirate's every second until, finally, horribly, he stiffened, gasping.

"This . . . is it," Merrick whispered, every word a labor. "I can . . . feel it. I'm—I'm—out of time. . . ."

Aunt Julia kissed him again, clutching the brooch to her heart. "I will never forget you," she whispered, and gently leaned his head back.

Merrick's blue eye flooded white. He flailed, disoriented. "Jewel . . ." He coughed one last time. And then Merrick the Monstrous, the terror of the nine seas, was done.

The words were there, on the tip of Fidelia's tongue: *I'm sorry* . . . The words that everyone says in moments like this. But she held them back, swallowed them down, and cleared her throat.

With a shudder, she sang the three notes of Cheapshot Charlie's mourning song, the one he had crooned when the *Jewel* had passed the Coral of the Damned.

Aunt Julia, with Merrick's head on her lap, turned to her niece with watery, red-rimmed eyes, and listened.

Fidelia was no singer—but she warbled out the three notes, and she concentrated on making them as strong and clear as Charlie's had been on the ship. She sang for Merrick, and she sang for Julia, and she sang for her parents.

She sang for herself, this simple three-tone dirge the only thing that brought her peace.

The rain dried. Night lifted from black to a hazy blue as the Undertow melted away. A few stars winked.

Through it all, Fidelia still sang those three droning notes, until her voice croaked and gave out and Aunt Julia ran out of tears. And Merrick's pocket watch still ticked, in time to the waves. The tide rushed in, the tide rushed out, and Arborley Bay was calm.

Until the next storm.

Ten Years Earlier

Julia sat on the boardwalk, a book propped open in her lap. She turned the page and closed her eyes, letting the thin sunshine warm her face. The heady exhale of the blush-pink apple blossoms mixed with the salty scent of the sea—the smells of springtime. A strand of hair fell from her tight bun; she let it dance across her cheek, tickling her skin.

Behind her, the pub was a symphony of noise and laughter and music. Before her, Stony Beach was also alive—families picnicking, children huddling around the tide pools, dogs paddling joyously in the chilly surf.

But Julia had a book in her hands, and so she didn't notice anything else. Nothing but the words on the page and the sun on her skin.

A new batch of books was due any hour—a set of almanacs that had to be stamped, bound, cataloged, and shelved.

She was here to watch for the *Jolly Dodger,* the merchant ship that delivered library goods from the mainland.

It had been a particularly long winter. The Undertow made hostages of all the islanders, but spring had finally begun its slow crawl to consciousness after its long hibernation. To Julia's eyes, the sky had never been so perfectly blue.

Ships sailed into the harbor, their crews leaping onto the docks to tie them off. All of them familiar vessels, familiar beams, familiar banners flapping from the masts. . . . Julia barely glanced up from her book to watch them arrive . . . until a lone ship anchored in the shallows of the bay caught her attention.

A strange ship.

She straightened her glasses, straining to see the ship's name, but its stern was clean of script. A no-name ship.

She frowned. The ship wasn't flying a flag, either.

A movement near the ship's waterline — the ship's longboat was rowing ashore. A tall bald man with dark skin and thick arms pulled the oars, and a second man knelt at the boat's bow.

A man with a sharp jaw and black hair absorbing the sunlight like cinders.

Even with the distance, Julia could feel the eyes of the

black-haired man on her. She blushed, finding the loose lock of her hair and tucking it safely back. Her book slid down her lap, her fingers losing her spot in its pages.

As the longboat drifted closer, she could distinguish the man's face—young, with oiled sideburns and a pair of moonstone eyes, sunken and piercing as the spring's rays. The back of her neck prickled. She tried to breathe in the sweet smell of the apple blossoms to clear her mind but found it difficult to operate her lungs.

Then the man winked at her, and her heart suddenly galloped.

She strode away from the railing, then slipped through the welcoming door of the candy store.

Once inside BonBon Voyage Sweets Shop, her heart tamed itself back to a nice, even pace. She tucked her book under her arm and walked straight to the chocolate aisle. She'd stay in here for a few minutes, give the man in the longboat time to dock and vanish into the port, and then she'd go back to the library and wait for her shipment there. There was plenty to do until the almanacs arrived—plenty of work.

Bells jangled as the door to the sweets shop opened and closed. She chose a brick of black chocolate and inspected its label.

"'Will have you swooning at first bite,'" someone behind her read aloud. "'The darkest chocolate available in Her Majesty's Kingdom. Made from pure grade cocoa beans, the blackest on the island.'"

She knew, the way she could often predict the endings in her books, that it was him.

Yes, when she turned around it was the man from the longboat, and she had to remind herself to stay standing, keep breathing, keep living. Up close she could see the details of his face—skin that had been battered by wind, burned by sun, chilled by arctic air. The skin of a sailor. A garden of whiskers grew along that knife of a jawline, and his blue eyes twinkled, as if concealing a secret.

He took the brick of chocolate from her, one of his calloused fingers brushing her pinky. "'The salt-spiked, bitter taste of this bar is an exotic, sensuous experience.'" His eyebrows danced. "You're a fan?"

Once, Julia had read a book about a mermaid who was brought onto dry land during a full moon and melted into a puddle of seawater on a fisherman's kitchen floor. If only.

"Hardly." She adjusted her glasses and jutted her nose into the air—the librarian's signal that all conversation should cease.

"Is that you, Miss Julia?" The elderly owner of BonBon

Voyage Sweets Shop stopped arranging a bouquet of buttery carnations and leaned over the counter. "Why, weren't you just here to stock up yesterday—?"

"No!" Her response came out a bit louder than she wanted, then resounded in her now hollow mind, sounding more and more ridiculous with every echo.

The man grinned—was he laughing at her? "Julia, is it?" She didn't move.

"Merrick Von Mourne," he said, offering his hand.

"Merrick of the good ship . . . ?" she prompted.

"Ah, well, we're all still getting acquainted with our ship," he said. "This is her inaugural voyage."

"Well. Nothing's more suspicious than an unnamed ship," Julia said. "Except maybe a ship with no flag."

"Then I'd better have my men pick up a flag at the warehouse," Merrick said. "We wouldn't want to attract the wrong sort of attention." He pointed at the book under her arm. "So, work or pleasure?"

Julia held the spine so he could see the title: *Library Trends and Research.*

He raised his eyebrows. "So, pleasure," he said.

"I'm staff librarian at Arborley Library," she clarified.

"Well," he said, "then perhaps you can help me." He finally broke eye contact with her and scanned the racks of candy around them. "We've just stopped at the chandler's to pick up a few things—tar and line and such. Then we hit the cocoa route, along with every other sea dog in the kingdom. It'd be nice to bring something aboard besides jerky and eggs. So what would you recommend, as an expert researcher? Besides the sensuous chocolate, I mean."

Julia straightened, willing her face not to turn pink. This man, she surmised, had decided she was the butt of some joke and likely wouldn't let her alone until she'd provided the punchline. She led him through the aisles, stacking the sweets into his open arms: apple crantruffles, kaleidorainbow figs, astrobloomers, and, for good measure, a bar of the sensuous black chocolate.

"There," she said when they reached the counter. "A sampling of Arborley's finest."

No sooner had she finished her words than someone outside shouted, "Pirates! At the warehouse!"

A line of constables ran past the window of BonBon Voyage Sweets Shop, their black trench coats streaming behind them. Cries of "Call the navy!" could be tracked all the way down the boardwalk to the chandler's warehouse.

"Pirates," Julia muttered. "They should all be hanged."

"Indeed," Merrick said, rustling through his pockets for green notes to pay for his sweets.

The sweets shop door jangled. A huge dark man popped his head in the doorway, a bead of sweat rolling from the top of his bald head down the length of his face. The man from the longboat—the man who had rowed Merrick ashore.

"Time to go, Captain," he said, panting. "They're calling reinforcements."

Julia's stomach twisted. She suddenly noticed the piercing in the bald man's nose, the scars across his knuckles, the pistol at his belt, visible through the rips in his tunic.

Pirates.

She gazed at the raven-haired man next to her with new alarm. A pirate, and she had been chattering with him as if he were just another library patron.

"I'll meet you at the gate," Merrick said to the man. "Get her ready."

The bald man left, and Merrick counted out exact change for his pile of sweets.

"Why bother paying for it?" Julia was surprised by her own boldness—certainly Merrick had his own pistol beneath his overcoat, and wouldn't hesitate to punish her for her lip. But something about the man made a flame flicker in her chest, made her words spill out without thinking.

But he gave her a crooked half-smile. "You like me."

Julia pursed her lips, but inside, the flame blazed. "Like you!" she repeated, incredulous. "You're a pirate. A scallywag."

"So what?" Merrick said. "You're a librarian. A common book pusher." He handed her the bar of black chocolate. "You don't hear me complaining."

Outside, the squabble got louder. Constables had swarmed the warehouse and were taking canal boats to the bay, where Merrick's ship prepared for departure. Someone fired a cannon.

"I'm afraid that's my cue." Merrick swept the pile of sweets into the pocket of his overcoat and nodded at her. "We'll see each other again."

Julia folded her arms, gripping the chocolate bar tightly. "What makes you think I have any interest in—?"

"Because," Merrick said, leaning so close that she thought for an insane second that he might actually kiss her—and that she might actually let him. "Because I saw you. I saw you reading, and I saw you ignore everything else around you. A sailor stumbled out of the pub and tossed his cookies three feet away from you, did you know? A rogue dog sniffed at your skirts. A fishmonger and a housewife nearly got into a fistfight over the price of shrimp, right within your earshot. And you ignored everything." Julia was certain he could see her pulse in her neck, hammering away. "You ignored everything in the whole damned world . . . until you saw me."

She swallowed.

Merrick opened the door but turned back. "We'll be coming through here again in two weeks," he said. "I'm sure you'll be out of chocolate by then. Perhaps I could bring you some? I'll be stopping in Canquillas for a night: they have this fig-infused black drinking chocolate—"

Another cannon fired, followed by the crunch of wood.

Merrick saluted her with a devastating smirk. "Good-bye, Miss Julia." And with a jingle of the bells on the door, he dashed away.

Julia stood there, chocolate brick in hand, listening to the gunshots and the cannons, listening to the constables' frustrated shouts when Merrick's ship got away, listening to the silence—the silence that made her smile, because it meant he'd gotten away.

"Good-bye, scallywag," she said quietly, and nibbled the corner of the chocolate, swooning.

The *Jolly Dodger* had arrived in the harbor; its captain was pacing the docks, searching for the librarian. Julia apologized for her tardiness and escorted him to the canal, where he loaded the shipment of almanacs into a boat.

"I'll be sending for another order tonight," she informed him as she stepped down into the canal boat. "An urgent order."

"Oh?" the captain said. Usually library shipments were months apart.

"Yes," she said. "I'll need it here in exactly two weeks' time."

We must learn nature's strange waltz, rising and falling by its cues. When our time comes to leave the floor, rather than trying to prolong the music, we must gracefully take our exit, and know that even after we've left, the dance goes on.

—*Exploring an Underwater Fairyland* by Dr. and Dr. Quail

Today

─────────◆─────────

March 20

First day of spring. First day of shark season.

 The tropics are somehow even brighter today, and life beneath the sea is teeming. From the trawler I can see a school of bluefin, weaving in and out of the reef. A few eels have poked their snouts out, catching some of the rays. It's as if they all know it's a beautiful day and that we're all lucky to be alive, and they're all out celebrating. Let's hope even the biggest fish feels like frolicking, too. I'm jotting all of this down as Aunt Julia steers the boat, so forgive my sloppy handwriting; I want to be sure to get every detail down exactly as it happened today. . . .

"Here," Aunt Julia said. "This is the spot."

 I slowed the new trawler, and she stopped immediately. At ten feet, she's not as big as the Platypus, *but we got her at a great price, and I rebuilt her engine myself. We've dubbed her the* Choco-Glomp —*the perfect name, since she's painted deep brown and has rounded sides.*

Beneath the sheen of turquoise, Aunt Julia and I both saw it—a black hole far beneath the waves, blurred, but still terrifying, like a mouth gaping from the sea bottom.

But we weren't there for the cave, or for Merrick. Today, we were there for me.

I pulled the new and improved Water-Eater from my rucksack. I still use parrot feather leaves for filtration, but now they have their own removable compartment. I've also shortened the chambers and made the mouthpiece more comfortable. I'd given the latest version a short test run in the shallows of Arborley Bay, but it was time for an extended experimental dive.

Aunt Julia pulled out the sack of plastic tags, and I placed one in my Track-Gaff (and a couple extra tags on the belt of my dress, just in case).

I secured the Water-Eater and diving mask over my head, then I tipped myself backward into the water.

It's only a hair cooler than the scorching air, but it felt delicious after sailing through the sticky, muggy islands of the tropics.

How different everything looked. How much crisper,

bluer, more beautiful now that I wasn't viewing it through the lens of fear.

My time with the pirates still feels like a dream. But it's long over. No more Merrick the Monstrous, yes—and no more Molvanian pirates, or stale old candy for sustenance, or navy blockades. No more treasure. No more Cheapshot Charlie or Bloody Elle, either. We haven't heard from them since the night Merrick died. "Just as well," Aunt Julia keeps saying, but I can see the sadness in her eyes when she thinks of them. When she thinks of her old secret life. "I expect they've moved on to better things," she says, and I hope she's right.

Here is what we know happened the night Merrick died.

Just the facts:

The Molvanian pirates took control of the Mother Dog. *The element of surprise was on their side, but so was the storm. The flagship was moored in the shallows, and the Undertow's strong, senseless, chaotic current towed the ship out to sea, tugging and straining the lines and sails. Its officers were too busy keeping the decks from flooding to be ready for the tiny Molvanian crew of five, who simply climbed aboard and took over the ship with their guns.*

Another fact:

The admiral reached the Mother Dog *in a dory, and shots were fired from both sides. It was too dark and rainy for any of us in the sweets shop to make out exactly what was transpiring.*

But here is another fact:

The Mother Dog *was suddenly cast off. Whether it was deliberate on Niccu's part or whether the admiral himself cut the ropes—or maybe the storm itself snapped the anchor line—the ship drifted out to the bay.*

A giant wave curled above the ship and froze.

The last image anyone had of the Mother Dog *—or of Niccu and his* pralipes, *or of Admiral Bridgewater— was the galleon's massive outline, silhouetted in a flash of white lightning. There was the ship, the wave above it, and then darkness. And then there was nothing but the anarchy of the storm.*

One final fact:

Bits of driftwood were found over the following days on the pebbles of Stony Beach. A few scraps still bore faint gilded lettering, but the sea salt had scrubbed out anything decipherable. The largest pieces were of the finest quality lumber—live oak, polished to the very definition of smoothness, navy-standard trim.

The treasure is gone. And both Aunt Julia and I think that's for the best. Now the stories of Merrick's legendary treasure can live on forever.

But back to the dive:

The Water-Eater worked marvelously—I filled my lungs with air and blew bubbles out my nose as I dove deeper in the water. There was the mouth of the cave—I loomed closer and tried to peek inside, but it was only darkness.

It won't be there forever, I mark. Sooner or later, the Undertow's tides will force water into the cave and bury the red daisies forever, and the world will forget it ever existed, except in the tall tales of sailors.

Just like the treasure, I think some things are better left to stories.

Just as I reached the carpet of algae along the sea bottom, a familiar shape enclosed me in shadow. The shadow I'd been waiting for.

I looked up, and there he was.

Grizzle.

He circled the reef, his caudal fins straight as canvas sails on a schooner, his mouth agape.

This was my third time seeing him in front of me, and of course I've dreamed of him for months — but my reaction is the same every time.

Scared and quiet and fizzing with joy, right under my ribs.

How could sharks not be my favorite?

The hollow spot beneath the coral is empty now, I could see — his little baby Grizzlings have grown and left the nursery. I hadn't expected to see them. Mom and Dad acquired very little knowledge about sharks' reproductive cycles, but they did discover a few things. Sharks don't mate for life. They are ovoviviparous — meaning they grow eggs internally, which hatch inside the mothers and are born live. The shark pups stay with their parents for a short time — maybe a few weeks — and then they say good-bye forever and leave.

No joyous return, like for baby sea turtles who fight their way through the terrors of the sea back to their homes. No family reunions, like for the colonies of arctic seals up north. It was a splintering. That meant Grizzle was now alone. His children, out in the world without him — without his protection.

I think of the scars that inspired Grizzle's nickname, and I hope that his offspring will be all right.

He approached me with caution. I wonder if he could remember me. My heart steadied, the Track-Gaff in my hands.

As he circled past, I raised my Track-Gaff and smoothly, carefully, tagged his fin. There. "Quail: No. 314," the tag says. I stayed just long enough to watch Grizzle cruise away from the reef, until he was just a silhouette in the turquoise water—a torpedo, a submarine, a vestige. A memory.

Then I surfaced and climbed back into the Choco-Glomp. *Aunt Julia was flipping through* Adventures in Science Engineering. *My Hydro-Scanner is on the cover of this month's issue—the patent office still wasn't keen on patenting any of my "doodads," but luckily for me a certain librarian researched the ins and outs of patent law, and now anyone who wants one can buy their own Hydro-Scanner and find their own Grizzle.*

"Well?" Aunt Julia said, and I spat out the Water-Eater's mouthpiece.

"Got him," I said. After I dried myself off, I wrote down his number: Tag 314, Quail shark.

Aunt Julia smiled. "You've finally settled on an official name. I like it!"

I flipped through my pages and studied the sketch I

made of Grizzle last fall, on that last day of shark season. The night I thought I'd lost everything.

"Will that be his scientific name, too?" Aunt Julia asked. "Carcharodon coturnix?"

I shook my head and ran my fingers along my drawing of his teeth, spectacular triangles of death, a ragged grin.

A beam of light hit my glasses, and I squinted. Sunshine reflected off the brooch pinned to Aunt Julia's collar. A pewter brooch, tarnished, the color of shadow.

"Monstrum magnificus," *I proclaimed.*

Magnificent monster.

We'll see if he shows up in Arborley this summer for another taste of our local halibut, which he loved so much last year. Or maybe he'll make a round-the-world excursion, same as us. Aunt Julia and I are heading to Crabmoore Shore as I write this, to watch the migration of the crabs. After that, to Molvania, to gather sea grass. After that, who knows? Maybe Canquillas, to see their famous lagoons? Back when my parents were alive, I thought I knew the world—I thought I had traveled its edges, seen every speck of it, knew of every creature that inhabited it. I hadn't even come close.

There are probably monsters even bigger than him somewhere, swimming the deepest, blackest reaches of the sea. The world is bigger than I can imagine—I know that now.

And I'm ready to see it all.

ACKNOWLEDGMENTS

Composing a list of people to thank for their influence while writing this book feels very much like a trip through the life of Lindsay, so I'll write this chronologically:

To my parents, who raised me in a household of books and stories and learning, who never once discouraged any of my kooky or nerdy pursuits, who always made sure the ink cartridge in the printer was full, and who literally and spiritually supported me while I found my footing in the publishing industry: thank you. Any success of mine is also yours.

To my siblings, who endured years of bossy big sister Lindsay ordering them around in plays, ballets, skits, home movies, and other productions so I could fulfill my need to tell stories: thank you. You are in the heart of everything I write.

To my second-grade teacher, Mrs. Howard, who assigned our class to read Ann McGovern's *Shark Lady,* triggering my lifelong obsession with sharks, and who also required daily journal writing and knew me as a writer before even I did: thank you. You are responsible for the shark Halloween costume, the shark posters, the shark business cards, and much more.

To the brilliant minds and brave explorers who inspired young me—Dr. Eugenie Clark, Valerie Taylor, Rodney Fox—and whose work brought the beauty of sharks into my landlocked home through books and television: thank you.

To my agent, Sarah Davies, who proves to be a wonderful guide through this adventure in publishing: thank you.

To the hardworking people at Candlewick Press—particularly Matt Roeser, the jacket designer; Hannah Mahoney, copyeditor extraordinaire; and Jamie Tan, publicist and human sparkle—thank you for making me look good.

To my dear editor, Kaylan Adair, who took a chance on this goofy author and said, "Sure, send over that one novel you've rewritten a dozen times—we'll publish *that* one next!"; who is patient with me, and trusting, and clever: thank you. There's no one I would rather have by my side on this publication journey than you.

To the many people throughout the years who read the various iterations of this book when it was still a disaster and kindly helped me find ways to make it better: thank you.

And to my husband and children: thank you. Kenneth, you are my safe harbor and my support. Finley, you are the rainbow sprinkles in my life. Clementine, you weren't even born yet, but I brainstormed plot-hole fixes while you gave me morning sickness, so thank you, I suppose. I love you all.